DEATH
IN
THE WOODS

THE REV & RYE SERIES

Death at Fair Havens
Death in the Woods

DEATH IN THE WOODS

A REV & RYE MYSTERY

MARIA MANKIN &
MAREN C. TIRABASSI

Published in the United States by Brain Mill Press.

Print ISBN 978-1-948559-82-9
EPUB ISBN 978-1-948559-81-2
MOBI ISBN 978-1-948559-83-6

Cover design by Ampersand Book Covers.

DEATH
IN
THE WOODS

1

RED CHILI SAUCE DOES NOT LOOK LIKE BLOOD. IT
spatters in a pattern that leaves inevitable clues, and
the smell is a dead giveaway. It's just as difficult to clean
up without a trace, though, and the spilling of Hardy's
homemade chili sauce was a crime. The punishment—
Rye's eyes streaming after she touched her face with
hands that had been doused in the oil of homegrown
Fresno chili peppers—fit the crime.

Rye was not known for her culinary prowess. As
she watched her father assemble his second pan of
enchiladas, she envied him his patience. He'd been
simmering the sauce all day and had made his tortillas
from scratch. She was half amazed he hadn't purchased
a cow to make his own cheese now that he was retired.

Of course, if Rye suggested such a thing, he might
consider it, and then the cozy apartment she'd made
in his barn would be turned over to livestock. Better to
keep her mouth shut and appreciate the fact that her
father was willing to cook multiple times a week. The
nights Rye oversaw meals, dinner was pasta with jarred
sauce and salad from a bag, or French toast. If she was

feeling ambitious, she might make chili in the crockpot. That was as close as she got to gourmet fare.

Hardy was gracious, if confused, about her lackluster skills in the kitchen. Rye's mother, Melanie, had abandoned them when Rye was in second grade, but on his own he had raised his daughter to be proficient, if not expert, at many things. For her tenth birthday, he had even built raised garden beds so that he could share his love of producing food and preparing it. The garden had languished under her care, but after a few disappointing harvests he took over, and the plants flourished and fed them long into the fall.

For her sweet sixteen, instead of a new car, Hardy had found her a project junker, and, although she was willing to put in the hours, Rye never had the deft touch with machinery that her father did. She could change a tire or pick a broken lock, fill her fluids, and replace windshield wipers, but when it came to the bodywork and engine repair, she glazed over. They slogged through the work together, Hardy doggedly teaching her which tools to use and which mechanic could supply parts for a deal, but the best part for Rye was the day they finished and she could begin to plan her escape.

On her eighteenth birthday, a month shy of graduation, Hardy had finally found a shared passion. As sheriff, he considered personal safety and responsible gun use to be paramount. He gifted his daughter lessons at the shooting range. Although she had no desire to own a gun, she was a natural markswoman, and after a few rigorous lessons—the only kind Hardy knew how to give—it was clear her talent for handling a weapon far outstripped anything else he'd taught her. Sure, she technically could make a quiche, but it was bland and uninspired. This, though—her ability to suss out a target and remain laser-focused on it—was a gift she'd inherited from him.

After she left town on graduation night for a gap year/escape, she'd kept up her lessons when she could afford it. She added bow training but refused the offer of a tracking course from an energetic young man at the range. That was when she discovered something about herself. She loved the excitement of targets—round ones, though, not those superimposed with deer or people. She would never own a gun or a bow. The memberships in clubs where these were available, and the lessons, were hobbies barely covered by the hours she worked at Killing It Bookstore. She had deferred her acceptance to Rice to save up, and after spending that time on her own, she appreciated her father's years of focused instruction and his patience with her decision to put her academic achievements on pause. Hardy might not have been the easiest parent to live with, but he'd gifted her life skills and freedom in abundance. He'd prepared her, and she was thankful.

Not as thankful as she would be when this cooking lesson was over, though. This was not exactly what she'd imagined when she'd mentioned to her father that she'd invited Andy over for dinner before they headed out to a movie. In retrospect, it should have been.

Rye looked down at her own pan. Hardy's filling was tucked snuggly into each wrapped tortilla. He was gently ladling sauce and had his cheese at the ready. Hers, in comparison, looked raked over. The shredded chicken was poking out of the sauce, and she'd used way too much cheese to cover up how badly her tortillas had torn.

Her father glanced over. "I see you're in a hurry." The comment and tone were mild, but Rye knew what he was implying. She wasn't giving the task at hand her full concentration, and the results suffered.

"Good thing we have yours to serve company," she replied, her tone a perfect match.

Rye saw the briefest smile twitch at the corner of his mouth. "That it is," Hardy said. He took her pan and placed them both into the oven.

"And now we wait," Rye said, jumping off her stool and stretching.

Hardy nodded toward the overflowing sink, counters covered with dishes and ingredients that needed to be refrigerated. He arched an eyebrow at her.

Rye gave a dramatic sigh as she reached over to give him a hug. "And now we"—she glanced up at him—"*I* get rid of the evidence."

2

IT WAS ONLY WEDNESDAY, AND WANDA ALREADY FELT over-clergied for the week. All morning she'd fielded calls about adjustments to the upcoming budget to accommodate a rotating homeless shelter that wanted to use their church one month a year. Her little flock was firmly in favor of opening the facilities for fifteen unhoused people, but they wanted to do it on a shoestring budget that wasn't realistic unless every member planned to contribute meals, toiletries, and a lot of time.

Tony, her music director, and Lisa, the church administrator, who'd been pushing Wanda for months to write more website content, both disagreed with everything she wrote about the project for the unhoused, Halloween, All Saints, Thanksgiving, and probably New Year's if she had gone that far, though she had not. The usually cheerful staff of Trinity Church was as moody as a middle school youth group.

Wanda and Lisa's relationship had been strained since the spring, when an investigation into a drug ring at Fair Havens Assisted Living and Rehab had put Lisa's three-year-old daughter within arm's reach of a desperate gunman. Wanda didn't blame Lisa for having a hard time bouncing back, but it made the office chillier.

Tony, one of Wanda's dearest friends, was rarely snippy—at least not with her—and not about something so trivial. She knew he had a new boyfriend, and although she thought it was going well, maybe something had happened between them and she'd been too busy to notice and inquire. It wouldn't be the first time. As adept as Wanda was at sorting out problems for her parishioners, she could be clueless with friends. She expected them to stay the same and give her sanity markers in her constantly changing profession.

By three thirty, she decided to take her Jack Russell, Wink, on an extended walk for a mental reset before the evening council meeting. They'd circle the high school grounds, head up the trail behind the parking lot, into the woods, on to the cross-country course, and finally home. She'd give Wink his dinner, then head back to the church with yogurt and a peanut butter and jelly sandwich to inhale before what would inevitably be a long night.

As Wanda pulled up her hood to shield herself from the light October mist, she could hear the cheers of a paltry crowd. Whoever heard of Wednesday afternoon football? Wanda knew that kids seemed younger every year, but these players looked painfully small.

A yellow school bus stood against the curb with the door accordioned open. Wink saw every open door as an invitation. "Wait!" She pulled back, but it was a retractable leash.

"Come on in, little fellow." The driver gave the dog a broad grin. "Come" was one of Wink's favorite commands, and he was up the stairs in a second, dragging Wanda to the door with his nineteen pounds of determination.

"I'm so sorry," she said, trying to catch her balance.

The man chuckled. "Can he have a treat?"

"Certainly, although he would happily scour the bus for dropped snacks."

A practically German Shepherd–sized Milk-Bone appeared, and Wink laid down right where he was and started chewing with delight, holding the biscuit between his two front paws.

"I'm sorry for barging in." Wanda reached out her hand. "Wanda Duff."

"I'm Ben." He looked in his early fifties, less paunchy than most commercial drivers of her acquaintance, and bald by choice.

"Is this the Loyola junior varsity team playing?"

"Freshman football."

"Oh, I thought they were …"

"Small? Yep, but tough. And before you start quoting statistics about concussions at me, I'll tell you I'd rather see these boys playing in a defined freshman league than desperately pushing themselves into JV."

She couldn't help but smile at his passion. He must hear questions like hers often. "I love football," Wanda said, "but it's true that we know more about its lifelong impact on the brain than ever before."

He nodded gravely. "Makes me glad more kids are getting into track. Fewer injuries, and it's not as expensive for families, you know? But sports—that's what makes a kid grow up right, knowing how to be a team, how to win and lose."

Wanda smiled. "Do you like driving a school bus?"

"I love it. I drive Uber and airport limos before and after my shifts, but this is where my heart is. I'm probably more of a dad here than I was with my own boys, but that's divorce for you."

Wanda, two-time loser in marriage, knew something about that. "Do you have a lot of trouble with bullying?

"Not on my bus."

Wink was licking his paws with a self-satisfied tongue, and she could see him judging whether more treats were possible. "Thanks for Wink's treat. Now we need to walk it off."

"Have a nice day, Reverend Duff."

She and Wink had already turned toward the tennis courts. Reverend? Was there nowhere she could hide?

Behind the school, there was a ropes course and a few climbing walls. As she headed in that direction, she could hear what sounded like a zoo, or possibly a commercial wild animal park. She craned her neck. It was the marching band. The brass was out and tuning up. The percussion was being carried across the parking lot. Wanda counted four bass drums, at least a dozen snares, several quad sets, three kettle drums, and multiple cymbals. If she took this route again, Wink might need noise-cancelling headphones.

The clarinets were drifting in—perhaps it was the instrument of choice of the perennially late. The drums had started with a cascade of intricate rhythms, though, and a steady unison crescendo of beats poured forth like a heartbeat. She could feel it coming up through the pavement. *Thump, thump, thump, thump.* Then it was cut off. The sudden silence was almost alarming.

Wanda shook herself and checked her hearing aids. Maybe she would turn them all the way down for the rest of the walk. She could use a break from listening to what everyone needed from her. She stroked the covers gently, recalling her splurge—autumnal colors with delicate gold vine tracing, and an amber enamel maple detail that coordinated with her gold curled-leaf earrings. When she was at her desk, they even matched her gorgeous crimson readers.

As silence descended, she let out a breath she hadn't known she was holding.

It was a liminal space, this trail through a strip of forest between the school and the back of a nursing home. As Wanda and Wink tramped over the fallen leaves, the darkness settled in rather suddenly. Autumn was a lonely time, but she came here to feel alone. Close enough to the road for most people to hear a truck cough, a car engine turn over, and the distant honking pilgrimage of geese, though for her they were whispers. Closer were the thin, sighing sounds she could imagine with her eyes—a chipmunk's hasty flight from its wild, small fears, the crunching of the carpet of detritus beneath her own boots, and, far above, a few yellow leaves stirred by the wind, thick, brittle, castanet, ready to let go.

After the time change, the fingers of darkness would gather evening in early. She and Wink walked slowly, savoring these early October days with slanted light and chill breezes. He stopped to sniff every few steps, occasionally wrenching her arm out of the socket to scare a rabbit. Although they often came here, she was struck today by a sudden feeling that they were not alone. Probably a deer watched her, wondering which way to run, or a coyote—a danger to house cats, but not to them. Wink caught her unease and whined at her.

She scratched behind his ears. "It's okay, Wink. Pretty soon, though, we'll have to give this path up until April."

Wanda shook herself like Wink coming in from rain and tried to regain the buoyancy she'd soaked up from the football players, friendly bus driver, upbeats of the practicing band, even the sudden heart-stop on the drums. No one was lurking—no one was watching.

And then she saw the hand.

It was white against a brown pack of leaves, palm open, fingers curled. Wink pulled toward it. Early Halloween prop, dropped from a backpack. Wanda took shallow breaths, glanced around, and stepped closer. Dark mound, clothes, dark...hair.

"Hello?" Her hand clenched around Wink's lead, keeping him close.

She knew a young man who lived rough out here, but this wasn't Dave. Wanda could tell that, even from the distance of a few feet.

"Hello?"

No answer. Wanda crept forward and crouched down. At the office, she had Narcan and knew how to use it, but not on an afternoon walk. No. She touched the hand.

Too late for Narcan if this was an overdose. Wanda's eyes filled with tears.

And then she felt it very strongly—the presence that she had felt before. Someone watching. Her hair stood up on the back of her neck.

She stood and backed off, fumbling for her cell phone while scattering doggie bags and tissues from her pocket.

"Nine-one-one. How may I assist you?"

Wanda's hands were clumsy as she turned her hearing aids up so they could connect to her cell. "I've found a body."

"What's your name?"

"This is Wanda Duff. I'm walking my dog behind the high school, and I found a body. It's so cold." Wanda forced herself to inhale slowly through her nose. She could feel panic welling up.

The dispatcher's voice was crisp. Wanda clung to the woman's calm authority. "I'm sending units to you now. Stay on the line, please."

Wanda's throat constricted as she spun in a circle. "I think somebody's out here with me."

Wink started to growl.

"Can you give me a more exact location?"

She could hear sirens. "Trail from the parking lot behind the school. Maybe a quarter mile in."

"The police will be there shortly. Do not hang up."

Wanda forced herself to kneel, to stroke Wink's warm body. It steadied her. "Wait. I have an alarm." She fumbled in her deep pockets, and more dog-walking paraphernalia dropped out. She finally found the little SLFORCE Personal Alarm antirape device and switched it on.

It made a deafening sound. She was sure the band director could hear her and was irritated. The dispatcher probably had permanent auditory damage. Poor Wink. But the police detail would find her more quickly. She wondered if Ben could even hear it from where he sat with his newspaper.

Wanda suddenly realized that she felt alone for the first time since she'd headed up the trail. She said a soft prayer of release and a blessing for this person lying on the ground, for whatever life this open hand left behind.

3

WANDA HAD ALWAYS IMAGINED IT WOULD BE embarrassing to sit in the back of a police cruiser with a plexiglass barrier and no interior door handles. The thought usually crossed her mind when she was protesting or involved in civil disobedience, but thus far she had not yet become a police magnet. Either they thought she was no danger to disturbing anyone's peace or they were worried she would start preaching and singing an off-key rendition of "Paul and Silas were bound in jail…" Of course, she couldn't completely discount her romantic history with the town's sheriff, although whether that made her less of a target or more of one, she wasn't sure.

In her current situation, the car put her in the eye of a storm. Wanda felt safer in the bulletproof police cruiser, and she had finally stopped shaking. Of course, she hadn't realized she was shaking until she stopped. Wink was glued to her side, probably more disturbed by the high-pitched key ring than the body they had found. Wanda would need to make a statement down at the station, but the police at the scene had pressed a water bottle into her hand and escorted them to the car farthest from the K9 unit.

The basset, Max, was new to the force, and he currently seemed more interested in Wink than in his duties. Wanda prided herself on being pivotal to the city hall testimony about the importance of replacing the previous K9, a coonhound named Sadie, despite the cost of dog and handler to the town budget. Wanda had testified to Sadie's importance in rescuing two preschoolers who had wandered away from their backyard in January and one memory care resident who had eloped and then been found in these very woods. The penny-pinching opposition maintained there was no violent crime nearby and that the force of a dog was unnecessary. Having been involved with a murder and drug ring sting a few months ago, Wanda was not so sure about that.

She leaned back against the seat and closed her eyes. The police had been quick to get to her, but while she waited on the line, Wanda had taken pictures of the scene. She'd been careful not to move her feet lest she disturb evidence, but she had turned carefully and grabbed as many shots of what was visible to her as possible. Wanda didn't see any reason to ignore the basic training of several how-to PI books she had checked out from the library this summer. Sermon research, she had blushingly called them.

She hadn't gotten her detective's wings in the spring for nothing.

THE OFFICERS AT THE SCENE NEEDED WANDA TO COME in to sign a statement, but she convinced them to let her take Wink home, claiming she also needed to lie down after the shock of her discovery. Tyler Phennen, department rookie and much younger brother of Wanda's former on-again, off-again flame, Sheriff Ryan Phennen, dropped her off at the parsonage.

He opened the door for her, and she clambered out as gracefully as possible. "Do you need me to take Wink to…do his business?" Tyler's tone was respectful, although he was blushing furiously at the mention of something as mundane as dog poop.

His discomfort gave Wanda a reason to smile as she shook her head. "No, thanks. We had a long walk, and he should be all set for this evening. I appreciate the offer, though. By the way, if you find dog baggies and biscuits at the scene, they fell out of my pocket when I was digging for the cell phone. They are not clues."

"I'll keep that in mind," Tyler said. "It was nice to see you, Wanda. It's been a while. I wish it could have been under better circumstances."

"Me, too." Wanda had always liked Tyler. Back when she and Ryan had first started dating, the brothers shared an apartment—well, Tyler had been crashing rent-free on the couch—while he attended police academy. He had been good company, though, and Wanda suspected she may have dated Ryan a little longer than she should have because dinner and a movie at his place felt more like family than anything else she had in her life back then. "I'm sure I'll see you tomorrow morning when I come to the station." Wanda paused. "Maybe you could give your brother a heads up? I know he doesn't love surprises, especially before he's had a cup of coffee or four."

Tyler laughed. He was a handsome man, but a great deal of what made him so desirable was the warmth that emanated from him. His joy was infectious. Wanda had heard that he was dating a teacher friend of Rye's, and she hoped they were happy together. "I'll do that. In fact, I'll tell him tonight, just in case he wants to iron his uniform."

"I'm sure that's not necessary." Wanda kept a straight face, but she was now furiously going over what was clean in her closet. She might not have feelings for Ryan, but it didn't mean she wanted to show up disheveled in front of her ex.

Tyler winked at her. "Of course not." He leaned down and let Wink lick his fingers, then gave him one last rub behind the ears. "See you tomorrow, Wanda. Get some rest."

WANDA TRIED TO REST. SHE LAID DOWN ON HER BED and stared at the ceiling. She got up and made toast. She threw it away and took a shower, soaping the hand that had touched the dead one quite superstitiously. She made more toast and ate it. She wondered what was new on Netflix. She watched five minutes of a very old episode of NCIS before deciding that was a monumentally bad idea.

It was about when she was brushing her teeth to get the taste of vomit out of her mouth that she knew she needed company to process what had happened. Another wave of nausea beset her when she picked up the phone and realized she didn't know who to call. Tony had a date with his new boyfriend tonight. She had met Greg Engstrom, a young librarian, a few weeks ago. Wanda knew that Tony bringing a date to the church meant their relationship had been promoted from casual to 'do not disturb on date night.'

Lisa? Definitely not. After last spring's investigation, Wanda certainly couldn't share news of another mysterious dead body. She hoped Lisa and her daughter were having movie night, even if it was *Moana* for the fortieth time.

Maybe Luke Fairchild would be willing to hear her out, but between his professional capacity as funeral director and his alter ego, Luca Fraticelli, fronting a band with regular gigs an hour from here, the odds he would be home were minimal. Wanda entertained a stray thought about why she, with her major hearing loss, had so many friends who were passionate about music. Maybe that was why she had enjoyed Greg's company on the occasions Tony brought him around. For all of his lovely qualities, Greg was musically illiterate. She drew her attention back to the matter at hand. Not Luke. The situation last spring had also raised dead body friction with him, and she desperately wanted things to get back to normal.

That left Rye.

The death of Niels Pond had brought Wanda and Rye together. Niels had been Wanda's parishioner, and his youngest child, Leslie, had been a junior at the high school, where Rye was the acting vice principal. First, Leslie had disappeared, which brought her under Rye's domain. A few days later, Rye found the girl on the floor of a school bathroom after she attempted to take her own life.

Rye was nearly two decades younger than Wanda, which meant that their social circles didn't exactly overlap. What had originally bonded Wanda and Rye had been their reticence to accept easy answers for Niels Pond's death and an unspoken commitment to putting themselves in jeopardy to uncover the truth. Of course, they also had been seeing each other's downward dog at yoga since before they had known each other in a quasi-investigating capacity, and if that wasn't a basis for something more than a professional partnership, she didn't know what was.

Wanda didn't think there was much of a mystery here. It was tragic, certainly, but people overdosed all the time. Rye would understand why it was troubling, though. She wouldn't laugh, and she wouldn't brush off Wanda's sense of unease or the suspicion that someone had been watching her when she found the body.

She also wasn't squeamish. If Wanda decided to show her the pictures, Rye would be intrigued. She might see something Wanda hadn't in the moment. Even better, she wouldn't judge Wanda for taking them in the first place or insist that Wanda turn them in to the police. Although Rye was a professional administrator, she harbored a strong streak of rebellion against authority.

It also didn't hurt that Rye lived in a converted barn behind her father's house, or that Hardy Rye, as retired sheriff, might have information about the body. Of all their friends, he was the only one who didn't actively discourage their interference. He had been the one to suggest Wanda check out a few books on detection from the library. While Hardy was a believer in independent investigation, he recommended they be knowledgeable about police procedure so they could stay out of harm's way and avoid contaminating evidence.

Wanda found it refreshing. Even more amazing was the fact that Hardy seemed to believe they could take care of themselves. When Wanda's car had been run off the road last year, he suggested she wouldn't be taken in by entrapment again. That attitude was unparalleled among male authority figures in her experience. Rye had simply smiled and said, "Welcome to Hardy Rye's 'clean up your mess' parenting seminar. He also teaches a bang-up course in 'cover your own butt.'" It was certainly one answer to helicopter parenting.

Wanda thought there was probably a balance somewhere between extremes, but she did appreciate his advice, and she suspected Rye did as well.

She didn't want to arrive empty-handed, so she phoned in an order to Wing-Time, which would be quicker than Locals, took yet another shower to get the stink of sick off of her, and made herself as presentable as possible. Twenty minutes later, she was in the car, driving the familiar route across town to grab her favorite takeout.

Fingers crossed that Rye wouldn't mind an unexpected visit if it came with a side of ranch.

4

ANDY WAS NOTHING IF NOT PUNCTUAL. AT SIX O'CLOCK on the dot, he stood on the porch, a six-pack in hand. Rye pulled open the door and reached out to take it from him as he leaned in to give her a kiss on the cheek.

"Ginger beer?" She pulled the cold bottles out of the damp cardboard sleeves and popped two open.

"I'm trying something," he said with a shrug.

Rye studied his face. Andy Soucek had become her best friend in the second grade, a few months after his mother passed away. He'd been raised by his grandmother, who, though strict, was not the teetotaler one might expect. He'd started drinking in early high school, just as Rye had. Nothing big—a beer stolen from a fridge, a drink at a party if it was offered—but still. She had never known him to abstain from the occasional beer or glass of wine.

But then, Rye reminded herself, she hadn't known Andy as an adult for all that long. When she left town after graduation, they were both wilder than they wanted to be. When she returned, they'd each taken their own path, though they hadn't diverged as far as she might have imagined.

She was an upstanding-ish high school vice principal. He was a nurse and surrogate father. Andy was deeply committed to his niece, Rachel, and his battle-ax grandmother. Rye was tolerating living back home with her father. She held up the bottle and clinked it gently against his.

"Cheers to growth potential," she said.

He smiled, the shadows under his eyes deepening. "To growth."

Rye shook herself to dispel the ghosts of the past year. Too often, it felt like they crowded in on her when she and Andy were together. It was probably what was keeping their tentative flirtation at arm's length. Every time they drew close, it felt like the heat of last spring's danger rather than of their own hearts.

"So," she said brightly, "we made enchiladas, as promised." She gestured to the counter, where both pans were on full display. "Bet you can't guess which one I made."

Andy laughed. It had been one of Rye's favorite sounds for many years, and one of the things she'd missed most during her years "abroad," as Andy called the time she'd spent anywhere but here. "Well, I know Hardy Rye would never leave a corn tortilla to burn around the edges," he said, examining the pans. "But I have to say, even if yours is a little"—he searched for the gentlest word—"haphazard, it smells amazing."

Rye gave him a side hug before reaching around him to grab the plates. She turned as her father came in, stepping back as though he'd caught them in a more compromising moment. "Hey, Dad!" It came out too brightly. "Join us?"

"Mr. Rye." Andy held out his hand. "Thanks for dinner."

"You haven't even tasted it yet." Hardy grabbed Andy's hand and pulled him in for a hug.

"If there's one thing I can count on, it's your cooking. And if you were here, that means I can count on Rye's as well." Andy sidestepped the towel Rye chucked at him.

"I'm not that bad!"

"Remember that cake you made for my birthday? How many tablespoons of baking powder were in that?"

Rye made a face. "Okay. That's fair. It was inedible. But in my defense, I'd never baked a cake before."

Andy's eyebrows shot up. "That seems like a major oversight in your culinary education."

"I'm a pie man," Hardy said solemnly, scooping himself some enchiladas before pulling a salad from the fridge. "She can make a mean key lime, if you ever get a hankering."

"I have one now," Andy said, raising his hand.

"Well then, you shouldn't have insulted my cake," Rye replied, grabbing her plate and leading the way into the dining room. "You'll have to get back into my good graces if pie is going to be on the menu."

She turned as she heard Hardy stumping up the stairs. "You're not joining us?"

He shook his head as he disappeared around the bend. "Three's a crowd, Prudence."

Rye stared after her father. He never—well, rarely—called her Prudence. Nobody did. Not Pru, or Prudie, or Priddy—not since her mother had left. The sound of her own name left a hot spot in her chest, as it always did. A dig, a remembrance of the woman who didn't want her enough to stay.

It was always "Rye" unless she was in trouble.

ANDY SAT ACROSS FROM HER, DEEPLY ENGROSSED IN his third helping of enchiladas. Since Hardy disappeared, the tension had returned, the feeling that there was an uncomfortable space between them. It ate at her, because she wasn't sure of the shape of the thing. She kept going through their last few dates—if they could even be called that, considering the absence of even the make out sessions that had marked their summer.

There had been a frenetic energy between them during those months after the shooting at Fair Havens. With school out, Rye had a lot of time on her hands, and while Andy had managed to dodge most of the legal troubles he was likely entitled to for his role in the operation, he'd put in a lot of extra hours at work while management tried to restaff.

When he'd been free, and free of commitments to his family, they'd snuck away and made out like a couple of teenagers. Nothing more, though. Something always seemed to come up right around the time something…came up. It was a line that neither of them seemed able to cross. Their history set them up for an epic romance, but something wasn't right.

"So are you going to tell me what's bothering you, or are you just going to keep shoveling food until you make yourself sick in the garden?" Rye asked.

"That happened one time, and I was fifteen. It's not my fault that adolescence clouded my sense of judgment when it came to your father's pot roast."

"I know you're holding out on me. Just spit it out."

Andy balled up his napkin and tossed it on the table. "Want to take a walk?"

"No. I want you to tell me what's going on."

He glanced toward the ceiling and then back at her.

Reluctantly, she pushed away from the table and followed him out the door and down the path. It was dark already, and cold enough that she wished she'd brought a sweater. He didn't walk toward her little apartment in the old barn, so she just hugged her arms to her chest and picked up the pace.

Andy stopped when they reached the birch tree that marked the end of the long driveway that led to the Rye residence. They'd spent many an hour here talking as teenagers, technically not breaking curfew—Rye's, at least—but unwilling to say good-bye. Its bark was just as smooth as she remembered as she leaned against one of the low branches that forked from the trunk. Andy studied the ground at her feet.

"We're breaking up, aren't we?" she asked, half kidding. Half kidding because this wasn't a real relationship. This was—she studied his face, so precious to her—misplaced traumatic energy, maybe.

Rye hadn't expected to move back here permanently after her father's health scare and early retirement. She had taken the job at Stoneridge because administrative positions were hard to come by, and she stayed because she found unexpected community. She had friends at work, and her relationship with her father—while not without its challenges—was healing a piece of her she hadn't realized had broken when she left so abruptly.

Sure, she had come back for the occasional holiday, but Rye had never really stopped to see what she had left behind. Her life in Texas was work, roller derby, partying, and love affairs that had gone out in a blaze of…well, not glory, exactly.

She had a lot more time on her hands now. Maybe that was why it had seemed smart to accept Andy's invitation when he'd asked her out in the spring. After the investigation into Niels Pond's death with Wanda, Rye had a lot of pent-up energy, and it needed an outlet. Her old friend had been the safe choice.

"Rye," he started, and then stopped.

She reached out and grabbed his hand, pulling him in so she could lean against his warmth. "It's okay," she said.

"Rachel is having such a hard time," he said softly. "Her dad's trial is about to start, and she keeps having nightmares about something happening to me." Rye gave him a little squeeze. "She's just... Her mother hasn't been in touch. I feel like she needs to be my focus, and honestly, being her everything is great, but—"

"But it's a lot of work to be the rock."

He nodded. She felt more than saw his head bob. "I don't really know what I'm doing. I just want to keep her safe. I don't want her to completely derail because I'm off having fun with you."

Rye sighed. "I could tell you that you shouldn't make your whole life about Rachel, and that it's healthy to have boundaries, but honestly, I've seen kids like her slip through the cracks so easily." She patted his chest gently. "I think you're right to put her first right now."

He was silent for a minute. Then he sighed, and the wall of tension that had been building between the two of them evaporated. "I thought you'd be mad."

Rye leaned back a little and looked at him. He had tears on his cheeks. He'd always cried easily. "Honestly, I'm not even all that surprised, so 'mad' would be a stretch." She smiled and wiped his tears away with her thumb. "I've loved spending time with you the last few months, and I hope you—and Rachel, if she wants—can still find time for me. But this"—she waved her hand between the two of them—"It's not clicking. Maybe if we didn't find each other in the middle of a crisis, we might have had something."

"Yeah."

She laughed. It felt good, like whatever had been off between them was right again. "For the record, I still think you're sexy as hell, and I hope that someday, when you have the energy for it, you find someone who will appreciate that as much as they do your sweetness and absolutely off-putting love of Monty Python."

"And my ability to bake a cake that's edible."

"Sure." Rye waved a hand. "Cake is good, too."

Andy leaned back against his favorite spot on the tree—a smooth section of trunk they'd carved into when they were ten and experimenting with whittling. He looked lighter. "I hope you find someone who appreciates you, too."

She shrugged. "I will."

"I like your confidence."

Rye just smiled. "I'm an acquired taste. But over the years, I've found a few people who taught me that's okay. They liked me, lack of cooking skills notwithstanding. No reason to think others won't."

She could feel his eyes studying her more intently, although it was so dark, she couldn't see his face clearly. "You've been in love."

"You know about Leila," she answered softly. Her chest constricted at speaking that name aloud. "And I think I told you about Patrick." Rye cleared her throat. Her past was littered with names she'd rather forget.

"I suppose I haven't found the time to make those big—"

"Mistakes?"

"I was going to say commitments."

She reached out and gripped her friend's hand. "You should. You'd be good at it."

"Thanks. That means a lot, coming from you."

Rye shifted upright and held out a hand for him to do the same. She pulled him in for a last hug, pressing her nose into his neck and taking a deep inhale. "Don't be a stranger, you hear?"

He laughed. She felt his cheek damp against her neck. "You, either."

5

RYE WAS FINISHING UP THE DISHES WHEN SHE GOT A text from Wanda.

> *Don't want to alarm you, but I'm in your driveway.*

She dried her hands and picked her phone up to respond but paused as the elusive ellipses appeared.

> *I found a dead body behind the high school.*

Rye was out the door without her jacket for the second time in an hour, but this time she didn't feel the cold at all. As she opened the passenger door to Wanda's car and slid in, a tantalizing scent washed over her.

"Your car smells like a chicken went swimming in hot sauce."

"Death and wings. It's kind of our thing, you know." Wanda held out a Styrofoam box.

Rye dug in as though she hadn't feasted earlier in the evening. Break ups made her hungry, and normally she would take spicy over sweet any day. But under the circumstances, her hand froze as she looked at her friend. "Are you okay? What happened?" She wiped her fingers on a wet wipe. She had a hundred questions, but one look at Wanda's face gave her pause. She put the box on her lap, then grasped her friend's hand.

Wanda shuddered. "I don't know. I was hoping your dad might have heard something about it. Might help to put my mind at ease about the whole thing." She forced herself to breathe deeply. The shaking had returned. "I was walking Wink behind the high school this afternoon in the woods. You know?" Rye nodded. "I had this feeling that something was off, that someone was watching us. I thought it was probably nerves. It gets dark early, and in the fall, ordinary can feel…occult."

"I thought you were getting better at trusting that gut of yours," Rye said.

Wanda put a hand over her belly. "I am. Or at least I thought I was. It's just been a rough week—month, really." Well, five months, but Rye didn't need to know that. "I saw this mound, and something white on the ground. I thought it was Halloween stuff."

"But it wasn't."

"No," Wanda said softly.

"Could you see a face? Did you know the person?" The questions were probing, but Rye's tone was gentle.

"No. It was just the hand. I took pictures." She handed her phone to Rye. She'd thought it would help to talk about it, but now, in the dark, Wanda felt more frightened than she had since the police arrived on the scene. She couldn't bear to look at the photos again.

"What made you take these?" Rye was flipping through them, food forgotten.

That was a good question. Wanda turned to look at Rye. "Instinct. It's not that people never die in unusual places, but something about this felt wrong. Bad."

"Can I ask you something?"

"Sure."

Rye paused, weighing her words. "Maybe it's not a question. It's just— Do you ever think about what happened in the spring, with the Ponds?"

"Of course."

"Me, too. I think about it a lot. I think about it so much that I let myself get into a relationship with Andy to…I don't know. Hold on to it? Make sense out of it?" She shook her head. "I'm not explaining this well."

"I don't think I realized you and Andy were a couple," Wanda said, hunting for a distraction from the death in the woods.

"We aren't." Rye waved her hand absent-mindedly, clearly also trying to make sense of what was running through her head. "We broke up an hour ago, but that's not the point."

"Are *you* okay?" Wanda interrupted.

"I'm fine, actually," Rye said. "We're still friends. It was a weird excuse for a fling, and both of us knew for a while that it wasn't working. He finally worked up the nerve to say so."

"Well, I'm sorry anyway. I like Andy."

"Me, too. Or, I like the idea of Andy—of a sweet, stable, compassionate more-than-friend who lets me feel a little flutter when he walks into a room. Andy and I have a history, though, and there's a lot of hurt there. I'm glad we tried, and I'm also really glad we're back to solid good-friend territory." Rye shrugged. "Sorry. I got sidetracked. You did that on purpose, didn't you? What was I saying?"

"You were asking about…me and Fair Havens."

"I don't want to see you hurt like you were when you got run off the road." Rye had never admitted to her friend how scary it had been, or how terrible Wanda had looked those first days in the hospital. After the cast came off her leg, Wanda had spent July, August, and September doing physical therapy. Rye hadn't seen her with the cane for a few weeks now, but she suspected the effects of Wanda's injuries, and of the scare, lingered. Rye looked down at the photos again. "And also, I trust you. If something felt off, it probably is."

Wanda took her phone back. "Maybe I *did* take these because something felt the way it did last spring." She didn't say it out loud, but she realized that was why she was here talking to the one person who understood, but who also had the amazing gift to be dispassionate and logical.

"You're freaked out, I can tell."

Wanda weighed her options. She could lie to Rye and claim she was fine, but what would that gain her? "It was awful. I've seen so much death. It is a part of my calling, and I didn't think a body could turn my stomach, but this was different."

They were both silent, staring through the windshield at the front porch, the lit windows, and across a length of lawn to Rye's barn apartment, a darker hole against the blackness of night.

"I'll ask my dad if he's heard anything, and even if he hasn't, I'm sure he will by tomorrow. If it took place on school property, Principal Mendoza will know. Why don't we meet for dinner at Locals tomorrow night?"

"Sounds good," Wanda said, the knot in her stomach loosening a little. "Seven?"

"It's a date." Rye started to open the door, then turned back to her friend. "Do me a favor? Please don't look at those pictures again, at least until we talk."

Wanda nodded. She wasn't even tempted.

"Jonathan Thorne," Hardy said when she came back in and asked. "Died in the woods behind the school. Seems he worked for the Drama Department on a contract basis."

"He's been hired twice a year—to help with the fall musical and the Festival spring play—for the last ten years or so."

"Can't make a living at that."

"He also worked at just about every regional and community theater within a hundred miles."

"So you remember talking with him?" Rye had known her father would jump on that. She had not won a prize for Ms. Congeniality in high school. "Good-looking guy?"

"My friends definitely liked him when he was the hot new teacher. He had that New York glamor and was openly gay. Those kinds of people were in short supply around here back then, so yeah, he was hard to miss."

"What about now?"

"I've seen him around for the fall musical. The theater department is more Principal Mendoza's domain. I should probably call him. He'll be devastated."

Hardy nodded to her cell phone, which was charging on the counter. "Check your messages first. Your phone was buzzing nonstop while you were outside with Wanda." Rye cocked an eyebrow at him. "What? I saw the car." Hardy dropped a kiss on her cheek. "Get some rest. It will be a tough day tomorrow. And thanks for cleaning up."

She realized she'd been tidying while they talked, a habit she'd had for as long as she could remember. It was one of a few that served her well.

"There's something else, isn't there?" Hardy asked.

Rye might have said no and let it go, but the memory of Wanda's face troubled her. Rye didn't know if it was shock or fear or PTSD. Wanda had been injured last spring, and her recovery had been slow—though, as she liked to say to her physical therapist, "the spirit was willing."

Then summer came, and with it a new relationship with Andy, as well as a long list of projects for her father. Wanda and Rye had only gotten together occasionally for coffee or wings. The last time they'd met up, Wanda had told Rye she was getting over the flu, so Rye hadn't thought much of how tired she'd looked. Tonight, she was shocked that Wanda seemed a shadow of her former self.

A compact woman with short, curly hair that often seemed to punctuate her enthusiastic commentary, Wanda was a well-known advocate in the community. She attended marches for immigration reform, headed a church that was a haven for the unhoused community, and was the unofficial chaplain of their local PFLAG chapter.

"Wanda was the one who found the body. In the woods behind the school," Rye said. Hardy nodded, so she continued. "She was walking Wink. She said she gave a brief statement to the police and has to go back tomorrow."

"I know." Hardy was in the loop, though Rye wasn't sure why. As the retired sheriff, he occasionally heard things on the scanner or caught the news early from an old colleague, but this was fresh—an ongoing investigation. Who would have reached out to him? And why? She studied his face but found only the bland stare he had perfected years ago.

"Were you planning to tell me Wanda was involved if I hadn't known?" Rye asked.

"Was she?"

"Involved?" Rye realized she was wiping down an already clean counter. "I don't think so. Not beyond what she's told me."

Hardy studied her face. "You haven't seen her much recently, have you?"

Rye shook her head. "I've been busy with school, and…things."

"Andy."

She shrugged. "My schedule's looking clearer on that front."

He added soap to the dishwasher. "I'm sorry to hear about it."

"But you knew," Rye said. He always knew. He never asked for details, but even when she'd lived two thousand miles away, he could tell when her relationship status changed—no Facebook notification necessary.

"He's a good man."

"That he is," Rye replied. "I'm lucky to have him as a friend."

"He's lucky to have you, too."

Rye could feel the blush creep up her neck, but when she turned to say more, her father was gone.

Disrupting the Woods 35

6

WANDA DID FEEL BETTER AFTER SEEING RYE. SHE WAS lonelier than she wanted to admit these days, and going home to an empty house, especially after finding the body, was hard.

Her first husband had been thrilled to have her pay his way through college and law school, at which point he dumped her for a younger, strawberry blond model who did not wear hearing aids. Wanda's second husband had been the best roommate she could ever hope for—they cooked together, loved the same TV, went to the movies and out dancing, and planned wonderful vacations. On a whirlwind British sightseeing tour, he found his own redheaded King Arthur, came out to Wanda, and, with tears that were a mixture of regret, guilt, and joy, told her he needed a divorce. Wanda had officiated their wedding—probably one for the books.

She stopped at Locals for a drink. "J&B, a double, splash of water, no ice." She had settled in to reflect on her day when a plate of pita triangles, hummus, and mixed raw vegetables arrived.

"I didn't order this."

"No. You never would." Cal, the bartender, knew her appetizer orders ran to more decadence. "He did." Cal gestured across the room.

Ever hopeful, she looked across the room and saw Harold Golightly, treasurer at the church. Wanda knew for a fact that his birth name was Harry Golightly and he had legally changed it to "Harold" to better represent himself as a financial expert. No more than thirty, he was a numbers wizard and a poker champ who used his winnings to help keep the Food Bank afloat.

This evening, he was with a group talking loudly over beer flights. His arm was around a young woman with extensive ink. Wanda waved her thanks and meant it. Another night, the appetizer might have been an invitation to join them, but they were in their own world tonight. He flashed her a bright grin and turned back to his friends.

Wanda looked down at her drink. A few months ago, she would have been mortified to be caught drinking in front of a parishioner, but with her leg in a cast for twelve weeks, Wanda's standards had slipped. She didn't like to drive far, even now, and it wasn't like the church expressly forbade alcohol consumption. When her friend Mitch had opened a second location of his bar, Laredo's, in town, Wanda had given up any pretense. She was a regular there for trivia night and drank freely at Local's as well.

Her Scotch was smooth, but she needed something to absorb it before she drove home tonight. She would really prefer the sobering effects of bacon cheddar potato skins, but she ate the pita and veggies and ordered a glass of water. She tried to listen to her latest library novel, Deanna Raybourn's *A Perilous Undertaking*, but even that was too dark for tonight. She settled on mindless scrolling until she felt that Wink could wait no longer.

She walked a satisfactorily straight line to the car. It was only a mile and a half home. She was worn out after the adrenaline surge, and putting alcohol on top of that had been a poor choice, but she wasn't impaired. She shook her head.

Wanda had just pulled out into the intersection when a screech of tires made her slam on the brakes. The other car swerved across the center line and then corrected all the way to the verge before pulling back into the travel lane. Wanda checked her rearview mirror before backing up into the parking lot to breathe.

Since the hit-and-run in the spring, she had continued weakness in her right leg, so she drove more carefully than before the accident. She was also averse to any close calls on the road, and she'd been careful tonight. She was aware of her own limitations, and still she hadn't seen it coming.

Wanda was stone-cold sober now. She turned off the car and got out her high beam flashlight. She could see where she'd stopped, angled into the turn, and the rubber laid down as the other vehicle crossed the road. She walked across the small highway. Only two other cars had come by since she'd left Locals. The skid marks continued into the brush a couple feet, but there was no ditch here to break an axle. She took a few pictures. Worried about her own ability to pass a breathalyzer, she did not call it in. She got in her car and drove so slowly that another traveler honked until she picked up her pace.

Thank goodness for Wink. She let him out into the yard as soon as she got home, then snuggled into bed with him without checking her phone again. He found his favorite spot behind her knees and slept with her all night.

NOT A PERFECT NIGHT. WANDA DECIDED TO SWIM away the night terrors and got to the pool at opening. If she'd arrived much later, not even half a lane would be free. She started with a steady-paced breaststroke, which meant keeping her eyes out of the water. She was an alligator swimmer, and, yes, she knew she could buy goggles, but it was hard to unlearn years of practice. Besides, it was the perfect way to keep an eye on the lifeguard in his chair. *Henry is your lifeguard. The water temperature is 84 F, and the air temperature is 84 F.* It reminded her of the whiteboards hanging up in hospital rooms. *Your nurse is…*

Henry looked like he could use a nurse. Usually he was wandering around the pool, putting away kids' toys, brushing water into the drain, or giving unwanted advice on sharing lanes. This morning, he was slumped in the chair, his shoulders sagging and his hands hanging limp over the float.

She finished her fifty lengths and climbed out at his end rather than by the locker room. She went right up to his elevated chair so that she could read his lips. It was impossible for her to hear a word in here without her hearing aids, and with the echoes of chatter and water splashing. "Morning, Henry. How's it going?"

He looked bewildered, obviously wondering how she knew his name. He wasn't clicking on all burners. "Fine?"

"You look a little under the weather."

He shook himself, a bit like Wink. "Yeah."

"Can I get you anything? Water? Or some tea from the vending machine?"

He shook his head. "No. Fine. I'm fine."

Wanda stared at him until the young man looked up. His eyes were puffy and as red as if he'd been swimming beside her.

Henry seemed relieved when the door slammed open and the high school swim team noisily filed in from the locker room. The downside to swimming at the public pool that sat adjacent to Stoneridge High School was that Wanda had to swim early, before the lifeguard needed to secure the two lanes students used every morning from six thirty to seven thirty. Henry jumped down and brushed past her, keeping his head down.

As she got changed and headed to her car, she couldn't shake the look on the young man's face. She'd worked with teenagers for twenty years. She knew what pain looked like in too many of its forms. What she had seen in him was fresh—maybe as fresh as a pale hand on autumn leaves. Maybe he knew the man.

WANDA STILL HAD NOT HEARD FROM THE POLICE when it was time to go to work, and she didn't want to make two trips to the station. She also knew that midday, as far from shift change as possible, was the most likely time to catch a police officer in a chatty mood. She did well with the police, since many of them interpreted the "confessional confidentiality" of clergy to mean they would never talk about anything they heard. Talk about a myth! If someone did not say, "This is in confidence," or at least, "Please don't tell anyone," anything Wanda picked up was fair game. She didn't like gossip, but her brief season of detection had allowed her to redefine chatting with cops as "selective prying."

The impact of touching that hand, and the feeling there was something wrong, had grown overnight. To her, it felt as though that hand had stretched up from the leaves asking for justice, for peace. Maybe it was foolish to feel responsibility for an anonymous dead body.

She felt a wave of empathy for law enforcement, always trying to maintain emotional distance from victims and survivors. From the stories told to her, it was impossible to completely put aside all of it—the death, illness, losses of cognition or jobs or relationships. It would be worse for cops. Homicide, accidental death, domestic violence, fires. They faced so many terrible things without the balance of wedding-excited couples or new babies to baptize.

Wanda pulled into the parking lot at Trinity Church by eight thirty. Hers was the first car there. Another rough preschool handoff for Lisa. Lily had been a shining star in day care, but since her near-kidnapping in the spring, she'd shown more anxiety when her mother left. It was a normal response to such a situation, and one that made Wanda feel terribly guilty. There was no way to change the past, but the ripples she felt from it and saw in those she loved weighed on her.

As Wanda unlocked the door, she spotted Lisa sprinting across the grass and held it open for the younger woman, preventing a crash.

"Thanks, Wanda. Sorry I'm late."

"I was just coming in myself."

Lisa brushed past her. "I'll check for messages and then scan emails for anything you might need to handle. Do you have any meetings?"

"Clergy cluster lunch at the new gym. I think Mel booked us all with a personal trainer and smoothies for lunch." Wanda sighed. "When I plan the clergy cluster, it will be exquisitely decadent. We might have multiple courses."

"Do we even have any restaurants in town that do that sort of lunch?"

"No. But I suppose I could settle for someplace with free fresh bread and a hefty dessert menu," Wanda said. "Besides that, I have a visit to the police station."

"What'd you do?" asked Tony. He had snuck in behind her, and she was embarrassed to admit that she jumped. He folded his tall frame so he could sit on Lisa's desk. The only chair he really liked was a piano bench. He looked like he grew there and could only perch anywhere else. He was tall, with the blond hair and blue eyes of his Icelandic mother and the oversized generosity of his Venetian father. And his hands were oversized, too, from stretching across so many piano keys. He was frequently early at the church, since he had to be at the high school from ten to five during the week and often until eight when there were rehearsals. "Did you chain yourself to a multinational's fence, or picket City Hall? Maybe burn a few bras?" She had told him about her first adolescent adventure into feminist counterculture in confidence, and he delighted in bringing it up at least once a week in public.

Wanda knew she would puncture the morning banter. "I found a body."

The silence held until Lisa took a deep breath and broke it. "Here?" She looked pale.

"No. Wink and I were on a walk in the woods behind the high school, and there was a body. I called the police." Wanda didn't want to scare them—especially Lisa—with more details, so she left it at that. "I need to go in and sign my statement."

"I've got a faculty meeting at nine," Tony said. "They called it 'hard news.' I wonder if it's someone from the school."

"Maybe," Wanda replied. "I don't know if they'll tell me anything, but—" She was interrupted by her phone. She pulled it out and showed Tony the display, which read, *Ryan—DO NOT ANSWER*. Tony had typed that reminder for her after the last of many times she and Ryan had broken up. She had no choice today, though, so she picked up.

"This is Wanda Duff." No big deal. Plenty of people spoke to their exes. Tony choked on the swig of coffee he had just taken. He recognized her professional tone—it was the same "no caller ID" voice that Wanda used in the office all the time.

"It's Ryan."

Wanda tried to decide whether the situation was too serious for her to answer, "Ryan who?" After a moment, she sighed and took the high road. "Good morning, Sheriff." Okay, so it was the high road with dust kicking up.

"You need to come down to the station, answer a few more questions, and sign your statement."

Wanda knew Ryan Phennen had never been one for small talk. He was the most taciturn man she'd ever dated, but it still stung that he didn't even ask how she was doing. She'd found a dead body, and he couldn't bring himself to inquire about how she might feel about it.

"I can be there at eleven." She bit her tongue before asking whether that would work for him. It was what worked for her. "See you then."

7

RYE PLANNED TO ARRIVE EARLY TO GET SOME WORK done before the faculty meeting and maybe an assembly, but she had overslept, and by the time she got to work she had to jog to catch up to her friends Camila and Ana as they headed into the teachers' lounge.

"Any news?" Camila asked as they found a spot in the back. Rye suspected her friends thought she might be holding out on them because of her father's connections.

"Nothing," Rye said. It was hard not to feel the effect this death was already having on the staff. As she glanced around, voices were low, and the general feeling was one of solemnity, if not grief. She imagined many of her colleagues were in the same boat—aware of the man but not friends with him. "I don't think we're going to find out much today, although if they deem it an overdose"— she held up her hands to forestall questions—"I'm not saying it was, but *if* it was, maybe they'll tell us." If it was an accident and not murder. Rye didn't say it, but the thought had kept her up for much of the night.

"What else could it be?" Ana asked.

Although Rye was reasonably certain no one was listening, she didn't want to be the one to throw grist into the rumor mill, so she settled on a shrug. "My dad knows something, but he won't talk to me about it. 'The police consider it an open investigation.' Makes me think there might be more to the story."

Camila nodded toward a young woman on the far side of the room. Rye glanced over and felt her face warm. Claudia Ramirez was a drama teacher. At the moment, her eyes were red, but her posture was straight as a dancer's, and she had a grace that Rye found captivating.

Claudia, like Wanda's friend Tony, was contracted on a yearly basis. She also directed at a local theater. Rye had seen one of her shows last year—a showcase of local playwrights—and thought that her talents were probably wasted working with high schoolers.

"She must be taking this hard," Camila murmured. She paused a moment before adding, "I wonder if she knows anything."

Rye rolled her eyes good-naturedly at Ana behind Camila's back. Camila Santos loved to talk. She was a consummate professional in her biology classroom, but she always had the best gossip about her students, their parents, and her colleagues. Especially the parents. While Rye only met with parents under the worst circumstances, Camila tutored after school and ran up against all manner of ordinary chaos. Rye wished she could say she didn't listen to the rumors, but her friend was an excellent storyteller. Brazilian-born, Camila had spoken Portuguese from birth, but she could drop her accent to imitate just about anyone, and it was impossible to resist once she dove in.

The more careful twin, Spanish teacher Ana was as far from a chatterbox as could be, but she loved her sister's stories as much as the next person. Rye respected the fact that, although Camila must know the details of her twin's love life—a topic of great interest to many when the three of them were out at a bar—she was a steel trap when it came to Ana.

Rye hoped, for his sake, that Jonathan Thorne didn't have a lot of skeletons in his closet. If he did, Camila would know, and that meant everyone would. She also hoped, for Wanda's sake, that the cause of death would turn out to be…what, exactly? Natural? No. It wouldn't be that, but maybe not criminal. She thought of the photos again, of the white hand against the dark leaves. She wouldn't tell Camila about it, much as she loved her. The man's death, or at least his repose, should be kept private.

Gerard Mendoza cleared his throat, and the room fell silent. "I know you're all aware that our community has suffered a tragedy, but you may not be aware of its scope." He looked around the room, his gaze landing for a moment on Rye. "Jonathan Thorne—" His voice caught. "My dear friend Jonathan died yesterday from what police believe to be an opioid overdose. I was not aware, obviously, of any drug use on his part, but the police have asked that if any of you know anything, to be in touch."

A murmur broke out in the room, but Rye was still. She knew her boss well enough to know that there was more, and she was right.

"Unfortunately, I am also tasked with telling you that another death occurred yesterday. Ross Jacobs—he graduated salutatorian two years ago, as many of you may remember—was found dead on Route 111 yesterday evening." He paused and wiped his eyes. "I know you will join me in mourning the great loss to both men's families, and to our family here. We will send out an email shortly with information for parents and students. Grief counselors will be made available to staff and students."

Mendoza needed one—that was Rye's first thought. Her second was that the email would be her job. She'd written them before, and she would again. She felt a pang of shame that she was grateful the second death was not a current student, nor a face she knew. Selfish, because she knew many students and teachers would be affected by the loss, but it wouldn't be another one that haunted her at three a.m. It wouldn't be her fault that these two men were gone.

TWO HOURS LATER, EMAIL SENT, RYE WAS CALLED TO Mendoza's office. She did her best to keep fidgeting to a minimum, but across the table from her, Gerard Mendoza was typing the slowest text in the world. He often made jokes about being all thumbs, but even Wanda could type faster than this, and at least she knew she could use Siri to dictate a particularly long or complicated message.

Rye didn't want to check her watch, but she was sure there would be calls to handle when she got back to her office. "Do you want me to come back?" Rye asked. "I know you're busy." It was the kindest way she could think of to say, *Get to it already*.

He finally looked up. His eyes were red-rimmed, and Rye realized just how hard he must be taking the death of his friend. "Sorry," he said, putting his phone away. "I wanted to be sure Elena and the girls knew I would be late."

"I could show you how to open Messages on your computer," Rye offered. "You can type texts, and it's much faster."

"Maybe next week." With a sigh, he looked around, a little lost in his own office. The room was cheerful, a contradiction, today, to the plump, dark man in front of her. The rug beneath her feet was lush, the deep red and gold flowers picking up the threads in the drapes his wife had sewn for him.

Gerard Mendoza looked like he hadn't slept. His shirt was rumpled, and his entire body seemed to sag as he looked blankly back at her.

"You wanted to see me?" she finally prompted gently.

"Oh, yes." He shook himself. "It's come to my attention that Jonathan—Mr. Thorne—that he attended a recovery program about three years ago."

"Okay," Rye said carefully. She'd heard the same, but when she'd checked his file, there hadn't been any mention of it.

"I didn't know," he said after a moment. "I didn't know anything about it. He never mentioned doing drugs, or even drinking. Not in the eight years I've known him."

"I didn't see any mention of it in his employment file either. Obviously, he went through all the normal background checks. There were no red flags. He never committed a crime—under the influence or otherwise—so legally a rehab center would not be required to disclose that information to us."

Mendoza nodded. "I know. I just— I don't know why he didn't tell me. It wouldn't have changed how I saw him. It was always wonderful to have him here. The students seemed to get along with him well, and I know Ms. Ramirez enjoyed working with him."

"Maybe he thought you would have to report it to the school board."

"Maybe." He paused. "He wouldn't have been wrong, although I don't think it would have been an issue."

"An openly gay man who has a history of drug abuse working with teenagers?" Rye snorted. "Parents here like to believe they're as liberal as they were when they were seventeen, but the fact is, they would have eviscerated him. It would have filled the letters to the editor, and even if he'd been able to keep his position, which is doubtful, it would have influenced how the students treated him."

"You think so?" Mendoza looked devastated by the thought.

"I know so. It would have ended his career," Rye said. "The drive for academic success has left compassion behind." The memory of her own suspension last school year was fresh in her mind. It had only taken one angry, grieving parent to cast doubt on Rye's qualifications and career.

He nodded slowly. "There's a lack of faith." Rye waited, since he seemed like he needed to say more. "There's a lack of faith in what we do, and in the ability of people to change." Mendoza rubbed his hand across his eyes. "We're in the business of growth here, aren't we? Teaching is all about giving our students the opportunity to learn and improve, and hopefully go out into the world equipped to use that knowledge. To adapt. To innovate."

"But we're under a microscope. I think parents want to protect and control so badly that they forget about the power of making mistakes and learning from them." Rye leaned forward. "It's about projecting a certain image rather than creating a system that values substance and truth. Personally, I think a person who has gone to rehab and stayed sober has a lot to share with our students. Maybe a few of them would think twice about the paths they're on, or about how casually they treat their bodies. Maybe it would open up conversations about nurturing mental health and emotional wholeness rather than GPAs and college admissions." She sighed. "And maybe we would just be depressed by the cruelty of the young, armed with such potent ammunition. I don't know." Rye reached out and grasped her boss's hand. "But I do understand why he kept it a secret, and I don't think it was because he didn't trust you, Gerard."

He met her gaze. "I know the last year hasn't been the easiest, but I'm lucky to have you." Rye sat back as he slid a folder over to her. "Your new contract. Take it home. Look over the terms. Decide if this is where you want to invest all that energy of yours." He smiled. "For the record, I hope it is."

"Thank you," Rye said, taking it and flipping the folder open. "This means a lot to me."

Five months ago, he hadn't defended her against Bellona Pond, although she knew he had spoken privately to the school board on her behalf. Now, he was asking her to commit—she flipped through the pages— for five years! Rye blinked. An eternity.

Mendoza nodded, then glanced back at his phone. "I hate to cut this short, but it looks like duty calls." He picked it up. Rye saw the words "Sheriff's Office" blink onto the screen before he answered.

She waved at him and let herself out.

8

WANDA WAS ALWAYS SURPRISED THAT THE POLICE station felt like a welcoming place. Jaz Malone, as the newest officer, often got saddled with receptionist and dispatcher duties, but it was a boon to the community because she always had a big smile for everyone. Most people who came through the door were in distinct categories—elderly but still driving, new to the English language, date rape victims, parents of kids in trouble, and people making or signing statements—the kind of folks who needed support. Jaz was there to give it. She sat behind bulletproof plastic to scan every person thoroughly, but her megawatt grin melted even that barrier.

The only downside was that she gave nothing up. Ever. Wanda had tried. Jaz didn't even let her guard down when she was teaching the self-defense class Wanda had joined after the events at Fair Havens last year.

Jaz set her up in an interview room, and Wanda was soon joined by Ryan and Tickle Lombard—well, Officer Tim Lombard now, and not thrilled that Wanda knew how he had gotten that nickname in her high school youth group.

Wanda dove in. "I know you have questions, but can you please tell me who I found?"

Ryan Phennen squinted at her. He needed glasses, always had, but Wanda knew he was a little too vain to wear them unless he was working on his computer. "You haven't heard?"

She stared at the man for whom she used to cook breakfast. Ryan was younger than Wanda by a decade, and he looked very good in his early forties—better than he had when they first met, in fact. She didn't love that he'd recently shorn his glossy dark hair close, though, and he'd lost weight since he started training for marathons. He was six foot two and lean, with bright green eyes. When Wanda had first met him, Ryan had worn a beard, but in recent years he'd favored a five o'clock shadow.

He had also gotten more tightly wound in the years she'd known him. "I didn't even see a face. It was just—" She paused. The image of that limp hand lasered into her mind made her queasy. She cleared her throat.

Tickle looked up from his notes with some sympathy at the catch in her voice. Ryan brought his chair legs back to the floor. "Jonathan Thorne."

Wanda waited. "Is he from around here?"

Ryan studied her for a long moment. "He was a designer for regional theaters, and he was working on a show at the high school. I can't tell you any more than that. I'm sure Vice Principal Rye will fill you in."

The sheriff had not been a big fan of Wanda's springtime investigation, and he had been even less pleased to discover it involved Prudence Rye. He'd gotten on all right with Rye's father, but he did not like the child she had been or, apparently, the woman she'd become. He cleared his throat. "Now, I need you to tell us everything you remember."

She gave them as much as she could—freshman football, bus, band, trail, then the dog dragging her toward the leaves and seeing the hand. Feeling for a pulse, calling, waiting.

"Did you see anyone else while you were in the woods?"

She shook her head. "I had a feeling that someone was watching, but I think that was just the woods."

Lombard and Ryan glanced at each other. The younger man cleared his throat to speak but closed his mouth when the sheriff glared at him.

"What is it?" Wanda asked. "Wasn't it an overdose?"

"Did you hear anything? Think about it. Wind, branches breaking, leaves shifting, a car starting up?"

Wanda shook her head. "I'd turned my hearing aids off."

"What? Why?" Ryan's eyes narrowed as though he thought she was a suspect. He probably hoped she was.

"Because it's my body," Wanda said icily. "And I have every right to take a break when and where I want to."

"In the middle of the woods?" Ryan said angrily. "That's just reckless!"

"It was four o'clock in the afternoon, Ryan. Give it a rest." She enjoyed watching his face turn that shade of red.

He pushed a picture across the table at her. The man she now knew as Jonathan Thorne lay uncovered, leaves brushed aside by paramedics and crime scene techs. His eyes were open wide, staring up into the trees. He looked like he had died in pain, or at least shock. Wanda's own eyes filled with tears.

"A man is dead, Wanda. And you found him. We're investigating all avenues right now. So, no. I won't 'give it a rest.'" He pulled the paper back and put it into the folder in front of him. "I'll ask you again. Did you notice anything unusual yesterday?"

Wanda sat back in her chair and tried to think through details that until now she had been trying to repress. The cold sensation of eyes on her back. The white hand on dark leaves. The scent of—

"Yes! I didn't think anything of it at the time, but I smelled weed."

"Not cigarettes?" Lombard asked, making careful notations on his tablet as she spoke.

"I'm sorry, what?" Tim's voice was just the range she found hardest to hear, second soprano, but she would never tell him that. "I didn't catch ..."

He faced her and repeated himself really loudly, with exaggerated facial expressions. "Not ci-gar-rettes?"

Maybe she should tell him he talked like a girl. The girl in her reminded her who would be insulted. "Not that I noticed. Someone had been smoking pot though, and recently. It was strong enough that I figured kids from the high school must have been on the path ahead of me."

"Anything else?" Lombard asked. Ryan was just staring at her, his pen *tick tick ticking* against the table.

She shook her head. "Just that feeling, like I said, that someone was watching."

"Too bad you didn't bother to have your hearing aids turned on at a murder scene. Might have learned something useful." Ryan pushed back from the table and made to leave.

And because he was sneering at her desire for a mental health break, she didn't tell him about the photographs she'd taken.

It was only after she had signed her statement and was in her car that she realized he had called it a murder.

A GLASS OF WINE. THE AFTERNOON SHE'D HAD CALLED for a whole bottle, but it was more acceptably consumed by the glass, so Wanda filled one to the rim. This particular vintage didn't have a "nose." No swirling and sniffing. No holding the stem. A peasant red is a pleasant red, her father always used to say, and a four-liter jug of Carlo Rossi's Paisano was what she bought when she did not need to impress anyone.

Only then did she flop on the sofa. She wanted very badly to accompany Maisie Dobbs on a cerebral journey through criminal activity, but the answering machine was summoning her. And ... no, she'd only had a few sips of the Paisano ... that was really twenty-six messages. She didn't know her landline answering machine could handle that many messages. Most people used her cell. She only kept the landline because she knew some of her parishioners still used the phone book.

She got out a notepad so she could keep track of this deluge of Luddites. The first message, noted at 9:00 a.m., was from her sister, Michelle. "Phone me." As was the second message, fifteen minutes later. And the third. The fifth message wanted her to participate in a survey. The eleventh suggested that she would learn something amazing about a cruise to the Caribbean. The fourteenth offered to sell her a chimney cleaning, patently unnecessary in this house. The twenty-second message warned her that she was in arrears on her college loan. All the rest were from Mickey. The tone of voice became more imperative around noon and sounded downright desperate about an hour ago.

No information at all about why she was calling. A family death seemed likely, though Wanda could not think who it could be. Wanda knew Michelle had her cell number, or at least had been given it multiple times, and she certainly knew what church Wanda was pastoring. It had a very helpful website and a prominent phone number. Lisa had suggested on several occasions the phone number did not need to be so easily found. Many churches buried it in hopes that casual visitors could find what they needed—say, Sunday service times—without calling. Wanda vetoed Lisa's request every time, insisting it should be easy to call a church. That number also gave any caller Wanda's cell for a pastoral response, so she was sure Mickey was doing her usual thing—expecting people to bend to her will to the point of blocking her own best interests.

It never helped to point this out. Mickey was the big sister, and she knew best.

Wanda had better just call her. Wink had come over and sat nicely very much in view of his food dish. Wanda wondered if she could hold Mickey off by implying that she had come in, fed the dog, and then needed to take him on a long walk. No, there were several aunts that she would genuinely want to know about if something had happened, and an irascible uncle Stephen whom she was always willing to bail out, if just to hear the story of how he'd landed in trouble.

She didn't have a chance to decide. The phone rang. She downed a soul-nourishing swallow and picked it up.

"Where have you been?"

"At work, Mickey. Where else?"

"Well, you've certainly left yourself with no time."

"And, 'How are you Wanda?' you might say, and then I would say, 'Doing okay, Michelle, given that I found a dead body yesterday.' And you would say, 'Oh dear, how terrible for you.'"

"There's no time for that. Besides, you see dead bodies all the time in your work. You need to get to the airport."

Wanda put down the wine glass. "Mickey, what are you talking about? I have an appointment at seven."

"So you're going to leave your own flesh and blood—and a child, at that—at the airport because you have some appointment?"

"Lance? Lance is coming here?"

"Yes, of course he is. He's coming to stay with you for the rest of the semester."

Wanda took a deep breath. She felt like she was sliding into an alternate reality. Lance (née Lancelot)Duff was her nephew. Mickey had moved to California to prevent Lance from having contact with her ex and his family, and Wanda had not seen him since he was in eighth grade. Spoiled, self-centered, and sullen was what she remembered.

"He won't be any trouble. He's a junior, you know. Just throw some food at him and make sure he does his schoolwork."

"Mickey." Wanda clenched her jaw. "I have no idea what you're talking about. Why is Lance coming here? Where are you going? Why isn't he coming with you?"

"I'm going to Italy, of course. I emailed you about all of this. I'm going to spend a few months with Enzo."

"Who's Enzo?"

"You're joking, right? He and I have been seeing each other for five months, Wanda."

"Wait, is this the guy you met on that cruise?"

"Of course."

Wanda sighed. "I still don't understand what that has to do with Lance coming here. You certainly didn't email me about it."

There was silence. "Well, I definitely meant to email you. Anyway, I enrolled Lance in a boarding school here, but it didn't work out. Obviously, he can't stay with his father—you know how Sean can be. I can't just leave him here by himself. That would be irresponsible."

"Obviously," Wanda replied dryly. "Why isn't he going to Italy with you?"

Mickey scoffed. "Can you even imagine? Enzo and I need time, just the two of us, to get to know each other."

"Mickey, how ..." Wanda stopped. It was futile to ask her sister how or why she thought it made sense to try to build a relationship with someone without her son around.

"So the bottom line is you've sent Lance here without asking me or making any arrangements. I have no legal authority to enroll him in school, much less speak on his behalf in medical or legal situations that may arise over the next two and a half months. Have you thought this through at all?"

There was silence on the other end. "Winnie, please. I really need your help."

Wanda winced. Although Michelle still went by Mickey, no one had called Wanda "Winnie" since their parents passed. It had been a joke when the girls were little—Mickey Mouse and Winnie the Pooh, their father had called them. She still had the photograph he'd taken of them dressed up in homemade costumes. It wasn't Halloween. He had just been up, and when their father was the life of the party, the girls had made the most of it, squirreling away the happy moments for when he crashed again.

"Michelle, if I'm going to do this, you need to get on a plane now. You enroll him in school, you bring me a schedule of what he does, what he likes, what he's allergic to—I want it all. Spend the plane ride writing down every single thing you know about your son so that I can take care of him properly. We will try this for one month. If it doesn't work, you'll come get him or I will have his father pick him up. Do you understand?"

"Don't do that," Mickey said.

"Send me your flight information so I know when to expect you," Wanda said. "Now. How can I be in touch with Lance?"

"I gave him your cell number."

"So you do have it." She'd avoided low blows like this with Ryan today. She wasn't a saint.

"Wanda—"

"Unless you're about to thank me for taking care of your son, I don't want to hear it right now." Her phone beeped. "And Lance is calling. See you tomorrow."

"Hi Lance. I just got off the phone with your mom." She didn't want to burden the child with the failures of the parent, so she left it at that.

"Oh, okay. I just wanted to tell you I'm stuck at O'Hare. They said I could take a flight to Manchester tomorrow afternoon or to Logan tomorrow evening."

"Take Manchester. It's much closer. Send me your flight info when you have it, and I'll be at the curb. I drive a red Fiesta."

"Thanks. I'll text you."

"Oh, Lance—do you want to touch base with your mom to let her know about your change of plans, or should I call her?"

"Would you?"

So that was how it was. "Sure. No problem. See you tomorrow."

Wanda checked her watch. She still had half an hour to make it to dinner with Rye. Plenty of time to panic scream into a pillow and then make a list of everything she needed to do in the next twenty-four hours. And call Tony to help her do it. He had at least *been* an adolescent male, even if it was two decades ago.

9

RYE SHUFFLED A FEW OF THE FOLDERS ON HER DESK and looked up at the clock. In the midst of arranging for counselors to come in, sending out information to families, and fielding calls from parents asking for more than she could give them, the workday had ended. It was after six, and she was going to be late to meet Wanda if she didn't finish up. She leaned over, turned off her computer, and stood up with a stretch.

The school had a blanket of silence over it, since extracurricular activities had been cancelled per police request. Nobody was rushing around the halls looking for friends or dashing out to make it to practice.

It was peaceful. Maybe with the death of two people connected to the school in twenty-four hours, Rye should feel afraid to be alone, but she relished it. As much as she loved her job, her friends, and (on most days) her colleagues, she needed to recharge with a little peace. It felt good to run long paths without company, curl up with a book, or binge a show on Netflix. She liked eating leftovers over the kitchen sink, staring out the window into the trees behind her father's house.

She took a deep breath as she locked up her office, then stilled when she realized wasn't alone. Rye walked across the foyer, so often filled with teen spirit, and pulled open the door to the auditorium. It had been ajar, otherwise she wouldn't have heard the piano.

Rye hung back in the shadows watching Claudia Ramirez play. She didn't recognize the song. She didn't have an ear for music the way Ana or Mike did. It wasn't familiar—or at least, the notes weren't—but the longing and the sense of melancholy were. She lowered herself into a seat in the back row. This piano sounded a little tinny, a too-small sound in a room built for grander theatrics, but Claudia clearly knew her craft.

As the song ended, Rye opened her eyes and studied the other woman. Claudia's dark hair was pulled back, and she'd cast aside the black sweater she'd been wearing at the meeting this morning. Rye could see it strewn across the back of a chair in the front row. It was a strangely intimate sight—such carelessness was rare for a person who would be used to projecting appropriate behavior to her students. Rye could imagine the woman's bedroom for an instant, clothes tossed on an armchair or the floor. Shoes kicked off, the top of the dresser a tangle of hair bands, moisturizer, old receipts, and Rye ached. She felt, in that moment, how long it had been since she'd experienced such intimacy.

It was a shock to realize she'd never felt that with Andy. Maybe it was because their relationship had remained so chaste, but she'd been in his home, in his bedroom. It had all seemed familiar, his habits ingrained in the back of her brain. He was tidy in just about everything he did. His shirts were all hung, his tees neatly folded. He recycled even small scraps of paper, and in his space, everything had its place. It was the same as it had been in the second grade—even then, his shoes had been aligned and his homework neatly stacked on the desk.

Rye felt an overwhelming urge to embrace this woman she barely knew, whose bedroom she imagined because of a sweater, to allow Claudia to let down her guard and weep if she needed to, or rest.

It didn't make any sense. Rye had never felt anything but cordial toward her before this, but for reasons she couldn't understand—the music, the darkness—something had cracked open in her.

She needed to leave. She wanted to slip out before Claudia knew she had intruded, but the door squeaked sharply as she eased it open, a blasted siren of her presence in the room.

"Hello?"

Rye winced. Claudia's voice was steady, musical and lovely. She clamped down on that thought and slapped on a more professional attitude. She forced herself to step out of the shadows. "Hi." She waved and regretted it immediately. "I'm sorry to bother you. I was leaving and heard the music."

Claudia walked up the aisle toward her. The room that had seemed massive a few minutes before shrank drastically as she approached. Rye prayed the dim lights hid the flush across her cheeks. "I stayed late in case anyone needed someplace to talk about Jonathan." She shrugged. "A few kids came by, but ..." She trailed off.

"It's hard to talk about this sort of thing." Rye felt her shoulders ease. This was something she knew, an area, sadly, of expertise. "Even if you want to."

"Later this week, they'll open up," Claudia said. "Most of them will be ready to process when the shock wears off."

"Some won't."

Claudia studied Rye's face, her chin tilting up in a way that Rye found immediately and painfully endearing. "That's true. All I can do is be here. Different people need different...distractions."

Rye wanted to agree, to say something profound about death or healing, but her tongue had turned to lead. She felt like she was sixteen. Her face was hot. "Thank you for staying," she finally managed.

"Looks like I'm not the only one," Claudia said with a small smile. She took in Rye's overflowing tote, jacket slung over one arm. "Your car is almost always here later than mine."

She knew which car was Rye's? That didn't mean anything. Oh, lord, what was happening to her brain? "I stay late some nights so I can meet up with a few friends after practices let out. It's nice to get a drink or a bite."

Claudia reached out and rested her hand on Rye's arm. "You should invite me sometime."

It was hard to think clearly with the sound of her blood pounding in her ears. "Yeah. I will. Definitely. I—Yeah."

Claudia pushed a strand of hair back behind her ear and smiled again. "Are you hungry now?"

Now? Yes. No. Yes. "I'd love to," she finally managed. "I—Oh, shoot." She glanced at her watch. Wanda would be waiting. "I'm so sorry. I have plans tonight."

She could see Claudia pull back just a bit. "Of course. That's fine."

Rye took a deep breath. She was not sixteen. This was not her first crush, and she would not leave this room feeling like a sweaty failure at life. "My friend Wanda and I are grabbing some dinner, but maybe later? We could get coffee? Or...a drink?"

"On a school night?" Claudia raised her eyebrows.

"Oh," Rye floundered. "Right. Saturday?" She took a slow breath to keep herself from blurting out other days of the week. "And how about a meal?"

"I'm out of town visiting family."

It wasn't going to work out.

"I'm chaperoning the dance next Friday, and Saturday I'm helping a friend move," Claudia said. "A week from Sunday would be great, though. It is a school night, but since it's the weekend, maybe we can give ourselves a pass just this once."

"Of course. The dance. I'm chaperoning too. Completely slipped my mind." That would be a disaster. Seeing this woman again, surrounded by the raging sea of hormones that was a high school dance? She couldn't very well back out now that she'd admitted as much.

"I know." Claudia gave Rye that searching glance once more before turning to go. "See you there." She disappeared into the shadows down by the stage, grabbing her sweater before jumping up and heading out the stage door toward her office. Rye stared after her.

She pulled at the offending door, its squeak now mysteriously gone. Wanda was waiting.

BY THE TIME SHE GOT TO LOCALS, THE RINGING IN HER ears had cleared, and her pulse had slowed to normal, but Rye still felt a glow in her chest. She saw Wanda sitting in a booth by the window and made her way over, pulling her coat off as she went.

"I'm so sorry I'm late." She slid in across from the older woman.

"I was, too. You're just…later." Wanda looked tired, but her gaze was sharp. "Are you okay?"

"What?" Rye laughed nervously. "Of course. Yes. I'm fine."

Wanda took a sip of water, raising her eyebrow. "I'm not buying it. Either you've already been out drinking, or..." She studied Rye carefully. "Did you just come from a date?"

"No!" It came out louder than she intended, and the waitperson who had about to stop by their table moved off quickly. "No," she said again. "I— No."

"Rye!"

"What?" Rye shrugged helplessly. "It wasn't a date."

"I forgot, you broke up with Andy. I'm sorry."

Rye just shook her head. "It's fine. I'm not upset about it."

"You look...dewy. How do magazines describe it?"

Rye looked at Wanda fondly. It had been too long. As she searched her friend's face, she saw the stress and exhaustion that she'd hoped she'd imagined last night. She stretched out a hand to brush Wanda's fingers and turn the tables. "Not to be blunt, but you look like hell. And I've seen you laid out in the hospital."

"And you think I look worse now? Thanks a lot!"

Rye shook her head. "I didn't mean it like that. I meant...I'm sorry. I'm sorry it's been so long since we've seen each other. I'm sorry it's taken a couple of dead bodies to make it happen, and I'm sorry that something's bothering you and I haven't been around."

Wanda sighed. She squeezed Rye's hand and pulled it back. "Thanks. I'm sorry, too. Life has been, well, life. Chaotic. Full of the usual."

"Four weddings and a funeral?"

"Unfortunately, it usually runs the other way, but yes." Wanda paused and adjusted her hearing aid. "Did you say dead bodies? Like, plural?"

Rye nodded. "This morning, Gerard Mendoza told us that the man you found was a contractor in the theater department. You probably know that by now. He works at the school every year during the musical. The police said it was a probable overdose and are asking people who knew him to come forward if they have any information." She took a sip of the water Wanda had already ordered for her. "But Mendoza also said a former student—he was second in his class the year before I started, apparently—also was found dead yesterday evening."

"Another overdose?" Wanda asked.

"No. A hit-and-run."

"Two sudden deaths connected to the high school in one day?" Wanda drummed her fingers on the table, clearly lost in thought. "Who's the other victim?"

"Ross Jacobs," Rye said. "Apparently well-liked. I know death brings out the saint in people's hindsight, but by all accounts, he was bright, friendly." She sighed. "I know his brother, unfortunately. Henry isn't exactly cut from the same cloth."

Wanda straightened. "Henry? Does he work at the pool over on Greenfield?"

"I think so. He's been in my office a few times recently. Smoking pot behind the school, cutting class with his girlfriend."

"I saw him this morning. I can't believe he went to work the day after his brother died." Wanda started shredding her napkin. "He looked awful."

"I can imagine."

"When I saw Ryan today, to give my statement? He used the word 'murder.'"

"For Thorne?" Rye asked. "Are you sure?"

"One hundred percent. I'm not sure if he realized that he let it slip. I may have riled him up a bit."

"Don't you always?" Rye winked.

Wanda snorted. "You know, his little brother said almost the same thing to me yesterday. Do you all know something that I don't?"

Rye rolled her eyes. "That Ryan's had a thing for you forever."

"What are you talking about? We broke up almost two years ago."

"And how many men have you dated seriously since? How many people has he dated?" Rye asked. "You two have been on-again, off-again for how long?"

"We're firmly off, thank you very much," Wanda said.

Rye just stared at her, one eyebrow raised. "I'm just saying, you two have a long history, and I can still see sparks."

"Yes, the kind that turn into a forest fire and destroy everything," Wanda said fiercely. "Trust me. I've had to rebuild a few times."

"Okay." Rye held up her hands in surrender. "I'm not rooting for you two. I'd much rather see you with that funeral director you're always giggling over."

"When have you heard me giggle?"

"Whenever you talk about Luke Fairchild, that's when."

"I do not!" Wanda insisted. "Besides, after what happened in the spring, he's seemed...distant."

"He has, or you've been?" Rye reached out to touch her friend's hand. "I know you went through physical therapy, but did you ever call that therapist my dad recommended? The one who specializes in PTSD?"

Wanda shook her head. "I've meant to, but it's been so busy at the church. A lot fell through the cracks while I was recuperating."

"It's been five months. You can't use that as an excuse anymore," Rye said gently. "I'm not trying to bully you into it. I've been seeing a therapist for years now, and after Leslie Pond tried to take her own life, I doubled down with my appointments. If I don't, I couldn't do my job." She pulled out the contract Mendoza had given her. "And since it looks like I'm going to be around for a while longer ..."

Wanda jumped up and came around the table to give Rye a hug. "Congratulations! We get to keep you!"

"It looks like it," Rye agreed. She had agonized over whether five years was too long to stay, but there was nothing waiting for her in Texas. "So, you see, I have a vested interest in your mental health. And finding you a boyfriend who doesn't hate me."

Wanda smiled. "Ryan doesn't love or hate—"

"I'm going to stop you right there. I don't want you to have such a massive lie on your conscience."

"You're not his favorite person," Wanda said. "And despite what you and Tyler seem to think, I'm not either."

"Agree to disagree."

"This is a little off topic, but can I ask you a favor?" Wanda took a sip of her water.

"Of course."

"I just found out that my sister's son is coming to stay with me for a while." She stared at a spot on the table in front of her. "They live in California. Apparently, Michelle is headed to Italy for an extended trip, and she doesn't want to bring Lance along." Wanda glanced up and caught the hint of a scowl on Rye's face. Self-serving mothers were a sensitive topic for her. Wanda chose her words carefully. "He's going to be at the high school, and I was wondering if you could keep an eye on him. Mickey mentioned he had to leave his boarding school. I'm guessing it wasn't for being a star pupil."

Rye straightened up. "I'm all over it. Lance, you said?" She pulled out a little notebook and scribbled down a few thoughts to remind herself of in the morning. "Is he enrolled yet? If he is, I can look at his file."

"She's supposed to fly in tomorrow to take care of that. Thank you. I'd just hate to see him fall through the cracks on my watch."

Rye leaned across the table, her eyes gleaming. It was ridiculous how energized she got at the idea of helping a kid she hadn't even met yet. "I've got your back on this," she said. "Now." She looked around and waved down the server. "Let's eat."

10

WANDA WAS SCRAMBLING TO SET UP THE HOUSE TO host a teenage boy on such short notice. Tony had managed to get away from school by taking a Rye-authorized two-hour lunch. They were both surprised that Greg Engstrom had been at Wanda's all morning with Tony's keys. He'd vacuumed the whole house, emptied the trash in every room, cleaned the bathroom, changed the guest room sheets, and thrown the Wink-furred ones in the wash with all the towels he could find. He had even removed a few ugly parishioner gifts from the guest room and stored them in the basement.

How dirty had the floor been before he vacuumed? Had anything gone off in the fridge, which he had also wiped down? She was profoundly relieved that Greg had not cleaned her room, since she usually aired out her bras and hosiery on a rack in the en suite.

"Tony," she whispered. "Is Greg for real?"

Her friend grinned broadly. "He is. Of course, he's a less than superlative cook. Just mastered his first PB and J last week."

"Ah, I see. Your culinary superiority is unchallenged, and you hope he moves in before the health authorities do."

"He has moved in."

"When were you going to tell me? When's the party?"

Tony lifted an eyebrow. "When you asked. And he didn't want one."

Ouch. Still, she put a hand on each shoulder and made him face her. "He's shy, or he's not sure?"

He shrugged. "Both?"

"I'm guessing he's sure about how wonderful you are and not so sure about some of your clueless friends."

Tony wrapped her in a hug. "For some reason, he likes you a lot. Of course, he only really knows you in your public persona." He smiled. "Oh, maybe that's why."

Wanda stuck out her tongue.

Greg stopped in front of her. "You guys doing a podcast, or can I get a little help here?" He thrust a power strip into Tony's hand. "By the bed. And Wanda, your impending guest probably doesn't want your summer nighties, skorts, and tank tops in his drawers."

"Greg, thank you. I couldn't have done this without your help."

"It's nothing. Just do me a favor and tell him to get a library card. It works for both towns. We have a robust teen program at our library. Maybe he could check it out."

She gave him a salute, and then she and Tony went to work. She hoped Greg liked pastries, because she was going to drop off a big box of Harvey's best at their house.

After they left, Wanda made a quick trip to the grocery store. She had no idea what Lance might want or like, but she'd spent a lot of time leading youth groups, and there was no question in her mind that he would run up a grocery tab vastly higher than her usual.

Back at church, she finished her sermon and helped Lisa with the bulletin, then wrote every weekly post on Facebook until the Holly Berry Fair. She cheated by using the basic format of last year's posts, but she was sure no one would remember. Wanda finished by three, with enough time to drop off the pastries at Tony and Greg's place. She was very curious but didn't go in. It looked like Lance's flight was running behind, but she didn't want to start off this new relationship by being late.

Lisa's response to her news about Lance had been, "You've been a helicopter pastor for years. You'll be great at the parenting thing." Tony's was, predictably, "Does he sing?" She had no idea. The anxiety about who this unknown young man was almost made her glad there hadn't been more time to prepare.

Wanda drove north on the Daniel Webster Highway to Manchester Airport. She was just on time, with five minutes in the cell phone lot before he called, and then she pulled around. Even though Wanda had not seen her nephew in person for years, she recognized him right away. He was texting, so she had a moment to consider this man-sized boy she was about to invite into her home. Her first thought was that she liked his blue glasses. Her second was warier as she considered his auburn hair pulled back in a bun. His hair was gorgeous, but the color—it was asking her to love the one thing she'd allowed herself to shift pain onto after both of her husbands had left her for red-haired partners. Though she did love the look.

Wanda pulled up and hopped out. An identical familial expression of panic crossed their faces as they simultaneously wondered whether they were supposed to hug. She settled for a quick one. "It's good to see you," she said, and looked around. "Any other luggage?"

"Nothing." He hoisted the backpack. "I mailed a box. I have enough clothes for a few days."

She gestured to the car door, and he folded himself into the Ford Fiesta. She walked around to the other side. They were silent as she carefully pulled back out into traffic and maneuvered her way onto the highway again. "How was the flight? You must be exhausted after sleeping at the airport."

Lance nodded. "The flight was okay. Late again today, but what can you do? It's Chicago. The new plane had arrived, but the weather was a mess."

"I haven't flown through there for a while, but I remember that."

Wanda was thankful for the classic rock station that covered the awkward silence that followed. As they got close to home, she suggested they stop for takeout. He said pizza, Thai, or Chinese would be fine. He ate everything except eggplant.

She handed him her phone, and he ordered, smiling at her ancient iPhone 5SE.

"I could update a few things for you," he offered.

"That would be great. Just don't delete the ReSound app. It feeds into my hearing aids."

He glanced at her ears and nodded. "I was just going to update the OS and see what other apps you might need, but I'll be careful. I'll check with you before I change anything."

"I appreciate that." Wanda smiled. She wasn't sure what she'd expected, but it wasn't this polite young man sitting next to her. He wasn't chatty, but there was a warmth to him that he definitely hadn't inherited from his mother. Speaking of whom. "Did your mom let you know when she's arriving tonight?"

Lance shook his head. "She said she called the school, and they told her she could enroll me online."

Wanda felt her face flush. "She's not coming, is she?" She could feel Lance tense next to her. She gritted her teeth to keep from spewing a few very inappropriate words about her sister.

"She said she's going to email you everything you need. She might have already. I'm not sure, since the last I heard from her was before I took off."

Wanda took a deep breath, then forced herself to take three more before answering. It wasn't Lance's fault that Mickey was like this. Wanda would not take it out on her nephew or make him feel bad about something he had no control over. "Okay."

"I'm sorry, Aunt Wanda."

"She can be her own worst enemy." She bit her lip. Wanda couldn't imagine what was going on in Mickey's head right now. The level of irresponsibility was unprecedented for Mickey, and it made Wanda anxious. "Can you tell me anything about her boyfriend?"

"Enzo."

Wanda waited for more. "Got that. Anything else?"

Lance shifted uncomfortably in his seat. "She's dated other guys. It's never been like this." He glanced at his aunt, then back out the window before continuing. "There's nothing left for me. For her friends. She quit her job. It's weird. I was glad to go away to school, just to be away from them."

"I hate to ask, but was he abusive to either of you? She's about to the leave the country with him. If I need to, I could talk to a few people I know who could give me some advice."

He shook his head. "He didn't live with us. Barely even talked to me, even though he's closer to my age than hers. I don't know if he asked her for money or anything like that. He never hit her or yelled."

"You weren't scared of him?"

Lance was silent for a long moment. "He made me uneasy. I couldn't put my finger on why, though," he finally said. "It's just a feeling."

"It's good to trust your gut."

"Maybe. My mom has been lonely a long time. I think she likes feeling special—all the dinners out, and gifts. This trip to Italy. It all seems…I don't know. Romantic. To her, at least."

"I get that." Wanda took the exit to the Thai restaurant. "And I'm happy to have you here. I just want to know that she's safe. My sister drives me up the wall, but she's the only one I've got."

Lance nodded. "Thanks for taking me in. I know it's a hassle."

"It was a surprise, for sure," Wanda said as they turned into the parking lot. "But we'll figure it out together, okay?"

"That sounds good." He waved her back in as she started to unbuckle. "I've got this one."

Wanda couldn't help but smile as she watched her nephew amble across the pavement to pick up their order. There was something off with Mickey, but Lance's kind gesture was redeeming Wanda's view of her parenting. A month or six with Lance might be exactly what Wanda needed.

11

RYE STARED AT THE BOY ACROSS FROM HER. LANCELOT? Really? Having been saddled with Prudence, she had sympathy for others whose parents chose unusual names. Inevitably, their own were common—Rebecca, Sarah, John, Matthew—and after a lifetime of being squeezed into a box with others of the same name, they rebelled in the way they imagined their children would appreciate. Spider. Vanilla. Zen. Rye had seen them all come through, and while she didn't think she could be surprised, Lancelot had thrown her.

Not the person. He was sitting up in at least an approximation of straight, and his face fell into easy, pleasant lines. He'd had the weekend to settle in before Monday's paperwork and introductions to classes. Rye had waited until Wednesday afternoon to meet with him so he could talk to her about how he was fitting in. She reread his file. She knew he'd been through a couple of high schools already, but she honestly couldn't have pointed to a compelling reason. He didn't have more than the most cursory write-ups, and his grades were decent, if not stellar. He didn't have any of the warning signs that would suggest drug or alcohol abuse, or self-harm.

Rye decided the straightforward approach would be best here. If he was going to be a problem, better to find out now than in six months when he'd stolen Wanda's credit card numbers and disappeared with a new identity.

"So, do you like to be called Lancelot? Or …" She left room for him to suggest an alternative.

"I go by Lance, thanks." He blushed a bit and ducked his head, as though he answered this question a lot but still felt as though it were an imposition to ask others to call him what he liked. Another tick she recognized.

"Lance, great. Do you know why you're here?"

"Here in this office? Or here in this town?"

Smart kid. He reminded Rye of someone. Oh, of course. Wanda. "Either. Both."

"My mother is in Italy. My aunt agreed to let me stay with her while she's gone."

"Wanda's a friend of mine, you know." Better to be honest. Regardless of what his test scores said, this boy was bright, and Rye knew smart kids didn't appreciate being lied to. Well, no kid did, but smart kids resented it and then retaliated.

"I know," he said. "You helped her solve that murder last year, right?"

Rye sucked in a breath. "She told you about that?"

"When she was in the hospital, the police contacted my mom. I don't think Wanda wanted her to know, but once my mother gets ahold of something, she's impossible to put off."

"She never came to visit Wanda." Rye surprised herself with the bitterness in her voice. She could tell from his face that Lance was surprised, too. She needed to rein it in. "I didn't even know Wanda had a sister."

"Like I said, I don't think she wanted my mom to know. Or come. They don't really get along. My mother is ..." He seemed to be at a loss for words.

"A hard person to love?" That was how Hardy had described Rye's mother more than once after she left.

"Yeah." He sagged in his seat. "Exactly."

Rye forced herself to breathe slowly and let the tension release from her shoulders. His issues with his mother were not her problem unless they became her problem officially. "I'm glad you're here," she said. It wasn't what she'd planned to say, but it was true. "I hope you like it at Stoneridge."

"Thanks," he said.

Rye studied the kid across from her thoughtfully. "How are you settling in?"

He shrugged. "It's fine. A school's a school. At least my mom's not around to date one of my teachers."

Rye made a face, then tried to school her features appropriately. "I doubt you'll have that problem with Wanda."

He laughed. It was a pleasant sound, and Rye couldn't help but smile at him. "No. My mother and Wanda don't really get along, but I know enough about her to figure that out. She doesn't seem like the wild type."

Rye put a hand up to cover a cough/snort/laugh. "I don't know if I'd say that," she replied. "But she knows a good boundary when she sees it." Rye stood, signaling the meeting had come to an end. "Let me know if you need anything or want to change or drop a class. You can email if you don't want to make an office visit. Individual teachers can tell you what you might need to do before finals."

"Thanks," he said again, pausing at the door. "Can I ask you one thing?"

"Sure."

"There's a girl my English class. Her name is Leslie Pond. Is she ... Is she related to the man who died?"

Rye felt her heart constrict. Her urge to protect both Leslie and this kid she barely knew was so strong. "Yes." She reached a hand toward him, then let it drop. "Please don't mention it to her though, okay? She's been through a lot."

"Oh, no. I wouldn't." He stuck his hand in his pocket and pulled out his phone. "I just ... She asked me if I was going to the dance on Friday? I kind of told her yes, but then I haven't said anything to my aunt about it. Or ... told her that Wanda's my aunt. I didn't know if I should?"

That was interesting. She was suddenly grateful she was chaperoning. "I think Wanda would be fine with it, but if she's a little weird ..." Rye paused. She didn't want to say too much, but to say nothing felt wrong. "It's a sensitive subject. What happened to Wanda was a big deal, even if she acts like it wasn't. So just ... be aware."

"Okay," he said uncertainly.

Rye came around her desk. "Listen. Your mom and your aunt are adults. You aren't responsible for making or keeping them happy. They have to make their own choices and deal with their baggage. We all do, right?"

"Yeah."

"I'm not asking you to take care of Wanda. She can take care of herself extremely well. All I'm saying is that she may not have told you or her sister the full story. Go to the dance. It's fine," Rye said. "And if Wanda seems upset or concerned when you tell her, and you want to know why, ask her. Or have her call me, okay?"

"If you say so."

"I do."

As soon as the door shut behind Lance, Rye was on the phone to Wanda. Wanda picked up on the second ring, which told Rye she'd been waiting for the call. Usually, Wanda took so long to find her cell that she had to call back as Rye was leaving a message.

"So?" Wanda asked.

"He seems great."

"I know, right? Isn't that weird?"

Rye laughed. "Weird how? What did you expect?"

She could practically see Wanda shrug. "Last time I saw Lance, he seemed like an antisocial brat. But to be fair, Mickey had dragged him across the country on zero notice, and she was on his case all the time. It was exhausting just to watch them together."

"He said she's in Italy? Is it a work thing? I know it's hard to place kids in schools abroad, but it seems like a fun opportunity."

"It's a romantic entanglement."

"For how long?"

"It's for as long as she can keep it up, or until this guy scams her." Wanda sighed. "Either way, when it ends, she'll be back expecting Lance to follow her wherever she goes next."

Rye's tolerance for generic bad parenting had become high—it had to be, since she had seen it all—but selfish parents? Wanda's sister better hope she didn't run into Rye. "She's done this before?"

"Not to Italy, no. But my sister's previous relationships have taken them all over the country."

"What about his father?"

"He's not a bad guy. He and Mickey were never married. They were together less than a year when she got pregnant. To his credit, he stayed for a while. I think he would have taken Lance when he left, but she refused to give Sean even partial custody, and the judge backed her up. Lance used to visit his father, but once his dad got married and had children, I think Lance felt awkward. Not unwelcome, but it was hard on him, and he realized that it upset the wife. That made it easier for Mickey to keep him away."

Rye tried to imagine that. For all she had struggled with her mother leaving, she'd at least known where she stood with her father. They might not always agree, but they were a team. He was her rock, her home, if she needed one. "That's rough."

"Yes." Wanda sighed. "I try to bite my tongue when it comes to my sister, at least around Lance. I don't want to cause any more trouble there. I just wish ... I don't know. That his life wasn't so complicated."

"Me, too," Rye said. "He seems like he's doing pretty well, considering."

"You read his file? No red flags?"

"Honestly, no. I can't tell you the details, but I think he'll do okay here." Rye paused. "I did want to give you a heads up though."

"Oh?"

"He mentioned to me that he wants to go to the dance this weekend."

Wanda laughed with a hint of relief. "That seems fine!"

"Leslie Pond asked him to go."

"Does she ... Does she know who he is?" Wanda asked.

"Hmm. Good question. He asked if she was who he thought she was, and I told him yes. I have no idea if she knows Lance is your nephew. I'm not sure how she would. You don't share a last name, and you don't look alike, beginning with a foot difference in height."

"Nicole, maybe," Wanda replied. "She was in church Sunday. She might have heard me mention it."

Rye's gut twisted. The investigation last year had been hard on Leslie and her family, but ultimately Rye thought they were grateful that they had uncovered the truth. Nicole might not feel the same. Her mother's involvement in the drug ring, however well-intentioned it was, resulted in Zoe Laferriere fleeing the country. Nicole, her father, and her siblings stayed.

"Do you think Nicole would mess with him? Or Leslie?" Rye wanted to believe their meeting was a coincidence, but she worked at a high school.

"I don't know," Wanda said. "I hope not. I've known her a long time, and I've always liked Nicole, but if we hadn't interfered, would her mother still be here? Maybe."

"Or maybe she'd be dead," Rye said bluntly. "Or in prison."

"I haven't talked to Nicole about any of it. Maybe that was a mistake."

"Okay," Rye said. "Let's not panic. I'm chaperoning the dance. I'll keep an eye on the three of them and see if there's anything off."

"They've all been through so much."

"I know. We have, too, and survived. If anything, it makes us better equipped to help them, right?"

"I guess." Wanda sounded surprisingly like her nephew.

"Listen. Just do me a favor?" Rye asked.

"Sure."

"If Lance says anything to you about the dance, or about Leslie, be honest with him. I sort of promised you would be. Not, like, brutally honest, but don't put on your pastor face."

Wanda gave a hiccupping laugh. "That sounds grisly."

"You know what I mean. You don't have to pretend you're fine all the time. We can handle it if you aren't."

There was silence on the other end. Wanda finally cleared her throat. "Thanks."

"I'll keep you posted, okay?"

"Sounds good," Wanda said. "Let's get coffee or …"

"You want me to stalk them and then tell all?" Rye asked with a grin. There was a knock at her door. "I'll see you at six thirty." She hung up before Wanda could make an excuse. "Come in!"

Claudia Ramirez poked her head in, glanced around, then closed the door behind her. Rye could feel a flush climbing her neck, but that was ridiculous. Just because Claudia was standing across from her, the room now smelled of…was that maple syrup? Who smelled like that? It was too Saturday morning for her.

She did recall hearing Claudia tell someone she loved oatmeal so much that she brought it for lunch in the winter and warmed it up in the microwave. Rye had seen a small glass container of syrup in the fridge. That was it. Oatmeal with syrup. Nothing alluring about oatmeal. "What can I do for you?"

"I was actually looking for someone. Lance Duff? He's new. Nicole Laferriere told me I'd find him here."

Nicole. Well, she seemed to be popping up everywhere, didn't she? "You just missed him. I think he was headed to—" Rye glanced at his schedule, still out on her desk, conscious of Claudia's shadow cast across the page. "He's in physics."

"Oh, okay. I can catch him after school."

"Is it urgent?"

"No. He signed up for my Intro to Drama class. We only go through December, so this is a really late registration. He already asked me about helping with sets for the show and adapting one of Jonathan's designs, so I gave him the benefit of the doubt and let him in."

"How's Lance doing, if you don't mind my asking? I know it's only been a few days, but still, he seemed to settle in quickly. And the rest of your students—anyone I should be checking on?" Rye had been reaching out to teachers all week, but the school's guidance counselor had taken care of the vocational classes and the Arts Department, since many of those courses were run by professionals who contracted with the school.

Claudia smiled. "Lance seems great. He saw the need to be helpful during a difficult time." She paused, then continued, "The older students are taking it the hardest. They've known Jonathan a long time, and he's always been a positive presence in the department. I think a lot of them are more shocked by how he died than that he did die, if that makes sense?"

"Sure," Rye said. "I don't think any of us knew he had a history with drugs."

Claudia cocked her head. "I did, actually. I thought Gerard knew, too. It seemed like a nonissue."

Rye didn't know what to say to that. After last year's inquisition at the hands of the school board, she had intimate knowledge of exactly how little understanding they had for anything controversial, and a part-timer in recovery connecting with students was on that list. They were barely on board with empathetic teaching approaches. "In my experience, especially in education, neither students nor teachers are given much grace when they fall."

"That's not what I hear about you," Claudia said. "You definitely have some fans."

Rye waved a hand away to deflect the compliment. "I love what I do, and I like to go to the mat for my students. Not everyone appreciates the way I go about it."

"I've heard that, too," Claudia said. The bell rang, and she glanced up. "I need to get to class, but I'd love to check in with you about a few things—maybe at the dance? If the kids are keeping it PG?"

Rye laughed. "Sure. Sounds good." She watched the other woman walk away, then sank down at her desk. Lance. Wanda. Claudia. Death, and more death. Only a week ago, she'd thought her breakup with Andy was going to be what consumed her energy. Who could have predicted that would be the easiest part?

She did have the urge to text him, though. His was always a measured response, even in crisis, and she already missed that balance. It felt as though the school's adolescent energy was sweeping her off her feet. She could imagine Andy reminding her to think *before* she acted. It had been the same when they were ten and she'd ended up trapped on his roof for hours in the rain after trying to fix the antenna on his TV. Even earlier, when they'd met in the second grade, she'd accidentally clogged up all the sinks in the girls' bathrooms trying to wash away the evidence of a slime experiment gone awry. "A Rye" was what Andy had taken to calling her predicaments. She hadn't always appreciated it, but now his steadiness seemed underrated and desirable.

Rye wasn't in love with Andy, but she missed him. He was her ballast. He was everybody's ballast, she realized. And, much as she wanted to reach out, she needed to give him a little space. Even she was savvy enough as to realize he might be hurt that she had a crush mere days after ending things with him, even if he had done the ending. He might tease her about it someday, but probably not today.

She sighed with relief when the next knock came moments later and Costa Alvarez came in. They were an exchange student from Colombia, and as sweet as could be. They had regular visits with her at her friend Ana's behest. Ana tutored them in English, but they enjoyed having someone fluent in Spanish to talk with when they felt homesick, and after spending almost a decade in Texas, Rye was close enough.

"Hola, Costa! ¿Cómo está?"

12

SHE WAS IN THE WOODS AGAIN. SHE SHOULDN'T HAVE come, but Wink had pulled her here. Wanda felt someone behind her and spun around. Wink's lead slipped from her tense fingers, and he went shooting off into the underbrush. She cried out and dashed after him. Wanda could hear the small dog, but he was too far ahead. She was frantic to find him and get out of here.

The feeling of a person's gaze between her shoulder blades only grew as she whisper-shouted Wink's name. She turned this way and that, trying to catch a glimpse of him or of the stranger. Nothing. She stopped, her breath ragged. It was all she could hear—gasping in and out. Even Wink's scuffling had ceased, because, because...she had turned off her hearing aids. She backed toward the path again and tripped, sprawling backward into the dried leaves. Her hand brushed icy flesh, and Wanda realized she had fallen over a corpse, its glassy eyes turned toward her. She opened her mouth to scream—

"Aunt Wanda!"

She woke gasping, tangled in a fleece blanket. She almost tumbled off the couch. Lance was staring down at her. She took a moment to take it in—the living room, her nephew, the muted TV she'd put on when she got home. Since she found Jonathan Thorne's body, her nightmares had turned napping into an everyday necessity, but this was the first time she'd had a dream about the woods during the day.

"Are you okay?"

She shook her head. "Just a bad dream. I'll be all right." Wanda looked out the window. It was already dark. She shivered, then took in Lance's outfit. Clean jeans and a slim-cut plaid button-down, untucked. He was freshly showered, too, hair combed and rewound. "You look nice."

He blushed. "Thanks. I'm headed to the dance. I was wondering if I could borrow your car?"

She was silent. She'd forgotten about Lance's date with Leslie tonight.

"Are you picking Leslie up or meeting her at school?"

"Her mom's dropping her. I was going to swing by and pick up Henry, though."

"Henry Jacobs?"

"Yeah." Lance shuffled his feet.

Wanda struggled to sit up. "You do seem to attract complicated people, don't you?"

He tipped his head to one side. "Yourself included?"

Wanda smiled. "You're too perceptive for your own good." In the week since he'd arrived, Wanda and Lance had fallen into an easy routine. She's never felt quite such an effortless connection to someone, but he made a great roommate. He'd already cooked two nights, and although his room was a disaster, he kept the rest of the house at least as tidy as she did. She noticed he didn't talk about his mom much, and when Wanda had asked whether he had spoken to Mickey, he'd been evasive. It worried her, but she also knew her sister—when Mickey was in love, she had blinders on. Wanda tried not to nag him. It had been…fun having Lance here, and she wasn't ready to rock the boat.

She stood and grabbed her keys from the table. "I'd rather have you take a Lyft, but I know on weekend nights they can be hard to come by, so I'm trusting you. I know it is an old model and not exactly cool, but it is mine. Please be careful."

"I will."

"What time does the dance end?"

"Ten. If we stay that long, I'll drop Henry off and then come straight home." Lance inched toward the door.

"And if you don't stay that long…?"

"I'll drop Henry off and come straight home."

"Good answer." Wanda waved him out, turning on all the outdoor lights as he closed the door behind him. Well, the nap meant she could test the honesty of his response. Still, she couldn't quite shake the dream, so she turned the TV back up and found a cooking competition to inspire some ideas for her next fancy dinner. Right. In her dreams. In the dreams she would like to have. It reminded her that she had planned to call Hardy Rye to fish for ideas about Mickey's situation.

Wanda muted the TV and picked up the phone. He answered on the second ring.

"Hello?"

"Hardy, it's Wanda Duff. Sorry to bother you."

He laughed. "No bother, Wanda. It's six o'clock on a Friday night. Rye's chaperoning a school dance, and I'm getting ready to dish up some biscuits and beef stew. I'm not exactly the life of the party."

Her stomach rumbled. That sounded wonderful. "I was hoping to pick your brain. I don't know if Rye told you my nephew moved in with me last week."

"I heard it was unexpected."

"Very. And I have some questions about my sister's situation, if you don't mind?"

"Not at all," he said. "I'll hold supper for you."

"Oh," she stuttered. "You don't have to do that. I can make an appointment."

"I'd rather have dinner with a friend, wouldn't you?"

Wanda wondered if perhaps the former sheriff, so accustomed to being in the center of the action, felt a little lonely sometimes, too. Early retirement certainly hadn't been his plan. Hardy had been an active member of the community when he'd had a heart attack and fallen off a ladder, shattering his right leg and shoulder. His recovery had been slow, and Rye had flown in to take care of him that summer when he had refused to have a live-in nurse.

Hardy was in his late fifties, and now that he had stopped using the cane he'd needed for close to a year, he seemed barely older than Wanda. His hair was sandy brown, without the distinctive auburn his daughter sported, and his eyes were washed-out blue. She had never seen him wear anything but jeans with a white T-shirt or flannel shirt. "What can I bring?" Wanda asked, shaking herself from her reverie.

"Just yourself and a little food for thought."

"Whoops, this pseudo-parenting is new to me. I forgot I loaned Lance my car for the dance."

"I'll pack all this up and come over to your place, then, if that's all right with you?"

"See you soon." Wanda said it brightly, glancing around the kitchen, the house ... then saw her hair reflected in the window.

SHE CHANGED QUICKLY INTO JEANS AND A CRANBERRY sweater, pulling her hair back in a messy bun to display her autumn earring / hearing aid cover combination before doing a frantic living room tidy that she managed to finish just as he arrived. She was also mentally planning a future Lance-gets-a-free-pass day, having discovered that he had straightened up the kitchen before he'd asked to borrow the car. She opened and closed the door to the landfill that was his bedroom to be sure that he was not a pod person.

Hardy's beef stew was a welcome balm, and the apple crisp was amazing. She waited until they were starting in on seconds of dessert to describe her sister's pattern with men and Lance's suspicions of Enzo.

Hardy leaned back and sighed deeply. "I should preface this with my own bias. I'm not sure how much Rye has told you about her mother."

"Almost nothing. She doesn't like to talk about her, or mothers in general."

He nodded. "She was very close to her mother when she was little, and it made my wife's disappearance much harder on her."

"Disappearance?" Wanda didn't want to push, but Rye wasn't going to tell her any of this, and both the friend and the minister in her hoped to know more.

"Melanie was ... She struggled. She was diagnosed with bipolar disorder when she was in her twenties, but by then she'd already been self-medicating for her depressive episodes with drugs and alcohol for years. When she was up, she was on fire. She could be the best mother in the world for weeks at a time, and then she couldn't." He stopped, and Wanda didn't push him to go on. He moved melted ice cream around on his plate for a minute before continuing. "Rye didn't understand any of this, of course. She was seven when Melanie left. I say 'disappeared' because it had happened before, and she had always come back to us. The last time, she didn't. Never called or sent a birthday card. Nothing."

Wanda didn't know what to say, so she got up and made a pot of decaf while Hardy collected himself. Wanda wondered what the search for Melanie Rye had entailed, although she was too tactful to ask outright. Surely Hardy had followed every lead like a bloodhound while simultaneously raising his daughter and working his other cases.

"When Rye was older, I told her about her mother's condition. I wanted her to be prepared in case she ever needed counseling or medication. She thought I was defending Melanie, giving her an excuse for leaving us. That wasn't it, but I could see why she might feel that way. We haven't talked about her mother since then. I know she thinks Melanie was a self-centered…piece of work."

"And she wasn't?"

He laughed. "Well, she could be. I loved her very much, but she did put herself first. It was learned behavior. Melanie's parents didn't take care of her the way she needed them to, so she learned from a young age to put her own needs above those of others. If she didn't, who would?"

"You don't think Rye's forgiven her for leaving."

"Rye told me once that she wished her mother was a terrible person so that she could just hate her in peace. I think the memories of when Melanie was up are more painful than anything else—the possibility of happiness torn away." He was quiet as she poured them each a cup of coffee. "But I was telling you why I'm biased."

"You're a single father who raised your daughter with complete and singular devotion under very difficult circumstances while working in a high-stress, high-profile elected profession. My sister is in the same parenting position—minus being a sheriff—yet she's left her son to gallivant across Europe with some Italian stallion."

"Not exactly how I would have phrased it."

"No, but it's true. I think what's bothering me, though, is that before this, I'd never have imagined her skipping out on Lance."

"The problem is that folks like Michelle can't imagine themselves as a 'mark,'" Hardy said. "Lance is seventeen, right? Practically an adult—and she's lonely. Maybe she's financially desperate or financially flush. We don't know, but chances are, something has changed for her recently."

"And she probably won't listen to me if I give her advice."

"Has she ever?"

Wanda laughed. "No. Not really."

"Well, if or when she calls, tell her not to cosign anything or lend her credit card to him. If he gives her jewelry, she should check to see if it's real. If it isn't, it might be a play to make her feel he truly loves her and has overspent for her. If it is, he may steal it and then accuse her of losing or selling a family heirloom, but he will 'promise' not to go to the police if she reimburses him. The most common scam is that she pays for everything because for some reason he cannot access his wealth, and when she runs through her money, he tells Mickey that he didn't intend for her to do that, and his family will not let him take the relationship to the next level." He shook his head. "In another country, her options will be a lot more limited—if she doesn't speak the language, even more so."

Wanda swallowed hard. Mickey was a pain in the butt, but this was scary stuff. And Wanda had no way of knowing whether her sister was having a little fun or in for a huge scam.

"Or maybe they're truly in love and will soon fly you and Lance over for their bijou wedding."

"I doubt it, even if he is legit. Lance, maybe, but she would not think of me as matron of honor material." She looked him in the eye. "She's embarrassed by my hearing aids. Always has been." She stood and started clearing the plates, grateful that he knew how to be silent. She decided to help him. "Me, I decided to accessorize wildly rather than hiding, and wore a T-shirt that said, 'I can read your lips.' It tripled my dating life." He laughed. "Thanks, Hardy. I really appreciate it. I'll try to call Mickey tomorrow."

"Don't be surprised if she doesn't believe you. All you can do is try." He carried his dishes to the sink. "And knowing you, be there for her if things do go badly."

"Can I at least say, 'I told you so?'" Wanda asked.

Hardy grinned. "The satisfaction might be fleeting, but as Rye says, you do you."

"High road it is," Wanda said, rolling her eyes.

She tried to hand Hardy his leftovers, but he took them and put them in her fridge instead. "You have a teenager now. You need this more than I do."

"That's true. Well, maybe we can do this again, and I will…Well, maybe not cook. This would be tough to follow. I do a mean delivery, though."

"I'd like that."

As Hardy drove off, Wanda wished she could have just one real date as pleasant as this antiscam tutorial had been.

13

RYE DIDN'T RECOGNIZE THE SONG PLAYING, BUT THAT wasn't unusual. She didn't keep up with what her students preferred to play, since she was generally fine with whatever was on as long as it was appropriate. The student council liked to have control over the playlist, and the school saved money by hiring former students for the monthly dances rather than shelling out for a more experienced DJ.

Her chaperoning duties were essentially to make sure everyone stayed sober and that brawls were contained. Fistfights were rare and much easier to handle than the emotionally charged verbal infighting she heard more frequently. Something about being over thirty made her invisible, and whole melodramatic worlds unfolded in front of her while she scanned the room.

"You look pretty tonight," Camila said, striding up with a cup of punch for each of them. She took a sip and made a face. "This is foul."

Rye laughed. "I know. If water bottles weren't so easily refilled with vodka, we'd all be a lot happier and more hydrated."

"Seriously." She strung her arm through Rye's. "How are you holding up? I feel like I've barely seen you this week."

Rye leaned into her friend. "I know. I've stayed late every night, and I'm still so behind."

"Did you know Jonathan Thorne well? I'm sort of embarrassed to admit this, but I'm not sure I would have been able to pick him out of a lineup."

"He started teaching here right before I graduated. I don't think I've run into him since I started working here, though," Rye admitted. She kept an eye on a couple sophomores hanging out by the back door. They seemed nervous, which was generally a sign that they were waiting on someone to deliver something they weren't supposed to have.

Claudia swooped in on them, and after a minute's conversation, the boys slouched out. Rye's eyes followed the other woman as she took up a semipermanent position by the door.

Camila followed her gaze. "So how are you feeling about things with Andy? I saw your text, but I never got to ask you what happened."

"It was the sweetest breakup you could imagine. No hard feelings. No drama. We're still friends, and we're both happier for it—or at least I am, and he suggested it, so it must be the right thing for him, too."

"Which isn't exactly the same thing as being happy about it," Camila observed.

"That's true, but Andy— I know you don't know him well, but he leans toward honesty. I think if he still had feelings for me and we'd only broken up so he could focus on his family, I'd know. This felt more like we both knew it wasn't the right fit."

Camila seemed to relax and smiled. "He seems like a great guy."

"He is. I'm glad we tried, even if it didn't work out." Rye's eyes scanned the crowd as the song tempo picked up, but the students seemed a little subdued tonight. "If we hadn't, I think I'd always be wondering, and it would hang over other relationships. But, hey! He's free, and you're free …"

"Hmm," her friend said, brushing a piece of lint off her skirt. "Any other prospects for you?"

Rye's eyes only blinked in the direction of Claudia, but she could feel Camila's attention sharpen. "Hadn't really thought about it," Rye lied poorly.

Camila generously let the topic drop. "I'm trying to talk Ana and Mike into doing a winter obstacle course. We need a team of four—it's a relay, and it's at New Year's, but totally fresh from the winter race that's been going on forever. I know it's not exactly your thing, but I'd love to train with you. Ana has gotten much faster than me since she started working out with Tyler, and Mike prefers to wing it."

"I'd like to see any of them try to beat you in a sprint." Rye chuckled.

"Oh, I'd leave them in the dust. It's just these endurance events in the freezing cold where they kick my butt," Camila replied. "I told you about how Ana and I are trying to run a race in every state, right? Whenever we sign up for a marathon, or even a half, she destroys me. But when it comes to the 5k and 10k, I power through. I don't hold back at all."

"That's the Camila I know."

"Luckily, the Rye I know won't be afraid to take on the sledding section of the relay," Camila said with a wink.

Rye laughed. "You mean I'm the only adult you know willing to throw myself down a hill on a flimsy piece of plastic."

"Yes." Camila nodded. "You have to join us. None of us can handle that. I've seen you sled on cardboard pulled from the school dumpster, so I know you have the skills."

"What do I have to do, exactly?" Rye felt, rather than saw, Claudia come up behind her.

"Sorry to bother you," Claudia said, "but I just heard a rumor that a bunch of kids have headed up into the woods where Jonathan was found. I didn't know if I should call the police or if we should check it out first to see if it's true?"

Rye sucked in a breath. "Let's check it out. We'll call it in if we see anything illegal." She turned to Camila. "Can you and Maxine hold down the fort here?"

"Of course," Camila said. "I'll text you the details for the relay."

"I didn't even agree yet," Rye cautioned her.

"But you will. Trust me, it's going to be fun," Camila said. "Now go bust some teens."

Rye and Claudia grabbed their coats and headed out the back door. It was only mid-October, but the night was bitterly cold. A light snow was falling, and under different circumstances it might have been romantic. As it was, Rye felt chilled to the bone.

Halfway across the parking lot, the sounds of the dance faded away, and they could only hear the occasional car passing on the street. Neither of them was inclined to break the silence, so they walked as quickly as they could, Rye in the low-heeled ankle boots she could stand in for hours without blisters, Claudia in soft velvet ballet flats that looked like they were going to be destroyed by the wet, icy trail.

Once they were under the trees, it was complete blackness, with only their phones to light the path. They heard voices raised in song. It was eerie cutting through the cold air, and the lyrics of the Charlie Worsham tune about wishing to be stoned when Jesus takes you home jarred her sense of decency, meaning she was officially middle-aged.

Rye could see light through the trees now, and although she hadn't been out to where Jonathan Thorne's body had been found, shreds of police tape proved they were near the site.

"A couple of my students are really into Americana. I've heard them singing a few arrangements that sound similar, though not this one," Claudia whispered. "I guess everyone grieves in their own way, huh?"

"I guess so." Rye refrained from saying that a song about drug use seemed in poor taste to honor a man in recovery from drug abuse.

"Should we break it up?" Claudia asked.

Rye didn't have a chance to answer. A scream cut through the air. Rye took off before the sound died. It hadn't come from the same direction as the music, and although she could barely see the ground under her feet, she pushed through the dense underbrush, frozen branches snapping as her hands reached out ahead of her.

She stumbled to a stop as her path met the trail and she almost fell over the girl flung across the ground. Rye could barely make out a body beneath her. She gently pulled the girl up. "Are you hurt?"

The girl just cried and tried to cling to the other body revealed on the ground. "Henry! Wake up, please. *Please,*" she sobbed.

"Tell me what's happened so I can help him." Rye was dimly aware that the boy at her feet was Henry Jacobs. She had seen him only a few days ago, when he and his mother had stopped by the office to pick up work for him to do at home while they made arrangements for his brother's funeral.

"He took something before we left the dance. I don't know what."

Rye pushed her out of the way and felt for a pulse. She knew even medics couldn't always find them, but at least this kid felt warm. She leaned closer and could hear his breath, although it was shallow. She hit the emergency button on her phone and turned the flashlight back on so she could see better.

"Nine-one-one. What's your emergency?"

"My name is Prudence Rye. I'm the vice principal at Stoneridge. I'm in the woods behind the school—south side of the parking lot. Not sure where exactly, but I'm on a cross-country path, and I think it's relatively close to where Jonathan Thorne's body was found, if that helps. I have a teenage boy, unconscious. Breathing is shallow."

"Do you know what happened?" the calm voice continued.

"The girl with him said he took something." Rye looked up at her. "Was it pills? Injected?"

"Pills," she whispered.

"She says he took pills."

"How soon did he collapse after he took them?" By this point, Rye had put the phone on speaker. She reached out and clasped the girl's hand.

She was shaking. "I don't know."

"Approximately? A minute? Five? An hour?" the operator asked.

"I don't know." She started crying again.

"How many pills did he take? Do you know what it was?

The girl just shook her head. "He got them from his brother's room," she said. "His brother— He died. He was hit by a car. Henry found them in Ross's drawer."

The operator jumped in. "Do you have any idea how many he took?"

The girl shook her head. "One with me. Probably at least one before he got here."

Rye could hear sirens in the distance. Who knew how long it would take to find them? She hoped Claudia had gone back to try to lead them in, or that she'd at least gone to the kids who were already in the woods.

"Was he drinking alcohol?" the operator asked.

The girl looked terrified. Rye answered on her behalf. "I can smell it on his breath. I don't know how much, but yes."

"Seizures?"

"He was shaking," the girl said.

"Is that when you screamed?" Rye asked. She nodded. "That was the right thing to do," Rye told her. "You helped me find you." She could see the girl's teeth starting to chatter. Shock was clearly setting in. She took off her own coat and wrapped it around the girl, pulling her close. "I think— What's your name?"

"Emma. Emma Reyes."

"I think Emma is going into shock," Rye told the operator. "I'm doing my best to keep her warm. Do you know how soon help might be here? Is there anything I can do?"

"Help should be there almost now," the woman on the other end of the line said calmly. Rye realized it was Jaz Malone and felt somehow better. "If you have a flashlight, make sure it's on. When the sirens stop, start shouting. If you can hear them, they can hear you."

Rye hugged Emma close. The teenager's body was shuddering. Rye prayed it was cold and shock, and not a second overdose.

What felt like hours later, emergency responders came running up the path toward Rye as she shouted raggedly, "We're here, we're here!"

She felt like she was in the center of a tornado of light and sound. She dimly saw a medic inject Henry Jacobs with what was probably naloxone and then go for nasal administration with Emma. Rye had never thought *Romeo and Juliet* was a romantic story, but if their deaths were anything like this— She was overwhelmed by a wave of terror for all children.

Amid the chaos, she felt a warm hand on her shoulder. She looked up to see Claudia's pale face. Rye forced her frozen legs to unfold. "I'm sorry I left you behind," she said, her breath white in the air.

Claudia reached out and hugged her tightly. She pulled the blanket the EMTs had given Rye tightly around her shoulders. "Can I help you down to the ambulance?"

"I don't need an ambulance. I'm fine." Her voice sounded odd, echoing inside her head.

"She needs to see someone," a paramedic said as he rushed by. Their focus was on Henry and Emma, loaded onto stretchers and headed down the path.

A police officer—Ryan Phennen, Rye realized after a moment—appeared at her side. "We need to take a statement from you."

"Surely we can do that down in the parking lot," Claudia said. "It's freezing out here." She looked at Rye. "You lost your coat?"

"Emma has it."

"Of course. Let's get you down to the school, and then once you can feel your fingers again, you can answer all the questions." She glanced up at the sheriff. "Right?"

He begrudgingly waved them away. "Don't leave the school before I've talked to you," he warned Rye.

"Even if I did, you know where I live."

"You know I do." He nodded in the direction they were headed. "Pretty sure your dad is down there already. Just a heads up."

"Your dad?" Claudia asked as they stumbled down the trail together.

"Hardy Rye, former sheriff. Current police scanner junkie."

"Sheriff Rye's your father?" Claudia whistled.

"*Former* sheriff."

"My mom had the biggest crush on him. She worked on all his campaigns." Claudia took on more of Rye's weight as they stumbled over another exposed root. "In another life, we could have been sisters." Claudia stopped to readjust her grip, slinging Rye's arm over her shoulder.

Claudia's breath was warm on Rye's ear, and it sent a much-needed burst of heat through her body. She hadn't been outside for very long, but it felt like her lower body had atrophied from sitting on the frozen ground. Her feet burned with the cold.

They limped the rest of the way in silence. The walk in hadn't seemed far, but it was an endless trip back to the parking lot, filled with its silent red and blue lights. By the time they arrived, the ambulances were gone, but a firefighter helped her the rest of the way into the school so that Claudia could head in to help with crowd control. All students were being held in the cafeteria until parents arrived to pick them up. Rye knew there would be searches of bags on the way out.

She was alone in the classroom adjacent to the cafeteria. It was hot and bright, but she still felt chilled. She could hear the rumble of voices through the wall. She wanted to be in there, comforting her students, but she knew Phennen would need to speak with her before she could go, and the adrenaline had drained away, leaving her exhausted.

The door opened. She lifted her head off the desk to see her dad standing in the doorway. Tears pricked her eyes at the sight of him. She pushed herself to standing as he came up and pulled her into a fierce hug.

"Dad?"

"Both of them were alive when the ambulances left. I'll find out more as soon as I can."

She let out a single sob of relief that he understood what she needed to know to keep going tonight. Rye clung to him until she felt the shivering slow. He eased her back into the wooden chair and pulled up another next to her. He held onto her hand until she pulled away and straightened, wiping her eyes.

"I don't know if you heard, but that boy is Ross Jacobs's younger brother. The guy who died last week. Not the teacher, I mean, but—"

"I know who you mean." Hardy's eyebrows drew together. "Ross Jacobs—standout student, graduated two years ago. Full ride to Brown. Delayed admittance a year. Hit-and-run on Route 111, suspicious lack of skid marks."

Rye hadn't known all of that. She had been so focused on handling the fallout from Jonathan Thorne's death that she hadn't sought out any details on the second victim.

"When you mentioned to me the other night that Wanda was questioning the official police report, I dug a little deeper," he said.

The door opened. Ryan Phennen stood in the doorway accompanied by a younger man who closely resembled him but was more striking. This must be Ryan's brother, Tyler. Rye hadn't realized Ana was dating a police officer. Ana said she'd met him at a boot camp class, though, and this guy had the physique.

"Hardy." Ryan acknowledged his former boss curtly. "I need you to clear out so I can take her statement."

"Of course," her father said. "I'll wait for you?"

"I'm okay." She was desperate to know what else he'd turned up, but knowing Ryan, that would have to wait awhile. He could be both pedantic and petty, and the current sheriff had never forgiven Rye for some of the completely harmless practical jokes she'd played on him when she was in high school and he was new to the force, or for when Hardy had beaten him at a pie baking contest and passed him over for a promotion Ryan had felt he deserved. Hardy and Ryan had come to terms with their own disagreements over the years, but she had never hashed things out with him. In hindsight, Rye knew their strained relationship was at least in part her fault, but this was not the time to admit that to Ryan.

"I have my car," she said. She took the paper cup the younger man slid across the desk to her. Hot chocolate from the vending machine. Better than nothing. "If I'm too tired to drive, I'll ask Camila for a ride, okay?"

Hardy hesitated for a moment, then nodded. "I'll wait up for you."

"Dad," she said, as he was about to close the door. "Wanda's nephew, Lance, was here tonight. Can you make sure he got picked up?"

"He's got her car."

"How do you know that?"

He just saluted and closed the door behind him.

Ryan inclined his head to her. "Do you need anything else before we get started?"

Rye sat up and stretched, checking in with her body. She felt drained, and she had a few cuts from running through the trees, but other than that she was fine, physically. She shook her head. "Are you Ana's Tyler?" she asked the younger man.

Tyler smiled, although Ryan looked surprised and a little annoyed. It was his default expression, so Rye didn't put too much stock in it. "I am," Tyler answered. "It's nice to finally meet you. She and Ryan have both told me so much about you." He smiled.

He had a warmth that his brother lacked, and Rye found herself grinning back at him.

"It's nice to put a face with the name," she said.

"Are we done with 'getting to know you'?" Ryan asked.

Rye wasn't sure what Wanda had ever seen in him. Maybe he was more charming to people who weren't her.

"What do you need from me?" she asked.

Tyler flipped open a notebook. "Tell us what happened."

Rye recounted the events of the evening to the best of her knowledge. She even mentioned the kids she'd seen by the back door who Claudia had sent packing, although she'd forgotten to ask her about them. They probably weren't involved, but Rye knew anything might be helpful.

"I don't know how or if this is connected to Jonathan Thorne's death," Rye said. Her hot chocolate was empty in front of her, and her whole body was slumped with exhaustion. Tyler pulled a bag of peanut M&Ms out of his jacket and slid them across the table to her. She smiled with deep gratitude as she opened it and popped a couple in her mouth. "Henry apparently got the drugs from his brother's room, but I haven't heard that there was a connection between Ross Jacobs and Thorne."

The brothers exchanged a glance, and Tyler ducked his gaze to his notepad. "It's an open investigation," Ryan said gruffly.

Rye perked up. "I was under the impression Thorne's death was a closed case." She didn't need to mention that Wanda had already told her it was murder.

"It was," Tyler said. Rye heard more than saw Ryan deliver a kick to his brother's shins.

"But it's not now?"

Ryan studied her face intently. "You haven't heard the rumors?"

Rye shook her head. "About what?"

"Jonathan Thorne having a relationship with Ross Jacobs." Ryan's eyes locked on hers.

She sat straight up. "What? No…with a student?"

Ryan held up a hand. He could clearly see where her mind was going. "Not when he was in school. Jacobs came back from Brown for the summer and was working at the Barndoor Theatre selling tickets. Apparently, he and Thorne met there. As far as we know, they didn't cross paths when Jacobs was at school."

"I thought Thorne was married," Rye said.

"So?" Ryan asked.

"So why would he be openly dating, seeing, *whatever* a twenty-year-old?" Rye asked.

"More importantly, why did they both die on the same day?" Ryan replied. "And what does his little brother know about it?"

Rye hid her shock that he was being so informative. He must want something. She shook her head. "Couldn't Henry have taken drugs because he's depressed about his brother's death?"

"Maybe." Ryan leaned back in his chair.

Rye started to speak, then stopped. She began again. "I appreciate your information. I'm glad you're trusting me with it, but I'm also not sure why. You said it's an open investigation."

"It is, and I expect you to treat this information with strict confidentiality. Gerard Mendoza hasn't been told this, and to be honest, you shouldn't be either." He rubbed his neck. "But the bottom line is, you know these kids better than we do, and we need information. If something more is going on, I need to know, and I need to know right away. I can't be here every day."

"You want an informant."

"Something like that," he agreed.

"Do you have a suspect? Or some leads? Anything to narrow it down from the eleven hundred students and seventy or so faculty and staff members?"

"Claudia Ramirez," Ryan said. "Aside from Mendoza, she's worked with Thorne the longest. Henry Jacobs and Emma Reyes are both current students of hers. She overlapped one year with Ross. She claimed to be in her office at the time of Thorne's death and in bed at the time of Ross's accident, but she was alone, so no real alibi."

Rye was sorry she'd asked. The information she probably could have gotten from her dad wasn't worth the price. "So you want me to spy on her? Interrogate her? What?" She thought of the new dress she'd purchased for their date.

"When we interviewed her in her office earlier, I happened to notice her wall calendar. Looks like you have plans tomorrow night?"

Rye could say a lot of unflattering things about Sheriff Ryan Phennen, but he was keenly observant and excellent at his job. She shrugged noncommittally.

"That's probably a good place to start." Ryan grabbed his hat and stood up, the action pulling his brother up in his wake. Sheriff Phennen strode out of the room, but Tyler held back as Rye levered herself out of the seat.

"She's not our only suspect," Tyler murmured to her, his look sympathetic. She wondered if he'd seen Claudia helping Rye in the parking lot earlier. It had felt intimate in the moment, but she was unaware of who might have seen or overheard them. The possibility of Ryan Phennen recognizing their personal connection and exploiting it filled her with rage.

Rye was grateful for the kernel of kindness. "Thanks," Rye said. "See you around."

He tipped his hat to her and followed his brother out. Rye could see what Ana liked about him. She just hoped he was worth the admiration.

14

Lance was quiet. Three pieces of baguette with honey was unlike his usual breakfast—either steel-cut oats or a fastidious meal that consisted of multigrain toast points and a soft-boiled egg in a blue-and-white porcelain egg cup he had brought from California in the seemingly bottomless depths of his backpack. There had to be a story about that egg cup, but she hadn't asked.

Wanda decided to turn off her audiobook, but not before Lance asked, "Is this book narrated by a dog?"

"Yup." Wanda grinned. "Well, it's the fictional personification of how a dog thinks. Every nap is the best nap. Every walk is the best walk. Ever bowl of kibble is …"

"Got it. And why?"

"Chet is the canine half of detective duo Bernie and Chet, written by Spencer Quinn."

Halfway to his mouth, Lance's fourth chunk of baguette was dripping on the table. "And the dog is the narrator, even though there's a human detective?"

"Yes, beloved narrator. Great books, clever murders."

"What is it with middle-aged women and murder?"

Revenge. "How was the dance?"

"Not great. You heard about what happened?"

Wanda nodded. "I did. Rye—Vice Principal Rye—called me this morning."

"The kid she found—it was Henry."

Wanda felt her chest constrict. She had only been at this foster parent gig for a week, and her nephew's only friend was a drug addict. "I didn't know. I'm so sorry."

"I didn't know he was into drugs." He could tell she was spiraling. Probably in Lance's experience spiraling turned into helicopter rotors. "He's just the only person I've really talked to this week."

"What about Leslie?"

He shrugged. "Leslie's really quiet. Nicole was talking to me nonstop. I guess I don't really have much in common with them. I sing, but that's not really enough."

"Not going to see her again?" Wanda tried not to let the relief show on her face.

"Probably not. I'm not looking for a girlfriend. The stuff with my mom—it's enough romantic drama for me."

Wanda resisted the urge to jump up and hug Lance. He occasionally showed a quiet maturity that she loved, but she knew a golden retriever approach didn't work with teenagers. "I'm glad you know what you need."

He brought his plate to the sink, glanced back at her, and then put it in the dishwasher instead. "Do you think it would be okay if I went over to see Henry this morning? We were going to play video games today, but I don't know if he can...or should." Lance leaned against the counter. "I mean, his brother just died. Last night *he* could have died." He shook his head.

"That's a lot for you to take on with someone you just met," Wanda said gently.

"Maybe the minister gene runs in the family." Lance gave a weak laugh.

Mickey would hate that. "Why don't you just text him and see whether he still wants you to come?"

"Because he would think I didn't want to and blow me off."

"Fair enough. I'll drop you—" She saw that he was about to protest and cut him off. "Nope. I need the car. I'll come in with you, and then if he's still feeling lousy, we'll both leave."

"Or if Emma is there, you need me for errands. I'll owe you a mocha."

"Deal."

Wanda got ready. Before she forgot, she texted Tony.

> *Lance told me he sings. Don't know what that means. Your move, Johann Sebastian.*

HENRY AND HIS MOTHER LIVED IN A MODULAR HOME in a neighborhood that was a mix of prefab and older houses. Wanda tried to connect this neighborhood with Ross Jacobs's acceptance to Brown, which in her experience drew wealthier kids.

Henry's mother invited them into the kitchen, and Wanda realized the family must have had money once. Autumn Jacobs's clothes were expensive, but even to Wanda's inexperienced eye for fashion they looked dated. The furniture was beautiful but well-worn.

"I hope we're not intruding. My nephew had plans with Henry today, but I wasn't sure if he was ready for company. I made Lance bring me along so I could be sure."

Lance blushed, but Wanda knew he was relieved to have her take control of this situation. "I can come another day if he's resting," he said.

Autumn shook her head. "He's out back." She gestured toward the window. There was a freestanding shed that must have been Henry's domain. It had wires running into it. "The doctor released him on the strict orders that he stay in bed and rest. I couldn't keep him in bed, but he's resting, I suppose." She opened the door for Lance. "Head on out. See if he's up for some company."

Lance glanced at Wanda. "I'll wait for a few minutes, if that's okay?" Wanda asked Autumn. Her nephew took off across the lawn, hands jammed in his pockets.

"Ross helped Henry work on that shed for months. It's even got a little alarm system that they built from a kit. No bathroom or fridge, so I at least see Henry occasionally." She poured Wanda a cup of coffee and put cream and sugar on the table. She waved Wanda into a seat.

The woman across from her was obviously smart enough to know that clothes could be old if they were well-made, but hair and teeth have to be perfect to stay in the privileged class. They were perfect. There was no wedding ring. The coffee smelled like heaven.

"I'm sorry about Ross." Wanda knew from experience that dancing around a tragedy would only make those affected feel worse, as though it was their responsibility to make others feel less awkward or sad.

Autumn's mask crumpled. She looked grief-stricken. "I can't believe he's gone. He was my shining star." She stared down into her cup. "He was my rock after the divorce. Without him, I don't know what Henry and I would have done." She glanced up at a family portrait on the wall. A striking young woman stood next to

Autumn, her face solemn. "That's Melissa," Autumn said, answering Wanda's unasked question. "I had her when I was in college. It's … complicated." Wanda just nodded. "She lives in Rhode Island. Runs a no-kill cat shelter with her partner."

"She's Henry and Ross's half sister?" Wanda asked.

"Yes. But she graduated from high school almost fifteen years ago. She hasn't lived with us since the boys were little. My relationship with her is … separate from the boys. Not my choice, but she knew long before I did that their father was a cruel person. She told me she wasn't going to stick around and watch him … well, that if I wasn't going to leave him, she would go."

"That must have been difficult for you."

Autumn shrugged. "She was right. But I had two young children and no degree. No source of income. At eighteen, she could choose to be free of her family. To her, it seemed straightforward." She took a sip of her coffee. "She understands better now."

"It sounds like Ross was the one who helped Henry through the divorce," Wanda said gently.

"He did his best. My ex-husband's business—he used to be in construction—was still very successful by the time Henry was old enough to notice such things. He was used to a much different lifestyle than we have now. After the company went under and we moved here, Henry was so angry. Ross was the only one who could really get through to him." She sighed. "Then, when Ross came out, my ex cut him off. Henry would come home from weekends with his dad and lash out at his brother."

"That must have been painful to see."

"Yes. Ross just avoided him, but Henry wanted his father to be the man he remembered. And he wanted me to take him back. There are things you just can't explain to children." Autumn wiped away a tear carefully with the edge of her napkin.

Wanda had seen, understood, and still she was always angry with those tears of guilt that abused partners shed. She could not yet do the math, but however long it had been, this woman still needed therapy. Blaming herself was no good for anyone.

Autumn looked up from her inscrutable contemplation of the empty coffee cup. "Didn't do a good job of it by myself, though, did I? Ross is gone. Henry could have been—"

"But he's not gone. He's here." Wanda had to repeat these words far too often. The rate of overdoses—both accidental and intentional—was still rising. At times, Wanda felt like she was being swamped by the calls and counseling she offered to those who were affected. "Have you thought about family therapy? Henry might benefit from talking to someone about all of this."

"I see my therapist weekly, and it's helped. Henry hasn't been willing to go."

Wanda nodded. If the therapist was any good, this woman must have been in terrible shape. And a child's death and near death? She promised herself to come back when she wasn't being a sort-of parent.

Wanda also knew she probably should at least call the therapist Rye had told her about. She was used to advising other people to seek help, but accepting that she needed it herself was a lot harder than pouring an extra glass of wine each evening. "Lance hasn't been staying with me for very long, but I can imagine how hard it must be to try to get a kid their age to do something they don't want to do."

Autumn's eyes closed for a long moment, as though someone had finally said aloud what she had been thinking for so long. "Exactly. I want to help him, but I don't want him to hate me." She cleared her throat. "Ross went to therapy for a while after he came out. Then there was rehab, and that seemed to work. I didn't even know he was using drugs. He hid it so well, but when he lost his job, he came to me. You knew he had to take a year between high school and college to work? Even with the scholarship?" Wanda nodded. Of course, she had not known. She knew now.

Autumn couldn't stop the tears. "He had a good sponsor, he told me. Ross said that made all the difference. And his freshman year was great, but then he quit ..."

"Had you met his sponsor?" Wanda asked.

"Oh, yes. Nice young man." Her face crumpled. "He died the same day as Ross. I don't know if you heard about it. I'm glad Ross didn't know. It would have broken his heart to know that Jonathan backslid like that."

Wanda felt her entire body go numb. Jonathan Thorne had been Ross's sponsor? Was this what Ryan had been keeping from her? But Jonathan had not backslid. It wasn't her place to say that his death was now counted as murder.

Thankfully, Lance came bounding up the steps to the back door. "Thank you for the coffee, Autumn."

"Anytime." The woman clasped Wanda's hand tightly for a moment before showing them to the door.

Lance was silent on the ride back from the Jacobs house. Wanda's brain was buzzing with all she'd learned, so she didn't press him about his visit. She dropped him at the house and headed for a home visit of her own to see a parishioner just out of the hospital. Then to the office to finish up a few things and make phone calls she had been putting off.

WHEN SHE RETURNED, THE HOUSE WAS TOO STILL. SHE had gotten used to the rustles of living with another person. The chirps of his computer games, the pinging of cell phone, the tap tapping when he did homework late at night. It was a comforting melody. Now, though, there was vacant silence. As her eyes adjusted in the dark of the fall afternoon, she saw him lying on the sofa asleep, his arm hanging off the edge.

The foolish boy, he had been mixing. She spotted an empty beer and the bottle of Canadian Club. She picked it up—about an inch missing.

Moment of self-reflection: Why did she know exactly how much alcohol was in the bottle? Why was she tiptoeing around her nephew when she should be reading him the parsonage riot act? Why, why, why was she tempted to let him sleep it off with no comment for fear of damaging their fragile new relationship? She thought of Autumn, a loving mother who was so afraid to be the bad guy that she was losing the only son she had left. Lance was not Wanda's buddy. He was her responsibility, and she loved him enough to call him on this. And she was relieved, because she knew enough about alcohol to know that if he'd passed out after a beer and a couple shots of the hard stuff, he wasn't a habitual drinker.

Wanda started coffee. She threw on all the lights and hauled Lance to a sitting position. He went from sleep to chatterbox in a disoriented moment.

"Hey, Aunt Wanda! Just having a little power nap. Are you back already?" He reached out and softly patted her hair with a smile. "It's so nice to see you." Lance wavered a little, looking a bit like a cartoon character with an imaginary circle of birds flying around his head. "Whoa, I think I'll just sit down for a moment." He didn't seem to realize he was already seated.

"Come with me." Wanda was a short woman—Lance had that foot on her—but she made up the difference in determination and the experience of sobering herself up on multiple occasions. Not recently, but that kind of memory does not die.

She should have cleared all the alcohol out, if not before Lance arrived, at least at the same time as she'd done the medicine cabinet. Wanda silently berated herself as she poured herself coffee with cream and sugar and left his black. He slumped into a seat on the other side and reached for the cream.

"Don't do it, or you'll see your stomach inside out."

He swilled it down without the cream and winced. "I'm fine." He rubbed his face and yawned. "Did you have a good date?"

Wanda cocked her head at him. "Date?"

He started to laugh. "Not date. I mean…I mean …" His gaze wandered off. She waited, but when he looked back at her, he seemed to be expecting her to fill in the blanks.

"Drink the coffee." He did. "Do you drink a lot?"

"Do you?" But he said it with a smile, as though he were making conversation with a stranger at a party rather than accusing his aunt of something. He focused on a point just past her ear, took another sip of the coffee, and made a face, pushing it away. "I think that coffee's gone off, Aunt Wanda."

"You're drunk, Lance."

He shook his head. "I don't think so. I only had, like"—he tapped his fingers on the table—"like, two drinks. And they did not taste good. I think your beer maybe's gone bad too." He made a face.

"Do you drink a lot?"

He shook his head. "I never get invited to those parties. I mean, I did, like, one time, but I brought a cake, and everyone thought I was weird. Can you believe that?" He leaned in, staring at her with an earnest expression. "Wouldn't you rather have cake than Jim Bean?" He licked his lips. "Beam? What's it called again?"

"So why did you do it today?"

Lance stared at her. "Do what?"

"Drink, Lance." Wanda was out of practice dealing with this sort of thing.

He took another sip of the coffee, gagging a little. "No, I'm good."

She took a slow breath in, then let it out. "Lance, why did you decide to have a couple of shots and a beer today if you don't normally drink?"

"Oh, that." He stared at her for a minute, and Wanda wondered if he'd lost his train of thought again. "Henry."

"Seeing Henry make you want to drink?"

"It felt…gross?" Wanda wasn't sure if that was a question, so she waited for Lance to continue. "Henry's sad about his brother's death, but he was also, like, really angry at him."

"For dying?"

"No, before. Like he was jealous. Like he wanted to hurt Ross."

Wanda tried to keep her tone light. "Did he?"

"Hurt him?" Lance shrugged. "I don't know. He was messed up. Not like at school. At school, he's been cool."

She could almost see his brain getting distracted by the rhyme. "So you didn't get this bad feeling when you were hanging out with him before?"

He shook his head, then seemed to consider. "Maybe when his girlfriend hung out with us at lunch, but otherwise, no. We've mostly just been playing *Fortnite* together. You know, online?"

She did know. Wanda might not have any interest in video games herself, but she'd run enough youth groups to know that those games, and the socializing that happened while kids were playing, was a huge part of adolescent relationships. "I do." A thought occurred to her that had nothing to do with Henry and everything to do with Lance's happiness here. "Have you been able to hang with your old friends that way, too?" Maybe that was why he seemed to adjust quickly the past week. He didn't have to leave everyone behind even though he was across the country.

Lance stared at her. He looked...sad. "No. I have a new character. Henry and a couple of other guys from school have let me jump in and play, but ..." He stopped and shook his head. "I thought Henry was going to be different."

"Different how?" Wanda kept her voice gentle.

"I have this, like, ability to hang out with the most messed-up kid. Every school. Every single one." Lance stood up and started pacing. "I'm not talking about the guys that party, either. No. It's the ones that are just...destructive. The ones that have to break shi...stuff. Or steal." He shook his head. "I always end up in the headmaster's office trying to explain why there's a car in the pool, or a cow in the cafeteria."

"A...cow?"

"It sounds funny, right? Harmless stuff. It always starts out as a prank. They have this idea it would be so funny, and then their dads can buy them out of trouble, and I'm sent packing." Lance wilted. "Henry seemed okay. Not like those other guys. But he might be worse, and now you're going to send me to my dad's—"

"What? Lance, no. I love having you here! I'm not sending you anywhere unless your mother forces me to, okay?"

He studied her face, his eyes a little clearer. "Really?"

"Really. You're stuck with me." She held out a hand, and he gave it a tentative squeeze.

Lance rubbed his chest and let out a loud belch, ruining the moment. "Sorry."

"It's okay." Wanda paused. "The burping. Not the drinking."

"Are you going to tell my mom?"

"Does she know that you drink sometimes?"

He shook his head. "I don't think so. You know she—" He cut himself off. "Am I a bad person if I don't want to be friends with Henry?"

"No," Wanda said. Her first responsibility was to her nephew, and that was what she would honor. When he sobered up, they could talk more, and she would loop Rye in about Lance's past as a sidekick and what he'd said about Henry so she could keep an eye on them both.

The coffee was gone, so she gave Lance water, and when the bread popped up, toast with butter, while she ate some soup warmed from the fridge. He ate and drank obediently.

"Feel any better?"

"A little. Aunt Wanda, I'm sorry."

"Me too, Lance. And just so you know, we will be talking about this again."

"I know."

"I'm also sorry about the plate of fried rice and bottle of soy sauce I found spilled all over the couch and floor. You have a date with the spot remover tomorrow morning."

Lance nodded sagely and winked at her, clearly not completely sobered by his meal. "So that's where that went."

WHEN WANDA LOOKED IN ON HER NEPHEW EARLY IN the morning, she reflected that he was appropriately somber, if not downright apologetic. Maybe he would nap this morning—she was not going to make him come to church. She was deeply grateful to God, and to Lisa's demanding organization, that her sermons now were done on Thursdays. She felt like she had been through a couple of lifetimes since Thursday. As Lance stared aimlessly into the fridge, she said, "Water. Juice. Ginger tea. Food."

"Yes, ma'am." One eyebrow was raised. The old Lance.

She had two mugs of tea at the table and sourdough toast with an over-easy egg and three slices of bacon. He drank and ate.

"Are you going to yell at me?" Lance asked as he wiped his plate clean.

"No, but I'm going to give you some advice. You have alcoholism and drug addiction on both sides of your family. I can't tell you what to do, but you could ruin your life easily if you use alcohol as a coping mechanism."

"You drink."

"I'm not underage, and I try to be responsible. Ready for coffee?"

"Yes, please."

"Look, I drink, and we have the same family. I work harder than other people not to lose the distinction between relaxing and drowning sorrow. Sometimes I miscalculate." She ignored the voice in her head whispering that in the last few months, that line had gone blurry. Wanda occupied herself with her English muffin and grapefruit marmalade. "Let's talk about Henry." She could see Lance mentally retreat. "Last night, you told me he was different. Angry. Maybe angry enough to want to hurt his brother."

Lance appeared fascinated by his coffee cup.

Wanda took a deep breath and tried to figure out how to explain how close love and hate could be, and how terribly abandoned a person could feel when someone died, especially if their relationship wasn't in a great place when it happened.

"Henry loved Ross. His mom told me that they used to be really close, but in the last year or two, they were having a hard time," Wanda said. "Henry might feel guilty if he was upset with his brother before the accident. That makes the grieving process much more difficult."

"It's more than that," Lance interrupted. "Henry kept saying that Ross always got everything he wanted, and he never did. His brother was gay, and I guess his dad is a homophobic jerk. But Henry also told me he liked having his dad to himself, even though he seemed kind of scared of him." He shivered. "The way Henry talked about him ..."

Wanda could see that whatever Henry had told Lance, it had disturbed him more than a casual comment should.

"Did you mean what you said last night? About it being okay if I decide not to hang out with him?"

"I do. And if you need to give him a reason, tell him that your mom and I talked about it and aren't comfortable with you spending time right now with someone who's struggling with drugs." Lance looked relieved. "I don't mind taking the blame for this one, as long as you promise me to talk with a counselor. I found one that does online sessions. Thought that might be more your speed."

"Therapy, huh? I'll do it if you will."

Wanda stared at him, speechless for once.

Lance shrugged. "You have nightmares. You went through something scary last spring. Your friends are all people you work with, and you seem to drink every day. Vice Principal Rye told me to let you and my mom take care of yourselves, but the thing is, I like it here." He pulled the hood of his sweatshirt up. "I think I'd better take a nap before I go finish up the sets. Hangovers are not appreciated."

If he was looking for a sympathetic chuckle, he didn't get it.

"Clean the couch and the rug. Then sleep." Wanda got the stain remover out from under the sink. Lance took it. "I'll be back at noon, and I'll make sure you are up by twelve thirty."

She grabbed her coat and iPad with the sermon on it. She didn't want to leave him, but she had to trust him. "Lance?"

"Yeah?"

"Walk Wink, too, okay?"

15

Rye put her phone on the dresser, speaker up. Wanda picked up on the third ring.

"Mmph—hey—hang on a second, will you?" Rye called. "I'm stuck in this dress." She could hear Wanda laughing on the other end, but the fact of the matter was that there were layers of fabric here that she hadn't considered, and she was getting caught in all of them.

"I can wait."

"Thanks. I think I'm almost there." There was silence on both ends of the phone until Rye emerged from inside the twisted fabric. "Sorry about that. I really didn't expect it to give me so much trouble."

"I've been there," Wanda said. "What can I do for you?"

"Skipping the small talk tonight, huh?" Rye asked.

"Lance and I are headed out to the movies," her friend replied.

"You convinced a teenager to be seen in public with you? Are you a witch? You can tell me, and I'll start collecting eye of newt." Rye stared at herself in her tiny mirror. Her tone was light, though she felt anything but.

"I've been called something that rhymes with 'witch,'" Wanda said. "Does that count?"

"Jury's still out," Rye replied. "Okay, well I don't want to keep you, since I imagine you'll have to release Lance from a salt circle before you leave, but I was wondering if you wanted an update or had anything. You know, since you stood me up this morning."

"I…did?" Wanda gasped. "I did! I'm so sorry. I completely forgot about coffee."

"It's not like you."

"I know." Rye heard Wanda sigh. "I'll fill you in later, but something came up."

"Lance?"

"Good guess. Can't talk about that now. I did chat with Hardy about Mickey while you were at the dance." Rye wondered if this was how her father had known that Lance had Wanda's car. "And Lance and I went to visit Henry yesterday."

"You did?"

"Yes. He and Lance had been hanging out last week, I guess," Wanda said. "I will definitely give you a full report."

"And I can tell you what I found out from Ryan."

There was a noticeable pause on the other end. "Really? Ryan actually shared?"

"Amazingly, yes." Now Rye could tell she had Wanda's full attention. She fidgeted with the collar of her dress. "He knows every button to push, though, doesn't he."

"That he does," Wanda said, although her tone had a hint of suggestion to it.

"Nope. No, no, no." Rye knew Wanda couldn't see her vehemently shaking her head, but she couldn't help it. "Just no."

Wanda laughed. "Just you wait—someday you'll be closer to sixty than twenty and realize that love, sex, and drama is not reserved for the young."

Rye heard a groan in the background and grinned. "I'm sure Lance enjoys learning that, too." She picked up her comb to try to tame her hair. "And just for that, I'm not telling you what he told me. You're going to have to wait until we get donuts tomorrow morning before school."

"Six thirty?"

"You better be there this time. And coffee is on you."

"That's fair," Wanda said. "Oh, and Rye?"

"Yes?"

"You'll have time to fill me in on your date, too."

"How did you know I have a date?"

"You get stuck in a dress often to watch TV with your father?"

"Ha-ha." Rye hung up.

She'd wanted to tell Wanda about Claudia and about Ryan's suspicions of her. She needed someone to tell her they were baseless. Rye absolutely wouldn't put it past him to derail one of her relationships just for the fun of it. Not that Ryan Phennen was cruel—it was more that the two of them had never seen eye to eye on anything, and there seemed to be no way to end the animosity that always bubbled up when they were in the other's proximity.

She smoothed the front of her skirt. It had been so long since she'd dressed up like this. Never for Andy. Their dates had been casual—more like glorified hangouts than anything particularly romantic—and before him it had been more than a year since she'd dated.

Moving back here had meant a lot of changes to her lifestyle, and dating had taken the biggest hit. Rye didn't want to be with anyone who might be a recent graduate, for example, or a person who had a sibling or child at the school. She related to the struggles Wanda suffered as a pastor, although at least her career didn't actively put her dates on edge. It was just hard to find someone she clicked with who also lived close enough that she could see them more than once a month and who was not on the vice principal restricted list.

The connection she felt with Claudia was one she hadn't felt in a long time. Rye had been in love twice before, although she rarely spoke to even close friends about it. After each relationship ended, she had been done. She did her best to wish them well, even when the pain was still fresh, and then trained herself not to think about them. Just to take the good and go.

Those lessons made her wary when looking for a partner. Rye was good at compromise. She trusted her instincts, and she didn't expect people she loved to be perfect. That might be what was troubling her tonight. She felt this immediate bond with Claudia based on nothing she could put her finger on. That was how it had felt before—not with Andy, who was emotionally safe, but with those she had fallen for deeply.

She'd once told Ana about her belief that the soul had many facets, and therefore many mates, and Ana had understood in a way that made Rye profoundly grateful. Everyone should have a friend like her, Rye thought, as she grabbed her keys and locked up. Ana had still waters that ran deep. Maybe Camila did, too, but she talked so much that the protective wall was high.

Rye had felt at the dance that Camila, who usually loved the juicy details, didn't want to talk about Claudia, but maybe Rye could tell Ana. She dialed as soon as her phone connected to Bluetooth in the car.

"Hey," Ana's soft voice came over the line with only a hint of static.

"Can I life-dump on you and get a reality check?" Rye asked. "It has to be quick, but if I don't, I think I might mess things up, and I really don't want to mess things up."

"Does this have to do with Claudia Ramirez?"

"How did you ... Did Camila say something to you?"

"She may have mentioned that it seemed like there was a vibe between you two Friday night she hadn't noticed before."

Rye smiled. "Of course she did."

"Okay," Ana said. "What's up?"

Rye paused for a moment. Ana was not a person to be bothered by silence. She would wait. "Claudia and I ... connected earlier this week. It came out of nowhere, actually."

"Probably not nowhere," Ana said. "You've worked with her for more than a year."

"I barely noticed her," Rye replied. "I think I had so much going on with my dad, and the Pond family and school board fallout. I didn't have bandwidth for anything else."

"And then you were with Andy."

"Yes," Rye sighed. "It helped me decompress. I never had to wonder with Andy. He's straightforward, you know? Not a lot of mystery there."

"Sure."

"Claudia—she's been honest with me. Or at least it feels like she has."

"What makes you doubt her?" Ana asked.

Rye chewed on her lower lip. "Friday night, when I was talking to the police, they said they had some questions about her."

"Do you trust them over your gut?

"Normally, I would say no. Ryan Phennen is not exactly my north star, but—" Rye hesitated. "But his brother was with him."

Ana was silent for a moment. "And?"

"And you trust Tyler."

"I do."

"So if he didn't disagree with what Ryan said, then he must have something to back it up with, right?" Rye asked. "Some evidence I'm not privy to?"

"Maybe. I don't believe Tyler would point a finger without just cause. But I've also been friends with Claudia for a while now, and she's never given me a reason to doubt her."

"Okay," Rye said. "But—"

"Listen, Rye. You already know what you need to do."

"Talk to Claudia."

"Talk to Claudia. If this feels like it could be something, be honest with her from the start. If you don't, it will weigh on you, and in a week or a month, it will become such a heavy burden, you won't even be able to look at her."

"Spoken like someone who's made that mistake before," Rye said.

"Well…all I can say is don't do it."

Rye let out a breath. "I know you're right." She twisted her cold fingers around the steering wheel as she pulled into the parking lot. "I'm scared, though."

"Of her reaction?"

"That if I am the one who's wrong, people will suffer, and it will be because I put myself before them." She turned the car off.

Her friend was silent. Then she asked, "Is what Ryan told you life or death?"

Rye thought about it. "Maybe." She pulled her scarf on, wrapping it firmly around her neck. She could see Claudia standing by the door of the Library Bar, her arms wrapped tightly around herself, her red wool coat a beacon. "But I still think she deserves to know the truth." She pulled her phone from the center console.

"Good luck, Rye."

"Thanks. Gonna need it." She pushed her door open against the wind that cut straight through her jacket, and she instantly regretted her short skirt. That is, until she caught Claudia's appreciative glance. The cold was worth it.

"Sorry I kept you waiting," she said as Claudia opened the door and a warm blast of air greeted them.

"I just got here," Claudia replied. "I had to swing by the school to check on the students and parent volunteers who were finishing up the largest set pieces. I'm lucky. People have really stepped up."

"That's great. The show's in just a few weeks, right?" Rye asked as they were seated at a cozy table in the back.

"Weekend after next." Claudia reached for Rye's jacket and hung both on the hooks across the back wall behind Rye.

"Are you going to be ready?"

Claudia shrugged. "It's been hard."

"I'm not sure if I've said this to you, but I am sorry for your loss." Claudia's eyes welled up, and she glanced away and gently blotted them with a napkin. Rye saw their server approaching. She waved her away.

"No, it's okay. Let's get a drink." Claudia signaled the woman to come back, and they both ordered one of the holiday cocktails. "I feel like we should be talking about something a little more first date appropriate."

Rye straightened her shoulders. "I need to tell you something before we do."

The change of tone brought Claudia's gaze up to meet hers. "Is it about Friday night?"

"Sort of. Why?"

"I thought you might be angry that I went and warned the kids having a vigil that the police were coming."

"So they could ditch their booze?"

Claudia shrugged. "No. Yes. Well, probably they did, but I went because I didn't think they were supposed to cross the police tape. I knew when I saw it that we should say something, but I didn't want them to get in trouble for finding a way to harness some of their pain." She paused. "I'm sure at least some of them were drinking. I should have told the police what they were doing, and I didn't. I don't think that endeared Sheriff Phennen to me."

"Probably not," Rye said. "He definitely has a zero-tolerance policy for underage drinking."

"I'm sure," Claudia said as their own drinks arrived.

"My dad told me Phennen's cousin was killed by a drunk driver." Rye took a sip of her drink. The cranberry juice was tart, but at least the bitterness was distilled enough to be palatable. "He had just joined the force. It's definitely informed the way he handles those situations."

"I didn't know," Claudia said. "I really don't make it a habit to go easy on my students when they're partying, even knowing that I was the same way and turned out okay. I'm just feeling protective."

Rye nodded, absorbing the fact that they had different ideas of 'protective.' "I appreciate you telling me."

"Selfish reasons. You were a hero the other night. I shouldn't have let you go alone." Claudia looked down at her untouched drink. "I think a part of me wants you to tell me it's okay that I was too scared to follow you."

Rye studied her face. "It is." There was no doubt in her mind that she and Wanda—people who foolishly ran directly at danger—were oddities. Caution was normal. Fear was smart. "My dad spent a lot of my childhood preparing me for emergencies. He never wanted me to be in a position where I couldn't help myself or someone else out of ignorance." She tried to smile and failed. "It was a hard way to grow up, but I'm grateful now. He gave me a gift."

"But maybe not enough hugs?"

"Maybe not. But he's trying to make up for it now. Nothing like ten years apart to make him appreciate me."

"Good," Claudia said. Her gaze was appreciative in a completely different way. "You deserve that."

Rye finished her cocktail in a hurry. "Listen. Sheriff Phennen said some things to me about you. He asked me to spy on you for his investigation."

"Really?" Claudia looked nonplussed, then thoughtful. "He *has* had me in a few times this week. I thought he was just being thorough. I knew Jonathan pretty well—better than a lot of other people."

"Was he having an affair? Was there someone else?"

Claudia shook her head. "Jonathan? I doubt it. He and Marc always seemed solid, like a unit. They have the sweetest dog, and they were always traveling to places I would love to go. Thailand, New Zealand—they even trekked across Greenland."

Rye reached for her glass, then remembered it was empty. "Maybe it's recent. Jonathan was in rehab for a few months, right?"

"Yeah, but—" Claudia shook her head. "I don't believe it."

Rye decided to keep any more information about Jonathan to herself. That would be all she was going to give Phennen. Claudia hadn't asked, and that way, Rye wouldn't be compromising the confidential part of the conversation.

"Does the sheriff think I knew about some affair?"

"I guess," Rye said. "I don't know all the details. I just wanted to be up-front with you. He tapped me for information. I didn't feel comfortable asking you how many siblings you have or what you might want to binge watch with me when we had that hanging over us."

Claudia winced. Rye wondered what nerve she could have hit.

"He put you in an awful position," Claudia said. "That seems unprofessional."

"I doubt he would have done it if my father weren't who he is," Rye agreed.

Claudia nodded. "You two have a history."

"It's not great."

"You've known him a lot longer than you've known me. I don't want to put you in a position where you feel compromised," Claudia said. "We can forget about…this."

Rye bit her lip. "I don't really want to."

"Me, neither." Claudia smiled. "I haven't felt this excited to be having dinner with someone in a long time. I want to tell you about this show I just started bingeing, and the school musical gossip, and my favorite dishes for Thanksgiving…and I want you to want to do this again soon."

"Me, too."

"So?"

"So tomorrow I'm going to text Ryan Phennen and tell him he can find another mole."

The full force of Claudia's joy was something to behold. Rye waved down the server just to keep from crawling across the table to curl up beside Claudia.

"Ready?" the server asked.

They both grinned. "Ready," Rye said.

This time, it was Rye who slept through her early morning coffee with Wanda, but she was grateful for the reminder call that got her to work on time.

16

"DO YOU KNOW WHAT'S WRONG WITH ALL THOSE mystery novels you like?"

Too many recipes? Too little sex? She didn't know, but she knew from experience that Ryan was going to tell her. He was sitting in her office on Monday morning, far too early. Lisa had pointed at her door with an exaggerated what-could-I-do? shrug, and answered Wanda's raised eyebrows by mouthing, "The Big R." Wanda had no choice but to paste on a gracious smile and go in.

Although he appeared to be relaxing in his chair, she could tell that he had been looking through the papers on her desk because they were straightened into neat piles, which was a habit of his she actually remembered fondly. What she did not love was his penchant for feeling he had the right to straighten up her life messes without asking permission.

"All those books present killers as smart," he continued without waiting for a response. "And they are not. Most homicide is stupid, unplanned, and just begging the perpetrator to give himself away."

"Or herself?"

"Well, yes. When it comes to murder, women are even more stupid."

"You should give a speech at a mystery convention. 'Talk with a Real Sheriff.' They would flock to you like seagulls to an open bag of garbage."

Of course, Ryan wouldn't recognize sarcasm if it froze his toes in the Yukon. He took her at face value and continued.

"Take these killings. The clumsiest attempts to cover up and misdirect that I have ever seen." He paused and regrouped. Wanda knew that move. He had given something away that he did not want to give. What was it?

"You're going to tell me more."

"Ross Jacobs was not killed by a hit-and-run driver." He paused for effect.

He had her attention, but she was not willing to hang on his words. That was personal. Everything in a small town was personal. "So he had arsenic in his system? The coroner found the mark of an elusive Latin American poisonous snake? Someone smothered him with a pillow?"

"He was killed by a single blow to the head, then left on the road to cover it up."

"How could you tell?"

"Only wound that bled freely."

Wanda sat down. "So someone thought they could cover up a murder by having an innocent person run over the body and take the blame for his death?" Wanda shuddered. "That's ... evil."

Ryan looked enlightened. "You know, that is possible. We were thinking the person who killed him was the same one who got in a car and ran him over to hide the evidence of the initial blow. Make it look like a drunk driving accident or a hit-and-run. I'll add your idea to my files."

Drunk hit-and-run. That jogged something for Wanda. "Now you think that there may be two people to find—the one who killed Ross, accidentally or on purpose, and someone else who thought they did."

Ryan stared at her thoughtfully. "What are you doing for dinner?"

"I have a date." Wanda had her fingers crossed under the desk. She would be in a restaurant eating a meal with someone. It was close enough. "You must have a reason for telling me this. What is it? Why are you here?"

"Officer Lombard found a rock not far off the road with blood streaks that match our victim. There were signs of a struggle once we were looking for it, so there was must have been a fight. Any tire tracks have been obliterated." He paused. "I thought, as clergy, you might want to sit with the family when they get the news that it wasn't a hit-and-run."

"I'm not buying it, Ryan. I've already seen Autumn." She held up a hand to keep him from interrupting her. "My nephew Lance is staying with me. He and Ross's brother know each other."

"Of course they do. I should have known you'd already be in it up to your eyeballs."

"You'd never have told me confidential information unless you thought you could get something from me in return."

"I know that you and Rye are investigating. I want to know what you know. I thought she would help out, but last night she texted to say she won't." His voice was steady, but she could see a vein in his temple bulging. Wanda understood why Rye had texted.

"I'm turning to my old…friend," Ryan said, "and in exchange for your keeping me abreast of what you know, I'm sharing information that we have managed to keep away from the media thus far."

"But not for long?"

He shook his head. "No. We have to hold a press conference later today."

Wanda studied his face for a minute before she relented. "Well, as a matter of fact, I can give you some information you don't have. On Wednesday night, after Tyler delivered me home, I went to Locals for a drink. I was heading home around ten, and I nearly got T-boned by a car speeding down Route 111. It swerved across the road, went onto the shoulder, then sped off without stopping. I wonder if it was your hit-and-run driver."

"Make of car? Color? Plate?"

"Sorry, none of that. There aren't any lights out that way."

Lisa blessedly interrupted them then with the arrival of a morning appointment, and Ryan got up to leave, promising to check in with her to find out whether she and Rye had anything else he could use. Wanda was noncommittal and glad to see the back of him. It was, in fact, a very nice backside, if he only he could keep his mouth permanently sewn shut.

But he opened it again, turning around. "Oh, did I mention? Jonathan Thorne? Not an OD."

He was happy to give her old news! She would keep that tactic in mind.

WANDA DID, IN FACT, HAVE A "NOT-DATE" ON MONDAY night. It was with a friend so handsome she'd thought more than once about how to convince him to drop the "not," but for the moment, she and Luke Fairchild were nothing for Ryan to get jealous over (or other friends like Tony and Lisa to waggle eyebrows at). Not that Ryan was jealous. Although he had texted her several times over the course of the day for insignificant reasons, and when she'd said she had to go get ready for dinner, he'd sent her that eye-rolling emoji she hated so much.

Luke Fairchild was a very attractive man. Not classically handsome—not with eyebrows that almost met in the middle even when he wasn't frowning at her and a pugnacious chin—but when he smiled, every straight woman and gay man in the room rotated toward him. As a funeral director, he tried not to flex that gift all that often.

His great-grandfather had changed his name from Francesco Fraticelli to Francis Fairchild to fit into New England. Francis, his son Vincent, and his grandson Antonio had not blended by marriage, falling in love with Italian women, but they had converted from Roman Catholicism to Congregationalism. Traditional in love but pragmatic in religion. Luke used his Italian roots to play incognito in a band as Luca Fraticelli. Wanda considered him one of her closest friends and often wished there could be more between them. He was forty-five—younger than her, but not *impossibly* young—and happily unmarried. Of course, he was also extremely private. Luke could have a wife in Jamaica, his favorite getaway, and no one would be the wiser, but Wanda doubted it.

He'd asked her out for dinner. They decided on Townsend House, which was comfortable and a close drive. They ran the risk of seeing parishioners or relatives of the recently deceased, but they were both busy. Wanda recognized she had not known what busy was until a teenage boy moved in.

Luke must have been telepathically eavesdropping as they perused the menu. "So how's it going with Lance?"

"I don't think he's fazed by the move itself, although we don't talk about his mom much." She shrugged. "He likes video games. He tried to explain one to me, and my eyes glazed over. My revenge—reading my sermon notes aloud."

Luke laughed. "That's great. Sounds like it's going as well as you could hope."

She nodded. "I feel fortunate so far. My friend Rye is the vice principal, and she's been keeping an eye on him for me, too."

"Nice to have eyes and ears around when you can't be."

"Exactly, although I know there's a lot going on at the school right now. Lance is helping in the theater department. Organizing props, last-minute painting. He's going to be a stagehand during the show. They're shorthanded right now. He seems to like it."

"Do you think he's too busy to help me out?" Luke asked.

"What did you have in mind?"

"A part-time job at the funeral home. Irregular hours, but the pay is above minimum wage."

"I don't know why not. Like every other kid I know, he needs more money than he has, and I told him that was his mother's domain. She told me she would drop a monthly sum in his account, and he can debit it until it's gone."

Luke nodded. "I could use someone on the door, greeting people at funerals. I need all the vehicles washed. I need an extra casket bearer for families who don't have enough. Probably no more than ten hours a week, but, if he likes it, it could grow to more."

"He doesn't have anything respectable to wear."

"I provide a new suit and a small stipend for shoes. If he sticks it out for at least three months, I eat the cost. If he doesn't, I dock his last wages."

"Seems more than fair. I'll send him by to talk to you if he's interested."

"Much appreciated, Wanda." Luke smiled at her. It made her squirm to have the full force of his approving attention. She avoided contact by motioning for a refill on her vodka gimlet. "And you know, I think he's good for you. You don't look so lonely."

She laughed. "Living with my nephew is not like having a good date, or even a bunch of mediocre ones."

"You're right. It's not," he said. "It's better. I think you could use more people like that in your life."

"Like you."

He paused. Her heart heard a whisper of hope … *Please, deny it, deny it! Deny it!*

"Yes, like me."

"I have friends. Tony and Lisa … and you."

"Three friends you can name, all involved with your work life, is not enough. You need other friends."

Maybe it was Luke who had the telepathic connection with Lance. He had just made the same accusation. How friendless did she appear? "I forgot about Rye," she said.

"I think she might be your saving grace right now. At least she and Lance aren't connected to the church." He sat back. "Of course, I would not be surprised to find out you two were making inquiries about the deaths that are sending such a tremor through our community."

Wanda looked away. "You've made your point. More friends and more distance from work."

"And something else," Luke said softly. He paused until she gave him her full attention. "Maybe more friends and less drinking." His comment sat between them for a long, awful moment before he decided to backpedal. "Look, Wanda, I'm just suggesting that you consider taking alcohol out of the landscape at home. Every kid in the world knows about watering the booze to bring it to its previous level on the bottle. Since you were nearly killed in the spring, I've seen you drink more than is...fun. You go out less and use work as an excuse more." He took a deep breath. "Listen to my advice or not, but I want you to think about it. You're parenting now. You have to at least consider that the adage, 'Do as I say, not as I do' is intended to be a load of crap."

Wanda nodded and swallowed hard. She could taste the lime. She wanted to reassure Luke that she was fine, but she couldn't have lied even if she wanted to—not without crying—and she was not about to do that. Could he possibly have known about Lance's drinking?

After a long moment, Luke simply nodded and started telling her a long, funny story about his parents, who had retired to Florida a few years earlier. Then they started comparing bad funeral stories...the director who fell in the grave, the minister who used the wrong name. By the time she regained her composure, the food had arrived, and she could pretend this was not an intervention.

17

THERE IS A BALM IN GILEAD, AND THERE IS A CHURCH afternoon with nothing to do. It was often a Tuesday. No hospital to visit, wedding couple to soothe, committee meeting to referee, or newsletter to finish. Empty afternoons made the wounded pastor whole and healed the work-sick soul. Wanda hoped God would forgive her implying that work was sinful, but sometimes it seemed like work was what kept a person from enjoying God's world. Also, naps. She loved the meme that went something like, One time in the Bible, Elijah the prophet got so mad that he told God he wanted to die. God said, "Here's some food. Now why don't you lie down?" So Elijah ate, slept, and decided things weren't so bad. Never underestimate the spiritual power of a snack and a nap.

She had just gotten to the point of wondering how she could work that into a sermon when Lisa buzzed her to say she had a walk-in.

"It's a rental request," Lisa said.

Wanda strode to the door and met a very short woman, shorter even than she was. She looked vaguely familiar, but Wanda couldn't place her. "Come on in. I'm Wanda Duff, the pastor." She indicated one of the comfortable chairs she had placed for informal meetings. "Please sit down."

The woman did and set her purse down before she spoke. "I wanted to meet you."

Wanda was confused. She always thought silence was safest when that was the case.

"I'm Jess. Jessica Thorne." She met Wanda's gaze with something akin to defiance. "Who knows how long Jonathan could have been laying there if you hadn't come along?" The woman paused. "I just wanted to tell you that I don't blame you anymore for not walking by earlier."

Wanda was transported back to that afternoon, to how impossible it had felt to stand there waiting for help. If Wink had not been with her, she might have left.

"Jonathan was ...?"

"My brother. I saw you at the graveside service."

"I came to pay my respects."

Luke had done a brief service for the internment of ashes, sharing not much more than had been in the obituary—a theater career with a couple off-Broadway appearances, then Massachusetts regional theater, his work with young people focusing on stage design and lighting. Luke added a few words about the gift of memory, then closed with a poem. Wanda had never heard one of his services, and she'd complimented him on how tasteful it had been.

"Well, it was nice of you to come." Jess gave her a wan smile. "I was wondering whether I might rent the hall here for a ... a celebration of life. Our thirty-fifth birthday is coming up. We'd been planning a big party at

Jonathan and Marc's place—you've met him, Jonathan's husband." She stopped to wipe her eyes. "Now Marc doesn't want to have it there. But we've already hired a caterer. I thought it might be …I don't know. Nice. On Saturday, October 31. I don't know if that's okay. On Halloween?"

"I think it will be fine."

"It was going to be this weekend, but I just couldn't do it. Not on our actual birthday."

Wanda felt her heart constrict. "You and Jonathan are twins?" Her professional training just barely kept her from jumping up and throwing her arms around this woman, who must be hurting terribly. Instead, she said, "The church would be happy to give you the hall free of charge but ask that you pay our custodian for setup and cleanup services. The downstairs sound system is not wonderful…"

"We can bring in our own. Thank you so much. That's very generous."

"I should tell you that we do not allow alcohol on the church premises. Will that be a problem?"

"Not at all. Jonathan was in recovery, and some of the people who are coming are friends from NA and AA, so we don't want to have it anyway. And this is a perfect excuse not to sound cheap." She took a breath. "Are you willing to be emcee? In case people want to share?"

Wanda could do it, but she hated the role because it was mostly crowd control. World Cup fans had nothing on those who grieve. She often couldn't decode what they were saying, mumbling into the mic, and she certainly couldn't consolidate it into her closing remarks the way so many of her colleagues did. But maybe she'd have a chance for closure and learn some things about the man she'd found in the woods.

"I'd be happy to do that. If you want, you can even give me a list of people to call on first, and then we will go to others as we have time." Wanda watched Jess take careful notes. "If there is anyone, particularly in the family, who anticipates being overwhelmed, have them type up their remarks so someone else can finish for them. Sometimes just the mention of that safety valve is enough to make it unnecessary."

Jess nodded. "Is four too late?"

Wanda wanted to say yes, that she wanted to get home for trick-or-treaters, but this woman had just lost her brother and was pivoting what was meant to be a milestone birthday party into something much grimmer. "It's fine."

Jess started to gather her things. "I can email you questions, right?"

"Of course. My email is on the church website."

"One more thing," Jess said. "I don't want any mention of Jonathan OD'ing or committing suicide. My brother was not using. Anyone who knew him knew that was long past. The police will not admit it, but my brother was murdered."

WANDA WAS SO GLAD THAT SHE WASN'T RESPONSIBLE for Lance's clothing budget. She'd assumed he would have grown out of being a human stain magnet when he reached high school, but she was wrong. He knew, though. Lance did his own laundry, and he had his own Tide stick, but if there was food or oil or mud or, in this case, paint, within ten feet of him, some trace would end up on his body. She had covered the upholstered chair he was fondest of with a blanket and replaced the new sky-blue bedspread she had bought for him with a navy one. The rug in his room was very old and thankfully only got more character with embellishment. Wink loved Lance both for his ear scratches and for his daily delivery of new scents.

They didn't eat meals at a set time, but Lance was more likely to eat supper when she was eating. He always appeared to be just wandering through and thoroughly surprised that she was sitting at the kitchen table. Tonight, he got a big bowl of chili and tossed some jalapenos, raw onions, and cheese into it. He grabbed the sour cream and pre-packaged guacamole out of the refrigerator and dumped a mound of tortilla chips on his plate.

"Looks great, Aunt Wanda."

She looked at him. There was green in his auburn hair. She should not trust redheads with her heart. He had a smudge of navy blue on his cheek and speckles of yellow and orange on simply everything. "You've been painting sets at the theater."

"Excellent detection skills."

"Ha! Is it a nice group of kids?"

His mouth was full of chili, and he kept it closed when he swallowed to effectively pretend that he had forgotten the question. She repeated it.

"It's just me. I'm the new scenic designer."

"You are doing it alone?" Wanda tried to remember if she'd seen posters up around town. "Is it *Peter and the Starcatcher*?"

"*The Addams Family.*"

"Halloween weekend, of course? And you're doing all the scenery?"

"Perfect, right?" He shrugged. "It's mostly projections. We get them from a service. The days of painting huge sets are mostly over, at least in high school. But props? So many props."

"But you're working on it all alone?"

"The stage manager is there, and if I need any help, the actors pitch in. It's okay. Don't worry."

Wanda mumbled around a big bite. "...not worrying. What about Luke's request? Are you considering working at the funeral home when the musical is over?"

"I've already been over and washed the hearse."

"Can you do both and study?"

"I can do both and get Bs and Cs. And be happier than not doing it and getting As."

There was the defiant teen lurking underneath, but Wanda didn't think it was such a bad thing. It was—what would a therapist say?—differentiation. "Works for me, Lance. What about the suit?"

"Measurements have been taken."

"Great." She was ready to get back to her chili, but he was randomly stirring and, since she knew it was very good chili and that he was usually ten-out-of-ten ravenous, there was something else. She waited.

"It's Jonathan Thorne. Everyone at school says that he couldn't have OD'd."

"I think they're calling it murder now." Surely it was out. Yes, Ryan must have announced it. "The police are following some new leads."

"The police don't think anyone who's been a drug addict could be anything but a lifelong loser. No second chances for them. If it looks like an OD, it is an OD. Someone should find out what really happened."

Wanda stared at him. Lance was angry. She had a flash of the young man who got in the face of authority, the one who didn't fit in at private school. The one who didn't listen.

Wanda wasn't naïve enough to reassure him that the truth would prevail. It often didn't. So she just nodded her agreement.

"Aunt Wanda, you found him. Don't you care?" Lance stared at her imploringly. "Last spring, you found out what happened to that guy in the nursing home, even when no one wanted you to. That's what Mom said, anyway. She said you nearly lost your job, but you wouldn't let it go."

"Let me think about it, Lance." Wanda stirred her soup. She hesitated, but only for a moment. "Because I think you're right. I don't know if I'm the right person to find out what happened, but it wasn't an accident."

Lance was eating again. Big bites. Loving her chili. She pushed her bowl away. She could feel heartburn climbing from the soles of her feet.

It had been a long day, but it was only a quarter to nine, so Wanda thought she was safe calling Rye. Lance was gaming in his room. He might not be studying, but at least he wasn't out roaming the streets. Wanda thought she deserved some credit for that much.

She poured a glass of Paisano and sank into her favorite chair. Wanda balanced her drink on the chair's armrest as she dug out her cell phone. Luke's concern about her drinking tickled the back of her brain. She glanced up the stairs toward where she knew Lance would be and put the glass just out of reach on the coffee table. At least for now.

Rye answered on the second ring. "Hi, Wanda. What's up?"

"How about a teenager with headphones on, a dog whose had his last visit to the garden, and me, minus a new book to read."

"And I'm the default?"

"Well, no. You are the de-tective."

"Joke, that's a joke, right?"

"I wanted to tell you that two people confided in me today that Jonathan Thorne could not have OD'd because his recovery was solid."

"Who told you that?"

"Lance says all the kids involved in the theater program think that the police were wrong and that Jonathan was killed by someone who wanted to make it look like an OD."

"I don't completely disagree with that, but it's high school. Our electricity is powered by the rumor mill."

"Second person. I was sitting in my office this afternoon, and Jessica Thorne came in."

"Who's that?"

"Jonathan's twin sister."

Rye whistled. "Well, that is interesting. Why did she come to see you?"

"She's turning what would have been a shared thirty-fifth birthday celebration into a wake."

"That's rough." Rye swore softly.

"I know. She wants to rent the parish hall and have me there to help facilitate."

"And you're going to do it?"

"I am. Ryan told me, before he gave the press conference, that both Thorne and Ross's deaths were murder." She paused and surveyed her now-empty glass before pouring another. *Oops.* "When I was in the woods, Rye…I wasn't alone. It felt…I can't explain it, but someone was there. Maybe someone found the body before me and didn't want to call the police. I don't know. But there's more to this. If there weren't, Ryan wouldn't be pressuring you to spy on Claudia."

"And you feel guilty."

Wanda sighed. "And I feel guilty. If I hadn't let Wink go into the school bus, if I hadn't stopped to watch the band practice, if I hadn't let Wink drag me to sniff every taco wrapper in the woods, Jonathan Thorne might not have died."

"If it wasn't an overdose, what would you have been able to do?" Rye asked.

"I don't know." Wanda knew Rye was right, that she wasn't a registered nurse or necessarily capable of stopping a cold-blooded murderer, but it still bothered her.

"If you'd been there earlier, maybe you'd be dead now, too," Rye said bluntly, as though reading Wanda's thoughts.

"Which means you have your own doubts."

"Of course I do!"

"So you'll help me?"

"I'm going to poke around on my end. I'll talk to Claudia again. Is Lance still hanging out with Henry?"

"Not really. There's something about Henry that has him pretty freaked out."

"Okay," Rye said. "That's fine. I don't want to use your nephew to get information anyway. We don't want to put him in any unnecessary danger if Ross' death is connected to Thorne. Two men, both gay, both in recovery, die violently on the same day a few miles apart? There has to be a connection."

"A hate crime?" Wanda asked. "Ross's dad was angry when Ross came out to his family."

"Angry enough to murder his own son?"

"It sounds impossible. I haven't met him. But I do know people who threaten that," she replied. "Maybe if he thought that Jonathan was somehow involved romantically with Ross ..."

"It's motive," Rye said. "The same could be said for Thorne's husband if Jonathan and Ross were having an affair. Husband finds out and kills both in a jealous rage?"

"It doesn't really jibe with what I've learned about either of the victims. And the crimes seem really different, don't they?" Wanda asked.

"I know. First one planned and second spur-of-the-moment. Everyone claims to have liked these guys, but they're both dead under highly suspicious circumstances, so either they're incredibly unlucky, or—"

"Or there's a connection."

18

WANDA DIDN'T GET A GOOD NIGHT'S REST. BETWEEN the wine and the rampant speculation with Rye, she went to bed anxious and sad. Then she dreamed again. Her imagination had conjured up the traffic accident that killed Ross Jacobs. She could see a figure hunched over, walking down the road toward…well, nowhere. Why was he out there in the first place?

In her dream, she wanted to shout, "Get a Lyft, for God's sake! For God's sake, for your sake, for your brother's and your mom's—even your homophobic dad must have some regrets now about the way he treated you!" The problem was that in the dream, she wasn't shouting at him at all. When that dark car came out of the night with its lights off, headed for the shadowy figure, the hoodie slipped, and it was her own face. She woke in a cold sweat.

Wanda would advise a parishioner to get some professional help, but she was too busy. Thankfully, coffee existed. She made a mental note to find out more about Ross's father. Wanda immediately felt better putting her detective hat on, so, before she went to the church, she got dressed and drove over to the entrance to the woods behind the school.

She remembered exactly where the body had been found. She had a hundred photographs taken on and around the spot. Some of her sleep troubles might be due to guilt over never having told the police about taking and keeping those photographs. She had not mentioned it when she signed her statement, and after that, what could she say?

October skies before a rain were so depressing. Without sun, the trees didn't cast shadows—they were just pools of dark. And in one of those pools of dark, someone was watching her. Again. She could feel it. First, she didn't look behind her. Then, damn it, she did. No one was there. There were houses visible on one side with sturdy fences separating out the wildlife sanctuary from the cross-country trails. Second-floor window and binoculars? Second-floor window and a scope? She looked up quickly—drone? No, no, and neurotic no.

Only in her mind did a body-shaped indentation remain where she'd found Thorne. Weather and foot traffic had disturbed it. But when she looked down, there was a syringe right where his hand had been. She knew it was the spot because it was where the coin had fallen. Half-buried in the ground, that quarter had probably been there for a long, long time, and apparently the police had not removed it. The syringe must be new, for the same reason.

Police should have noticed a coin. She hadn't noticed it when she was standing vigil over the newly dead young man. She only saw it later in her pictures, and she had thought, *Isn't it odd that people are still carrying cash?*

Wanda pulled out her phone. "Is Sheriff Phennen in?...Wanda Duff...I'll hold."

As soon as Ryan answered, she blurted it all out. Her walk. The syringe. She held back on the pictures, acted as if she remembered the coin. He said he would send a car. She should go to the nursing home parking lot at the other end of the path and wait. But his tone of voice made it very clear that she was wasting his time. Before she left, Wanda crouched down and took a photo.

Wanda expected that Sheriff Phennen would make her wait a long time, but the car was there by the time she arrived. Ryan had sent his brother.

She explained again to him everything she had said on the phone. "I know you'll find it weird that I came up here."

He started to deny it, and Wanda raised her hand.

"It *is* weird. Honestly, ever since I found Jonathan Thorne, I've been having terrible dreams and a feeling that if I'd arrived earlier, it would have been different. I thought maybe if I walked up here it would just be a woodsy trail with sad memories, and I could let it go."

"Witnesses do that all the time," Tyler said. "It's normal to be feeling a lot of stress right now, especially with an unsolved case."

"Thanks." She led him the rest of the way in comfortable silence. But when they got to the spot where she had seen and reported the syringe, there was nothing.

"I'm not … Somebody has taken it. I felt like someone was watching me." Could she dig herself into a deeper hole?

"Are you sure this is the place?"

"I knew where I was going when I walked over here, and I returned to the exact spot with you now. Do you see that coin? It was right next to the syringe."

Wanda went into her pocket for her cell phone. She showed him the photo. He looked around and down at the coin.

"Sure looks like the same spot. It's not a coin, though, you know. It's a chip. Twenty-four-hour aluminum chip. AA or NA." He knelt. "You do know that it couldn't have come from the time of the murder? We covered this ground."

"You missed it, then. It was here when Thorne was killed."

"Someone is messing with you," Tyler said gently.

"I can prove it. But I think we better go see Ryan." She held up her phone and flipped to the photos she'd taken of the body. Tyler studied the pictures, blood draining from his face.

Wanda had a confession to make, and the sheriff had probably better hear it, too. She hoped Ryan would settle for yelling at her, because she did not want to think about what the legal penalty for suppression of evidence in a homicide might be.

Then again, she wondered how thorough the officers had been if they had missed the chip. Had they made up their minds about the overdose too quickly?

Tyler took his own meticulous photographs of the scene, then bagged the chip, and they walked slowly back to the parking lot, resigned to Ryan's well-deserved wrath.

19

ON FRIDAY, SOPHIE, THE SCHOOL ADMIN, CALLED OUT
sick, so Rye was taking a turn signing people in and out
of the office after sanitizing all surfaces. Reminded of
what New England autumn was like, she was making
an appointment for a flu shot when Jonathan Thorne's
husband, Marc Dubois-Thorne, arrived.

He was not what she'd expected. Jonathan looked like
he should play Jesus in the next production of *Godspell*,
with his creatively patched overalls and black hair pulled
into a ponytail at the nape of his neck. His husband was
all business. His navy suit was exquisitely tailored. His
hair was close cut and neatly trimmed, as was his beard.
He reminded Rye of a venture capitalist on the prowl,
dangerously hip and prepared to bring on new investors
at a moment's notice.

Rye couldn't deny he had a charismatic pull. Marc
shared that with his husband, at least. There was a
magnetism that suggested that under either collar or
paint-speckled coveralls they were men meant to be
noticed. She found his masculine energy a little off-

putting, but she had plenty of friends of either gender who would swoon for this guy.

He dropped his keys on the counter and grabbed the pen to sign in on the clipboard. He had obviously been here before, although Rye couldn't remember ever seeing him. Maybe she had assumed he was somebody's father. He gave off such self-confidence that, though he'd be a young dad for a high schooler, he could assume that role without wrinkling his suit.

"Purpose of visit?" Rye asked.

He brushed an imaginary piece of lint off his wool coat. "I'm picking up a box from Claudia Ramirez."

"Okay," Rye said, closing her laptop. "I'll take you down."

"I know the way, thanks."

She smiled her most ingratiating smile. "I'm sure you do, but staff members have been asked to be more vigilant with guests during this difficult time." They'd been asked no such thing, but Rye wasn't letting this guy out of her sight. "I'm sure you understand."

He clucked his tongue in exasperation but stepped back as she came around the desk and led him out into the foyer, closing and locking the office door behind her. She flipped the sign to let others know she'd be back shortly and led him toward Claudia's office behind the auditorium.

"I'm sorry for your loss," Rye said to fill the silence stretching out between them. "I didn't know Jonathan well, but he was beloved here."

"Thanks," Marc said. "I never understood why he wanted to work with children, but he liked it."

Rye rolled her eyes. Five minutes in this man's company, and she was already irritated. She couldn't imagine being married to a person like him, though maybe this was his reaction to grief. Not having met him before, she couldn't, or shouldn't, judge. But, oh, did she want to.

Claudia's office door was open, but Rye knocked anyway when she saw that Claudia was on the phone.

"Let me check in with you about that tomorrow, Tony. I'm happy to run the songs again, but we need to have costumes in place before we do." Claudia smiled at Rye, then noticed who was standing behind her. "Tony, I've got to run. Sounds good. Bye."

"Sorry to bother you, but Marc Dubois-Thorne is here to see you." Rye prided herself on her excellent memory with names, but she was surprised to see Marc throw her a dirty look when she introduced him.

Claudia stood up and came over to embrace Marc. She gave a Rye a raised eyebrow over his shoulder, though, so she had seen it too. "Of course. I'm sorry I haven't had time to stop by the house with Jonathan's things." She gestured to a small box by the door. "I've been meaning to, but we've been swamped here. Jonathan set us up for success, as always, but we're scrambling."

"He was one of a kind," Marc said.

Claudia patted his arm. "I know it could be hard on you to have him here on top of his other work, but we appreciated him so much. The kids really miss him."

Marc shrugged, a remarkably elegant gesture. "He did what he wanted. Jonathan was a free spirit. I knew that when I married him. I may have eaten a lot of dinners alone, but at least when he came home from the school he was happy. That's more than I can say about some of his regional theater gigs."

"Marc, you get to do what you love every day," Claudia said. "Not all of us land our dream jobs right out of college. It can take a little searching. Jonathan was ... he was trying. He told me once that he wished he could be more like you—excited to do something steady, more mainstream—but his heart wasn't in it."

"What do you do, Marc?" Rye asked.

"I work in marketing. My office is in New York. That's where I met Jonathan."

"But you live here?"

"The train goes into the city. I work in the office three days a week and from home the other days."

"That sounds exhausting," Rye said.

"I like to keep busy," he replied coolly, stooping to pick up the box he'd come for. "I have to get going. I have a meeting to plan Jonathan's wake."

"I can walk you out," Rye said.

He waved one hand in the direction of the door across the hall that led out toward the back parking lot. "I'll go around." He strode off before she could argue.

"Well." She turned to Claudia. "Marc from marketing does not like me."

"No, he doesn't."

Rye leaned against the doorjamb. "Is it just me? Or is he always like that?"

"I might be biased, because I find you extremely likable, but he's usually not quite that . . . unpleasant. Of course, grief does strange things to people."

"He seems very different from his husband."

"Oh, yes—theirs was definitely an opposites attract situation. In fact . . ."

But Claudia didn't go on.

"You knew them as couple, then?" Rye asked. "Because I know when I mentioned that Jonathan might have been seeing someone, you were surprised."

"I've been to their house. Christmas parties, barbecues, that sort of thing. Always a lot of people around, of course, but they never seemed unhappy to me." Claudia tilted her head thoughtfully. "It's funny, though. I just realized that those were mostly Marc's friends I met. I think Jonathan's friends were people he got high with, and when he went to rehab, the people he met there were—not friends, exactly? More like a support group? Then there were friends from meetings and people he sponsored in recovery. They wouldn't have mixed well with Marc's crowd."

"That makes sense," Rye said. "I imagine you have to get comfortable being vulnerable, especially if you're serious about sobriety. Of course, he certainly wouldn't be the first person who slipped up. And if he was having an affair—" She held up a hand to forestall Claudia's denial. "If he was, the stress of that might have been the tipping point."

"Maybe I shouldn't be telling you this. Claudia leaned a little closer. "But Jonathan wasn't really interested in sex. It was something he struggled with, and it was in rehab that he finally admitted he was okay with that being a part of who he was."

Rye rubbed her hands together. This office clearly had the same issues as hers in terms of heating. "Was his husband okay with him being Ace of hearts?"

Claudia snorted. "I don't know the details of how Marc was handling it, but I know Jonathan talked to him before he talked to me. I asked."

"What about an emotional affair? Maybe his relationship with Ross Jacobs wasn't about sex, or maybe even romance," Rye said. "If they'd been in rehab together, it could be the basis for a connection Jonathan wouldn't be able to find with Marc."

Claudia stared past Rye. "You don't think Marc would have hurt Jonathan, do you?"

Rye laughed a little hollowly. "Not liking me doesn't make someone a villain."

Claudia laughed more naturally. She looked as though she were about to say something but changed her mind. Instead, she asked, "Are you still stopping by tonight?"

"You did promise a special libation. After the day I've had, that's impossible to pass up."

"And here I thought you were coming for the company!" Claudia teased.

Rye grinned. "Well, she's not so bad either." She ducked out of the office as Claudia sent a stuffed bat from her desk flying at Rye's head.

HARDY AND RYE ATE HIS DELICIOUS TURKEY MEATLOAF together, but both were absorbed in their own thoughts. It was the best thing about living with him, Rye thought. Conversations were never obligatory.

"Have you talked to Wanda lately?" Hardy asked as Rye stood to clear the table.

"I have." She was supposed to meet Claudia in half an hour and wanted to have time to change before she left, so of course this was when he wanted to debrief about the case.

"How's she doing?"

Rye straightened from loading the dishwasher. "Lance is settling in well. She seems happy to have him here, although I know she's worried about her sister." In fact, Rye had been pleasantly surprised to see the change Lance had brought when he moved in. Wanda still looked exhausted, but she also seemed lighter. Rye knew it was in Wanda's nature to take the grief and pain of others to heart, but she also had a wonderful capacity to love, and Lance seemed to have renewed that sense of herself.

Hardy nodded. "She's right to be concerned. It sounds like a classic scam." He handed Rye his dish and glass. "How is she handling the case? She seemed shaken up after she found Thorne."

Rye glanced at her father. Was he blushing? There was a note in his tone that she didn't recognize. "She should be in therapy, if that's what you mean."

"I was just wondering if she was feeling any better, that's all."

Hardy had averted his gaze, but he wasn't the only one who could direct his laser focus onto a misspoken word. "You could call her, you know," Rye said. "She even has a landline number you could look up in the phone book." She gestured toward the book gathering dust in the corner. She was always trying to recycle it, and her father was always digging it back out.

"I have her number already."

"Oh?" Rye asked, eyebrows going up. "Do you to hang out often?"

She heard him mutter something, but it sounded a lot like "none of your business," so Rye let it go.

Of course, *Hardy* never would have, if their positions had been reversed, but she had to practice what she preached if he was ever going to learn about the importance of butting out. "Well, if you do see her, remind her that she should call Dr. Lindstrom."

He made a face at her. "Where are you going tonight? Seeing anyone special?"

"Nobody you know, Dad."

"It's a school night, so don't stay out too late."

Rye rolled her eyes. Sometimes she understood how her students felt when they sat in her office with their parents. Would she ever age out of cringing at her father?

"Don't wait up," she said as she brushed past him and out the door.

BY THE TIME SHE KNOCKED ON CLAUDIA'S DOOR, HER fingers were nervously pulling her hair down and trying to calm out the errant waves. She had changed into jeans and a V-neck black sweater. Simple, but effective.

Claudia opened the door, and Rye felt a smile spread across her own face in response to the other woman's welcome. Claudia looked stunning and a little sleepy— in Rye's experience, a dangerous combination. She wore leggings and an olive green Henley tee that brought out her deep brown eyes. Rye allowed herself to be pulled inside.

The furniture was covered with cozy throws in jewel tones. A yoga mat was spread out under the window, and there was a ukulele beside it. Across from the kitchen table, Claudia had an old upright piano and a cello. A flute had been put down on the coffee table, presumably just before Rye arrived. Sheet music covered most of the surfaces, and even the bookshelves seemed to be succumbing to the collection, although Rye could see that beneath the bulging folders Claudia had collection of well-thumbed biographies. She itched to know what lives held her interest, but Rye resisted walking over to browse.

The building was old—not charming or historic, just on the edge of run-down, but Claudia had created a little home for herself. Rye could see the unmade bed through a beaded curtain, the type she'd hung in her college apartment. By the door, a coatrack was challenged by the sheer number of cardigans and jackets the woman owned. Rye carefully added hers.

"I'm glad you came," Claudia said.

"Me, too." Rye had to keep her hands in her pockets to hide some nerves.

"Can I make you a drink?" Claudia gestured to a small cart overflowing with bottles.

"Sure," Rye said. "What's your specialty?"

"For tonight, how about a French 95?"

"Don't you need to open champagne for that?"

Claudia smiled at her. "What better opportunity?" She went to the fridge and pulled out a bottle, popping the cork with a practiced hand.

Rye blushed. She handed Claudia the bourbon and simple syrup, then wandered over to the bookcase to wait. She gently shifted a stack of music aside to get a better look at the titles. She recognized a few, but the most loved copies weren't familiar to her. She pulled one down and started reading.

"Have you read it?" Claudia asked, as she handed Rye her glass.

Rye allowed her finger to slip out and closed the book. "No. I've heard Janet Mock speak, though."

Claudia nodded. "My brother transitioned a few years ago. My mother took a while to get on board, but this was one of the books that helped. I gave it to her after a disastrous Christmas when my brother announced he wouldn't come back to her house again." She reached out and touched the book's cover. "We were a close family. It broke my mother's heart to lose 'her.'"

"And now?" Rye asked.

"He bought the house next door to her after he got married. She watches his daughter while he's at work." She handed Rye a framed picture of herself with a dark-haired toddler. "My niece is the most spoiled, adorable little troublemaker."

"Do you see them often?"

Claudia nodded. "We have dinner every Monday night. I usually see them on the weekend, except when we have a big production at the school." She gestured to the couch, and Rye took a seat next to her.

"Didn't you go out of town last week to visit family?" Rye asked. It sounded like Claudia was surrounded by a big family right here in town, at least by Rye's standards.

"My grandfather lives in Bar Harbor. He and my grandmother never officially divorced, but he worked as a lighthouse keeper, and she got tired of the isolation. He's retired now, but he can't give up his proximity to the sea."

Rye's drink was fizzy and perfect, light on her tongue. "It must be nice to have so much family around," Rye said wistfully. "It sounds like you worked a little magic with your mom."

Claudia shook her head, the dark waves streaked with indigo spilling around her face. "No. I'm just persistent."

"Persistent in the pursuit of justice."

"Wasn't that your dad's campaign slogan?"

Rye laughed. "Not exactly. That was a poorly managed smear campaign against him. We had T-shirts made, though."

"Sometimes enemies make the best press agents."

"Well, they at least come up with the best catchphrases. My dad never would have thought of that one himself, although it does describe him to a T."

Claudia finished her drink and snuggled closer, pulling the empty glass from Rye's fingers. The couch dipped beneath them as Claudia leaned forward to kiss her. She brushed her fingers through Rye's hair, pulling her closer even as Rye felt her phone vibrate.

She successfully ignored it the second time, but when it buzzed for the fifth time, Claudia pulled back, cheeks flushed. "You should probably check that."

"Yeah." Rye fumbled for her phone to check her messages. "It's my dad. I'm sorry." She typed a quick response to let him know she would be late. As she glanced up, she caught sight of a picture by the sofa that she hadn't noticed when she came in. It was Claudia with her arm around a striking woman with short, straight black hair. It must have been recent, because Claudia had her nose ring in, and Rye had heard from parents of current students about the buzz around that first faculty face piercing.

Claudia followed her gaze. She pulled herself to the edge of the couch and reached out to grab the picture. She wiped dust off the top, then put it back on the table. "My girlfriend Veronica."

Rye froze. She had been cheated on before, and it was a line she never crossed, no matter how attracted she was to someone. "Your...girlfriend." The words sat in her mouth like ash.

"She died in June," Claudia said. "She OD'd."

"I'm so sorry." The words hung heavy in the air, any earlier effervescence gone.

Claudia bared her teeth in the approximation of a smile. "She went to rehab. The same one Jonathan did, actually, though they weren't there at the same time." Claudia's hands were balled up in fists. "Sobriety didn't suit her. She tried for a while, but ..." She shrugged. "I actually asked Jonathan if he would be her sponsor. She'd tried a few people, but none of them had been a good match. I knew she liked him, and it seemed like he might be able to help her."

"But it didn't work out?"

"He was part of a group of sponsors who only worked with other gay men." There was anger in Claudia's voice, in addition to sorrow. Rye reached out to put a hand on Claudia's arm, but the other woman pulled back. "I'm sorry. I got over it, but ..." she sighed. "I'm sorry. I've totally ruined the mood."

Rye didn't want to agree—wanted to kiss Claudia again, and for the rest of the night—but she stood reluctantly and let herself be led to the door.

"Talk Monday?" Claudia asked as she handed Rye her jacket.

"Sure."

As she pulled the door closed behind her, Rye swallowed back tears. The air felt frigid against the flush of her cheeks. She hurried to her car.

As she got in, she looked up to see Claudia standing at the window.

She pressed the button on her phone and said, "Call Andy."

RYE PULLED UP OUTSIDE ANDY'S HOUSE AND TURNED the car off. He sat on the front porch waiting for her in a heavy jacket, his hat pulled down over his eyes. Rye closed the door of her car softly out of respect for the dark house behind him and the silence hanging over his neighborhood.

She zipped up her own jacket and pulled on her gloves. Andy didn't make a move to stand, so she sat down on the step next to him, leaving a few feet between them.

"What's up?" he asked, his voice pitched low. He glanced back at the house, then at her, and Rye nodded her understanding.

"I'm sorry to call," she began. "I shouldn't have."

"And yet here you are," he said gently.

"Here I am."

They sat together staring out at the flakes of snow that had begun to swirl again. It would be lovely holiday snow if the upcoming holiday wasn't Halloween.

"I want to be supportive," Andy said, "but my body is freezing into an ice sculpture while you sit there not telling me why you've been crying."

"How could you tell I was crying?" Rye asked.

"I've known you since the second grade. Your face gets red and puffy, and your nose runs for, like, an hour afterward."

"So you're saying I'm a beautiful crier?"

"I'm saying that if you don't get to the point in five seconds, I'm going inside to drink the world's largest mug of hot chocolate while sitting on the radiator."

"I met a girl, and I like her, and also she's totally messed up," Rye blurted out. "I shouldn't have called. You and I broke up last week. You're my oldest friend, though, and I just … when I found out that her last girlfriend died—"

"It reminded you of Leila."

Rye wrapped her arms tightly around herself to stifle a shiver. "Yes."

"How did her girlfriend die?"

"Overdosed."

Andy scooted over and wrapped an arm around Rye. She dug her head into his shoulder. "Did you tell her about Leila?"

Rye shook her head. "She was so upset." She sat up. "Besides, I barely know her. We've been on one date."

"Where did you meet?" Andy's tone was genuinely curious.

"School. She's the drama teacher."

"You never mentioned her before."

Rye looked at him. His shoulders had tightened even though his voice was relaxed. She gently patted his arm. "You know I'm not a big theater buff. I promise I wasn't harboring a secret crush on her while we were together."

"I know."

"Andy." Rye waited until he made eye contact with her. "I repeat—I didn't break up with you for her."

"I broke up with you."

"It was mutual."

Andy cleared his throat, but his body had relaxed. "Whatever you have to tell yourself."

Rye rolled her eyes, but it made her feel better to hear the laughter in his voice. "I didn't...expect her. With you, it felt like...I don't know. Like I was coming home to a place I had forgotten was special."

"But there was no spark."

"I wanted there to be one. I know my dad did. I think he's ready to exchange me for you, in fact."

"Hardy's a good egg," Andy said. "I'll miss him."

"Maybe you could bring Rachel over to spend time with him," Rye suggested. "I don't even have to be there. I know she doesn't like me much."

Andy looked like he was going to protest, but he changed his mind and nodded. "You're too alike."

"Hardy's really good at connecting with people who are lost. Especially kids."

"He did win me over when I was little, and I was about as big a mess as you get."

"I don't know about that, but he loves you, and I think he and Rachel would get along. Maybe he could help her see herself as something other than a victim of circumstance."

Andy looked thoughtful. "I don't hate that idea."

"Good. I'll tell him to call you and set something up."

They were quiet again. The sky was purple with the promise of a silent storm.

"Do you think you'll talk to—"

"Claudia."

"Do you think you'll tell Claudia about Leila?"

Rye studied her boots. "I don't know."

"Because you don't trust her?"

"I do," Rye said. "I did."

"I'm sure she trusts you, or she wouldn't have told you about what happened. Like you said, you've only gone on one date. You can't fault her for keeping some things to herself."

"When I'm doing the same thing?"

"Exactly." Andy patted her knee. "You have to give people a chance."

"I do!"

He laughed then, and Rye realized how that laugh was his signature. "You absolutely don't. You were wildly defensive in high school, and now you're …"

"Jaded?"

"Maybe a little."

"I'm realistic," Rye said. "That pain doesn't disappear just because you look up one day and feel a spark again." She laced her fingers together to stop them from trembling.

"But you like her."

"Yeah."

"I can't tell you what to do here, Rye."

"I know."

He heaved himself off the porch and reached down to give her a hand up. They both stood stamping their feet as feeling slowly burned its way back into their frozen limbs.

"Thanks for letting me come over," Rye said. "I know it was insensitive to even ask, but no one else here knows …" She hesitated. "I'm sorry to put you in an awkward position."

"You've been doing that since we were little. The only difference is the apology," Andy said. "And honestly, I don't want to hurt your feelings, but I'm not even jealous." Rye narrowed her eyes at him. "Okay, I'm a little jealous, but not because you like someone else."

"Oh?"

"I was thinking about what you said the other night— about how you thought I'd be good at being in love. I'd never given it much thought before, but all of sudden I can't stop thinking about it."

"You're welcome."

He gave her a little shove. "Except that there isn't anyone I'm interested in."

"Well, if you ever want me to set you up, I know at least"—she paused to count—"one to two eligible women who might be interested."

"Not exactly a social butterfly, are you?"

"How many do you know?" she responded with a snort.

"Who don't have dementia, you mean? Good point. I'll let you know." He gave her a hug and turned to head inside. "And Rye? Let me know how it goes with Claudia. I'm here if you need me."

As she pulled away from this last stop on a long day, she remembered one thing. Jonathan had turned down the opportunity to sponsor Veronica, but not Ross. She tried to recall if Ross had come out before or after he went to rehab.

Maybe there had been something between them after all.

20

RYE SLEPT LATE. SATURDAY AND SUNDAY MORNINGS were delicious, but this time she woke knowing that she had been dreaming something unpleasant. It was gone in the daylight, and she pasted on a big smile for Hardy's pancake breakfast. It was only after she pushed away from the table fuller than was comfortable that she remembered her meeting with Marc, which had been overshadowed by everything that followed.

She had been playing phone tag with Wanda. It was infuriating that her friend would barely text, instead choosing to call and leave a voicemail in response to a text Rye had sent her. Rye had gotten the first message after she'd texted about the unpleasant encounter with Marc DuBois-Thorne, knowing that Wanda would have to deal with him at the wake, and maybe before. Wanda had left a message that she had a meeting with him today, but when Rye had called her back, there had been no answer.

It wasn't like Wanda not to answer. She hated to miss a call, knowing it could be from a parishioner having an emergency.

"Maybe I'll just stop by the church," Rye told her father, who was headed out to the yard to check on the chickens.

"Maybe I'll call the sheriff," Hardy said. Rye started to protest, but he raised a hand. "Just as a precaution. To give him a heads up."

"I'll just tell her to make plans with Marc Dubois-Thorne by phone." She glanced out the window at the freezing rain that had already demolished the pretty snow. "She can use the weather as an excuse."

She waved, slid into her car, and headed for the church slowly. The roads were icy, and the last thing she needed was a fender bender—or worse. Rye took a deep breath. She was probably blowing this out of proportion. Marc had been rude. That wasn't a crime.

Rye had zero proof that Marc was anything other than what he seemed—an uptight exec who had just lost his husband—but she used hands-free to call Wanda again. Still no answer.

She took the turn into the Trinity parking lot too quickly and slid on a patch of ice. Rye eased her foot off the brake and tried to gently correct, but she hadn't bothered to get snow tires yet, and her 1996 Camry didn't have four-wheel drive. She kept sliding, her heart in her throat, completely at the whim of her vehicle.

All of sudden, she realized she was on a collision course for a man striding across the parking lot. She spun her wheel desperately while pumping the brakes. He began to stumble backward, suddenly aware that she wasn't in control of the vehicle, and as her car came to hard stop against the curb, he was only a foot or so away from it.

Sheriff Ryan Phennen stared at Rye through her windshield.

Shakily, she unbuckled her seatbelt and eased out of the car. Her hands were shaking as she stumbled toward him. His mouth was open, but before he could speak, Rye threw herself into his arms and wrapped him tightly in a hug. "I'm so sorry," she said through chattering teeth.

He remained frozen for a long moment, then squeezed her back tentatively. "Are you okay?"

Rye stepped back and caught herself as she almost slipped again on the ice underfoot. "The roads were fine. I wasn't expecting that icy patch in the parking lot." She held her hand up to forestall him again. "I should have." She looked him over carefully. "Are you okay?"

"It was too close for comfort," he said, "but I'm fine."

"What are you doing here?" Rye asked.

"I was about to ask you the same thing."

"I'm looking for Wanda." She glanced at the church building. "She has a meeting with Jonathan Thorne's husband, and when I was talking to Claudia—" She paused. "I was worried about Wanda going to visit him."

"What did Ms. Ramirez have to say?" Ryan asked sharply.

Rye lifted her chin a bit defensively. "I just didn't like the idea of Wanda alone with him. She can be…indiscreet."

Ryan huffed. "Reckless as hell, you mean. It's like she doesn't even care that two people have been murdered—"

"And you think whoever did it might be a danger to Wanda."

He shook his head. "I can't tell you that. But she's been a danger magnet recently, and I know for a fact that she's poking around in this case." Ryan glared at her. "As are you, of course. Even though you should know better than to play amateur detective."

"You asked me to," she shot back. "You practically begged me to spy on Claudia, and I know you wouldn't have done that if you weren't desperate." They stood glaring at each other. "Ryan, you know me. You know I'll keep my mouth shut, but I don't see how I can really help you if you don't tell me anything."

"I can't," he said through gritted teeth. "You know I can't."

Rye pushed her hat up and scratched her forehead impatiently. "Can you at least tell me if Ross was DOA?"

Ryan paused. "Yes."

"And you know the cause of death for both men?"

"Yes."

"Were either of the deaths drug-related?"

"Rye—"

"I'm going to take that as a no."

He grimaced but didn't contradict her. "I can't say anything."

"You still haven't told me why you're here," Rye said.

"I was checking up on Wanda. Like you said, she can be …" He trailed off. "But she's not here. Her admin is in to catch up on a Saturday with her little girl, and she said Wanda's gone to Marc Dubois-Thorne's house." He cleared his throat. "I'm sure she's fine, though."

"She's not answering her phone. I've called her about ten times."

Ryan's whole body tensed. "I need to visit Marc anyway. I have some … paperwork for him."

He turned and strode toward his car.

His personal car, Rye noted. Not the cruiser.

21

WANDA IGNORED HER CELL. IT WAS JUST RYE. SHE could catch her up later. The home that Marc and Jonathan had shared was striking. It was a small barn set on a hill with a sweeping view of late autumn meadows and dark green pine forest. Wanda had briefly dated a man who worked for Yankee Barn Homes, and she knew more than she wanted to about the advantages of open-concept post-and-beam construction. Most were in the wrong place and stuck out because of it. This one was in the perfect location, and she knew the sunset view would be extraordinary.

"Come in!" was the shout from somewhere above her. "Come up the stairs. Down there is the 'barn.'"

Not really something she liked to do with someone she had never met, but Wanda climbed to the next floor, took a deep breath, and opened the door.

Hygge was the Danish and Norwegian word for a style of coziness with hints of contentment. This house was practically a magazine spread for it. There was a basket of wool knit socks to put on by the front door, a furry blanket on the sofa, candles everywhere (not yet lit), and a fireplace (lit). Even the mugs that surrounded a teapot on a fondue fire were steaming perfectly.

Wanda kept her shoes on, wondering if this room had been staged for her to enjoy before meeting her host. It was lovely coming out of the cold October slain—that unfortunate nickname for this awful wintry mix—but it also felt calculated.

The dog won her over. Great-great-grandma must have been an Irish wolfhound, but the next few generations had diminished in size until this shaggy love only took up half the hearth on an oversized dog bed.

"Oh, you darling! Do you want some attention, or should I wait for your person? I have treats in my pocket, but I think Jack Russell Milk-Bones are just cupcake sprinkles to you."

"Paddy-pup is not particular at all. All treats are enthusiastically received." Marc DuBois-Thorne padded in, himself in wooly socks, leggings, and a sweater that was either Irish to match the dog or Danish to match the decor. "Jonathan was his person. I am an acceptable substitute, but he keeps going to the door when I get home to see if he is coming." Marc took a deep breath and steadied his voice. "He does need to be bribed a bit before completely fawning all over a woman, but a Jack Russell treat would work for that."

Paddy condescended to be bribed and then appeared to offer unconditional adoration. He swung his huge head around, and Wanda was relieved to have avoided needing a knee replacement by half an inch. Marc handed her a steaming mug of mulled cider, which she gratefully accepted.

"Thank you, Marc. Jess didn't tell me much about what you need for the memorial, so why don't you tell me what I can do for you?"

He seemed intent on grinding his cinnamon stick into a nub with his bare hand. "I don't really know what she wants from me. I told her this event is a bad idea. But she's persistent. Jonathan always called her the bossy twin."

"She mentioned that you were planning the memorial together," Wanda prompted gently.

"With Jonathan. When it was a party, not ... this." He stared out the window at the sleet. "I wanted to cancel. We had the graveside service with Mr. Fairchild. We don't need to do it again."

"Have you told Jess how you feel?"

"Yesterday. She's adamant. I can't tell her what to do when it comes to Jonathan. Twins are ..." He trailed off. "I can't tell her how to grieve for him."

"I'm sorry. I missed that?"

This time, he almost shouted. "I can't tell the— *her* how to grieve for him."

"But you'd rather not participate?"

He turned away from her. "It's not up to me."

Wanda couldn't hear him, but she guessed and nodded. Since he was looking out the window, she put her phone beside her drink and set the amplification for her hearing aids on full. "Why don't you tell me about Jonathan."

"I met him when I was promoting an off-Broadway short run of a British show he was lighting, and I fell in love. He was the one. I was barely out of the closet, only one other relationship, but Jonathan had been out forever. I don't think there was a time when he didn't know, and his family was fine with it. My parents took longer to come around, but they loved Jonathan, too."

"He sounds like he had a gift for truth," Wanda said.

"And for performance."

"They go hand in hand."

Marc smiled a little at that.

"When did he start using, if you don't mind my asking?"

"He fell off a stage ladder about two years before we met. Common story, as I'm sure you know. Painkillers are hard to quit." Marc paused. "He spent almost a year as a completely lost soul."

Wanda nodded. She knew the story far too well. Fell off a ladder. Fell off the wagon. Funny how the expression suddenly meant something. "But he went to rehab."

"He told me things got really bad. He couldn't even work. It was after he was in recovery for the first time that I met him. I had other issues that made me vulnerable. We were wild about each other. He moved in. We got married. It was the dream."

Wanda allowed Paddy-pup to snuggle his head into her lap. She stroked his ears as she waited for Marc to collect himself.

"But it fell apart about three years ago. I didn't like to leave him to go to my office in New York because I was afraid of what I'd find when I came back." He paused, then continued softly. "What you found." He rubbed the cuff of his sweater across his eyes. "I couldn't take it. I told him he could go to rehab or I would leave him, but I couldn't stay if he was going to kill himself."

"And he went."

"We were separated for a few months. I sublet an apartment across town. I had to let him know that I meant what I said. It was the worst time of my life." Marc put his mug down on the coffee table. "I thought it was, at least." Paddy left Wanda's lap and came over to put his head on Marc's knee. He pulled away and tucked his legs up under him, and the dog settled on the floor by the couch with a sigh. "Rehab was the best place for Jonathan. He took to it like a duck to water. He made new friends. He got clean. He became a mentor and was working part-time with a program to help others get clean. Jonathan was all in. He was…He was my Jonathan again."

Wanda sat in the silence. She could do that. Years of practice helped her to make friends with this kind of pause.

"Do you know what I think?" Marc leaned forward suddenly. "The only way Jonathan died of an overdose is if a couple of big guys held him down and force-fed him pills. That's what I think. Not that anyone cares."

"I do," Wanda said. The quiet stretched out.

Marc took a deep breath. "But he was a very good actor."

"I know that this…celebration of life?

"Party," Marc replied.

"Party, then, is for Jess. It's what she needs to say good-bye to her brother. I can see that it's not what you want, and I wish I could tell you to stay home, but we both know you'll have to get up, get dressed, and face the music, so to speak." She finished her cider and put her mug down. "It's going to hard, and you'll probably hate it, but keep an open mind. You'll be surrounded by people who loved Jonathan too, so it might not be all bad."

The loud knock on the door was so unexpected that Wanda spilled the dregs of her cider. The dog immediately lumbered over to lick it up as Marc stood to answer the door.

Wanda was still brushing the big tongue off her skirt when she turned and froze. Ryan stood in the hall, dripping. His features looked tight and angry—worried, she realized. He didn't even make a pretense of being surprised to see her, just nodded curtly in her direction. "You should check your messages," he muttered. Then he turned to Marc. "Sorry to bother you at home, but we got some new information about the toxicology report, and I wanted to talk to you about it." He glanced over at Wanda. "Can we speak privately?"

Marc apologized to Wanda and then escorted Ryan into the only room with a door. It must have been an office, with a barn door that slid closed but didn't do much to deaden the sound. Wanda gave the dog a pat and made her way near enough that she could overhear.

Ryan's clear tenor was unmistakable as he detailed the results to Marc—that there had been trace amounts of fentanyl, not in Jonathan's system, but on his clothing. It had been enough for the department to make its initial assessment. "It wasn't an overdose."

"I told you," Marc said, his tone very different from the grief-stricken one he'd used with Wanda. "He's been clean for over two years."

"Once we ruled that out as cause of death, I asked the ME about his stomach contents. He died from anaphylactic shock."

"Milk?"

"You knew about his milk allergy?"

"Of course I did. But he has an Epi-Pen— Oh." Marc's voice trailed off. "He used it about a month ago. I kept reminding him to get another one, but I don't think he'd picked it up yet."

"He didn't keep a spare?"

"That was his spare. He was so careful about everything he ate. He'd used the other one a few years ago when we were in Paris. He didn't see the point in having two when he was so cautious. It was incredibly rare for him to eat anything we didn't make in the house."

"Who would have known about his allergy?"

"Everyone. It wasn't a secret—just the opposite. It was safer for people to know." Marc sounded angry, but Ryan's voice was calm and controlled.

"Who would have known that he wasn't carrying an Epi-Pen?"

"Besides me?"

"Besides you."

"I don't know. Maybe Jess? He's always been this way, casual. She used to carry one for him when they were kids."

"Anyone else?"

"I don't know!" Marc exploded. Wanda took a step back from the door. She put her hand down on the dog's head for comfort.

"Sit down." Ryan's voice carried now. "I'm trying to help you here. Right now, you're telling me that the only two people who knew about the fact that he was casual about carrying his Epi-Pen are you and his sister. Is that correct?"

"Do you think I killed my husband?"

"If I was convinced of it, we would be having this conversation in a different location. I'm doing my best to get all the information we need to solve this case. You can either help me or you can come answer questions down at the station."

"I'm calling my lawyer," Marc said.

"No more questions now, but you might want to alert them."

Wanda was sitting primly on the couch when he slid the door open, and she was grateful that Marc's back was to her. Ryan gestured to her angrily. She quickly picked up her coat and bag and followed him down and outside.

"I'm not going to pretend you didn't hear that," Ryan said as they stood getting soaked by her car.

"Hear what?" Wanda tried her best to look innocent.

"Stay out of this, please." Ryan looked like he wanted to yell at her, and the effort was causing his cheeks to flush. "No matter what you think, you're not a detective. You have no business poking around murders, and if you keep doing it, you're going to end up dead."

"It's nice that you still care," Wanda said, fishing her keys out of her purse.

"Of course I care," he said as her eyes fastened on him. "I don't want to see anything happen to you. Again."

"Did the card fall out of your get-well bouquet last spring?" she asked sharply. "Did you forget where I lived? I don't remember you stopping by to see I was okay. But now you're worried?"

He stood there silently, wet snow starting to stick to his lashes. She was sorry she'd noticed.

"You were busy. You were working on a case. You had a thing," Wanda said. "I've heard it, Ryan. You have time for me when it's convenient for you."

"I'm trying to help you," he replied through gritted teeth.

"And I'm trying to help you. Looks like neither of us wants help right now." She waved back at the house. "Now go find out who killed those men so I can sleep without dreaming about a car running me down."

She should not have said that last bit. Ryan opened her door for her and stood glaring until she got in.

When she glanced in the rearview mirror, he was standing with his arms folded tight, watching her drive away.

22

Rye cursed Wanda's entire generation on the drive over to her house. They treated their cell phones as optional communication rather than essential. Rye knew for a fact that Wanda often turned the ringer down so low she couldn't hear it. Of course, it pinged her hearing aids, so that excuse only worked with people who did not know her well.

Rye hadn't grown up with cell phones either. In fact, she hadn't gotten her first one until her sophomore year of college, but it was so much more economical to use it as her primary phone that she couldn't remember the last time she used a landline outside of her office. Even her father recognized the benefits of instant connection.

The lights were on at Wanda's house. A huge bubble of relief floated up through her as she jogged to the door to ring the bell. She was obviously still going to give Wanda a piece of her mind for poor phone etiquette, but she'd also give her a hug.

A face appeared in the window at the top of the door. Wanda's nephew Lance peered out at her. Rye felt her gut tighten again. She'd forgotten that Wanda wasn't living alone anymore. She gave him a half-hearted wave as he unlocked the door and let her in.

"Is Wanda here by any chance?"

Rye's last shred of hope dissolved as Lance shook his head. "She said she would be home for dinner, so I expect her soon. Would you like to come in and wait?"

Most of her students would have looked for any excuse to shut the door in her face so they could get back to doing whatever it was they did before the adults in their lives got home.

"That would be great, thanks, Lance." She came in and took off her soaking jacket, hanging it by the door. She slipped off her boots and put them to dry by the radiator. Her neck was sweaty and cold with rain at the same time, as were her clothes, and it was a relief to take off layers in this warm house.

Rye glanced around. Lance had only been here a few weeks, and already the house looked more like a home. Wanda didn't spend much time here, so it made sense that her office was the space that was the most reflective of her personality, but Rye liked this. The shoes and hoodies, the stacks of homework and half-finished projects with doodles in the margins. The TV was on, paused, presumably when Lance got up to let her in.

"Is this *Avatar: The Last Airbender*?" she asked, plopping down on the couch. He came and slouched in a chair covered with Wink's hair. Wink had jumped down when Rye entered, but now he happily settled back on Lance's lap with a sigh.

Lance absently scratched his ears as he stared at the television. "Yup. It's my go-to show when I need to get some work done but I'm also feeling burned out from the day." He glanced at her. "You've seen it?"

"I love it," Rye said. "I watched it for the first time maybe five years ago with a friend in Austin. I've probably rewatched parts of it three or four times since then."

"It's so good, right?" Lance reached forward, and Wink jumped off his lap, indignant as only a small dog could be. He stalked off to find a less mobile hot spot as Lance handed Rye one of his notebooks. "I like to doodle some of the animals."

"These are amazing! No wonder Claud— I mean Ms. Ramirez is so happy to have your help." She handed them back to Lance. "How much of that is natural talent and how much is practice, would you say?"

Lance looked at her with that particular head tilt teens got when someone asked a question that broke through the noise of irrelevance. "I've always loved art, and I must have been good enough when I was little because a lot of people told me they liked what I did. I think whether or not I was actually good, it gave me confidence to work at it."

"I get that. The affirmation feels so good that it primes you to work harder on something?"

"Right." Lance nodded vigorously. "And then at some point, it's nice to have people like it, but it just becomes, like, something you do even if they don't get it."

"Yeah, exactly." Rye leaned back against the blanket on the back of the couch. She knew Wanda wouldn't get to keep him forever, but Rye hoped Lance stuck around long enough for her to get to know him better.

"Do you have something like that?" Lance crossed one long leg over the other. "And you aren't allowed to say anything that has to do with work."

"Why not?"

"Because even if you love your job, you still get paid to do it, so there's motivation to improve beyond just loving it."

"But what about actors and musicians? DJs?"

"They probably still have hobbies."

"Hmm. Fair point." She thought about it. "I'm not sure I have a hobby. Growing up, my dad taught me how to do a lot of things well, and I liked some of them, but none so much that I do it in my spare time." Rye pulled her damp hair off her neck and wound it into a bun she could wind a hair band around. "Well, I run, I guess. But my friends like it more than I do."

"What about what you do with my aunt? Like ... detecting, or whatever?"

Rye realized this very bright boy might have had an ulterior motive for asking her in while his aunt was out. She sat up. Where was Wanda? The sick feeling stole back in as Rye realized she'd relaxed in the air of coziness Lance exuded.

She sighed. "I don't know if I'd call it a hobby, but you're right that it is something I do for myself. Certainly no one else except Wanda seems to be thanking me for sticking my nose where it doesn't belong."

"And you're good at it?"

"Better than some," Rye said. "Why?"

Lance straightened up. "I know I wasn't here when Mr. Thorne died, but Aunt Wanda is pretty messed up about it. She won't admit it to me, but I know it's haunting her."

"What makes you say that?"

"Everyone thinks it's so suspicious. They don't think it has anything to do with rehab." Rye noticed he hadn't answered her question about Wanda.

"Wait." She held up a hand. "Kids at school know he was in rehab?"

"Yeah, why? Was it a secret?" Lance asked.

Apparently only to the administration. "Some of his friends didn't know, that's all. I guess I shouldn't be surprised that a bunch of teenagers would. Can I ask who told you?"

Lance shrugged. "Henry Jacobs. The one whose brother died?"

"How did he know?"

"His brother, Ross, told Henry that he met Jonathan when he was in rehab." Lance played with the zipper on his hoodie. "Ross recognized him from school, so when he needed a sponsor, Mr. Thorne offered. Emma told everyone at school about it after Henry told her." Lance looked at her. "I feel really bad for Henry. His family has had a pretty bad time. The divorce was terrible, they lost all their money, and his dad was so pis— *mad* when his brother came out. And Henry's just this boring kid, you know? Maybe that's why he and I got along—we both kind of get what it's like to take care of ourselves because our parents are too busy to help, and then we get into trouble."

Rye nodded. "I have a friend like that, too. I've known him since we were seven, and he got too good at keeping his head down. I was the one who was always stirring things up, dragging him into trouble." She winced. "Probably shouldn't have told you that last part."

"It's okay. I won't blab it around school. Mostly, kids actually think you're pretty okay."

Pretty okay. For a teacher, that was high praise. For a vice principal? Rye felt like she'd just been awarded a medal of honor. "Thanks."

"I told Henry he shouldn't have gone out with that girl Emma. Her sister dated Ross when they were in high school, and then when Ross came out, the sister freaked out on him. I think Emma is just messing with Henry and plans to drop him, as, like, revenge or something." Lance shrugged. "But he says no. That she's cool." He shook his head. "I don't think he ever even smoked pot before they started going out."

The door opened, and Wanda came in, stamping her boots on the mat and shaking her coat.

"Hey, Aunt Wanda," Lance said. "Hope it's okay I let the VP in while you were gone?"

She met Rye's gaze and held up her phone, mouthing, 'Sorry.' "It's fine, Lance. She's housebroken."

Rye stuck her tongue out at Wanda, relief flooding through her. She wasn't going to make a scene in front of Lance, but she also couldn't very well leave now that she'd been sitting here for fifteen minutes. "Need some help with dinner?" she asked, standing up.

Wanda looked exhausted, but there was also a contentment beneath the surface that Rye hadn't seen before. She watched her friend out of the corner of her eye as she chopped veggies for a salad. Wanda was making what looked like way more pasta than three people could possibly eat, but considering one of them was a teenage boy, maybe it wasn't enough. Hence the garlic bread in the oven, Rye concluded.

He might not have been here long, but Wanda had adjusted to having her nephew in the house. Rye knew that a part of Wanda wished her life had been just different enough to allow for children, but Rye also thought this was a better arrangement, with no diapers or expensive preschools. Just all the spaghetti Lance could eat, and a few awkward talks about human sexuality.

Piece of cake for Wanda, who had probably had just about every uncomfortable conversation imaginable with parishioners over the years.

Lance put his headphones on and started *Airbender* again.

"I met Marc yesterday," Rye said. "He didn't exactly make a great impression, and when I went to the church looking for you and you weren't there, I panicked." Rye carefully scooped cucumbers into the bowl.

Wanda stepped closer to Rye and lowered her voice. "Ryan showed up at my meeting."

Rye flushed. "I know. I need to fill you in on a few things."

Wanda eyed her suspiciously. "Did you sic him on me when I wouldn't answer the phone?"

"Not…exactly." Rye could feel Wanda's eyes boring into her back. "Okay, yes."

"Hmm."

"He was looking for you at the church. Lisa was the one who told him where you'd be. I was worried about you. Maybe he picked up on that."

"Maybe?"

"Okay, he definitely did. And we are not going to dissect that, just so you know."

"Well, as it turns out, it was a blessing in disguise." Wanda stirred the huge pot of boiling water and started the sauce simmering on low heat, the smell of garlic filling the steamy kitchen. "Jonathan died from anaphylactic shock. He was allergic to milk, and he didn't have an Epi-Pen with him. Apparently, he didn't eat food he hadn't prepped himself, so he wasn't always careful about having it on him."

"So it wasn't murder, then? Just an unfortunate accident?"

"That wasn't the impression I got from Ryan," Wanda said. "My guess is Ryan suspects someone poisoned him, then rubbed fentanyl into his clothes, hoping it would be an open-and-shut OD. The thing is, people knew about the allergy, but Marc told Ryan that Jonathan has been without an Epi-Pen for about a month, and that he wasn't sure if anyone else knew."

Rye washed a handful of cherry tomatoes and tossed them into the bowl. "Well, I've heard enough at this point to know that Marc and Jonathan didn't have the picture-perfect relationship people told me about right after he died."

"Who does?" Wanda replied.

"That's more jaded than I usually get from you."

Wanda carefully poured the pot out over the strainer, then dumped the fettuccine back in with the sauce. "I didn't mean it like that. I know many happy couples, but none of them would describe their relationships as perfect. Marriage takes a lot of work."

"Especially if one person is an addict or in recovery," Rye pointed out.

"Exactly. Or if the other is a judgmental prick," Wanda agreed. "But I'm pretty sure Marc loved Jonathan. And he wouldn't have admitted that only he knew about the Epi-Pen—that doesn't make sense." She paused. "I actually liked him, and he has a great dog called Paddy-pup."

Rye set the table, lining up each utensil carefully as she chose her words. "Claudia told me that Jonathan wasn't into physical relationships, so it seems more likely it was an emotional connection, or possibly an innocent sponsor-sponsee situation. But Marc could still have been jealous. The man I met definitely seemed like he could have an explosive temper."

Lance chose that moment to saunter in. "Smells amazing in here. Should I wash up, and do you need help?"

"Wash up. It's all done. You can do dishes later." Wanda set out the food on the kitchen table. She gave Rye a look behind Lance's back, but it was unnecessary.

Rye had already pumped this kid for information. She wasn't about to go dishing about a double homicide in front of him. She rolled her eyes at her friend and mouthed "duh" at her as she sat down. "Everything looks delicious," she said.

Lance helped himself to an enormous serving before dropping into the chair next to Rye. "Yeah, it does. She's a great cook, you know?" He nodded to his aunt with a full mouth.

Wanda blushed. "Not really, but I have a few dishes on rotation that are solid."

"Taco night and any of her soups are the best." Lance used a hunk of garlic bread to wipe up some sauce.

"It's a good thing the meals I know how to cook well can serve a crowd," Wanda replied with a laugh.

Lance patted his belly. "A crowd of one, with no leftovers."

Rye laughed. "I might have to start coming over more often. Wanda and I usually grab a bite out, but this is wonderful."

"Maybe you could have Hardy whip something up and join us," Wanda said. "My cooking has nothing on his."

"Or you could invite Ms. Ramirez," Lance said, his eyes darting toward Rye, then back to his plate.

Rye choked on a bite of bread and used it as an excuse to hide behind a napkin for a minute. When she looked up, Wanda was staring at her, clearly amused.

"There's nothing to— I mean…no." Rye sighed, then turned to Lance. "Why don't you tell me what you've heard?"

He shrugged innocently. "Didn't hear anything. I saw you two at the dance. I mean, I'm acing Chemistry for a reason."

"Remind me who this Ms. Ramirez is?" Wanda, who knew perfectly well, was having a good time playing with them both.

"She's the drama teacher at the high school," Lance piped up helpfully. "She's pretty cool. I was late like three times last week, and she only marked me down for the last one."

Rye laughed. "Nice to know what passes for cool."

"So are you going to tell me more?" Wanda asked.

Rye shook her head. "I think I'm good."

She made a gesture like she was texting and Lance just laughed. "You guys are so old sometimes."

Wanda patted Rye's hand. "You heard it here first, dearie. You are officially as old as I am. Make sure you grab my copy of AARP on the way out."

"You get AARP?" Rye couldn't stop herself from asking.

Wanda threw a napkin at her. "You are officially uninvited from this dinner."

Lance grinned at Rye and stage-whispered to her. "Don't take it personally. She's up past her bedtime."

"You just cost yourself half of my leftover slice of cake," Wanda said haughtily.

Lance bit his lip. "Uh …"

"Don't tell her you ate her cake if you want to live," Rye warned.

"I did…not? It was Wink!"

Wanda leveled a look at both. "Joke's on you. The piece I left in the fridge was sugar-free leftovers from a meeting yesterday. Tony brought me a slab of homemade chocolate cake this morning that's still in my bag." She waved her fork at each of them. "None. For. You."

Rye put on her best puppy dog face, and Lance hummed a Wink-inspired whine, but to no avail. Wanda pulled the Tupperware out and ate it slowly while they watched. Revenge was a dish best served with ganache.

Only Lance was willing to even field a question. "Why did Tony give you cake? It's not your …"

"It is not and never will be my birthday. My birthday is how astronomers discovered there were black holes." Wanda licked the back of her fork. "It was sheer gratitude—I told him you sing."

"That was between us!"

"Lance …"

"Boundaries, Aunt Wanda! Just because you heard me singing in the shower doesn't mean I'm joining the choir!"

Rye grinned, loving this.

"I'll tell him myself if you won't," Lance warned. "I like Tony. I've gotten to know him at school."

"But you don't want to get up for church every Sunday?"

"That seems like a good enough reason to me," Rye mumbled under her breath."

"Not really, no," Lance said. "But that's not it. I just don't sing anymore. I'll shake the maracas. I'll even learn the tambourine."

"What about the bells?"

"Don't push your luck." Lance used his long arm to try to snag a bite of the cake before it disappeared. Wanda covered it with her arm and stuck her tongue out at him.

"I heard you owe Greg a favor."

"Who's Greg?" Rye asked.

"Tony's boyfriend," Lance told her. "Greg's great. He got me a copy of Klingelhoefer's *The Art and Craft of Scenic Design* with interlibrary loan. It's like sixty-five bucks online."

"Wow, I'm out of the loop," Rye said. "Last I heard, Tony was dating that guy from Maplewood—the gymnast." In deference to Lance, she refrained from quirking her eyebrow at Wanda, as had been their custom when discussing Tony's previous crush. He had been beautiful, double-jointed, and dull.

"Ah, yes, the stunning Dusty Moran!" Wanda wiped her mouth primly on the napkin before using her finger to scrape the plate's remaining frosting. "They split. Tony and Greg have been together for a while."

"And he's a librarian, I gather?"

"And a sweetheart. I have to admit, I haven't spent as much time with them as I should," Wanda said, "but he seems fantastic."

Lance gave a little sigh as Wanda stood up to clear plates away. She rolled her eyes. "Fine. There's another piece in the bag, but you have to share it with Rye."

"Softie." Rye handed Lance a knife to slice it.

"You don't have to get cake, you know."

Rye popped up and grabbed her plate before Lance could make a move to take it back. She shoved a huge bite into her mouth. "Now that's where you're wrong," she mumbled, spitting cake crumbs at her friend.

Lance started to laugh so hard he choked, and Wanda had to pound him on the back while tears streamed down his cheeks. He finally swallowed. Rye finished her cake to a soundtrack of helpless giggles, although when she tried to relieve him of the rest of his slice, Lance sobered enough to grab it and run.

"Don't forget you're on dish duty!" Wanda called after him as she showed Rye to the door.

"Ten bucks says you do them yourself." Rye pulled on her scarf.

"I have a secret weapon," Wanda replied.

"Oh, yeah? And it works on teenagers?"

"Better than anything."

"Pray tell!"

Wanda grinned. "I change the Wi-Fi password every day. I leave it for him after school if he's done all the chores we agreed to. If he hasn't, he gets it when they're finished."

"That's actually brilliant."

"As a side benefit, it keeps me honest about my own share of the household responsibilities, too," Wanda confessed in a low voice. "Wouldn't do to get called out for slacking."

"Yeah." Rye laughed. "He might disconnect the landline on you."

As she shut the door, she could her Lance cackling from the stairs.

23

THE CORRECTION ABOUT JONATHAN THORNE'S CAUSE
of death had gone public to anyone interested in a two-
week-old presumed overdose death. Which few people
were, if the two paragraphs on an inside column that the
story was given in the Sunday edition was any indication.
The authorities were late, but there was no reason for
publicity. There were not very many ways that murder
by milk could be solved through reader and listener
input. Wanda thought the fentanyl on Jonathan's clothes
and the chip were suspicious. It meant someone who
was using had been there at the scene, probably trying
to deflect investigation. And the later addition of the
syringe and taking it away? It made it seem less like an
accident.

Wanda was happy, though, that Ryan had listened
to her and given the newspapers a brief version of the
coroner's findings on Ross Jacobs:

> *...the recent early morning accident*
> *victim on Route 111 appears to have*
> *been dead before the car struck him. Jacobs*

suffered a fatal blow to the head and was then dragged into the road, possibly in hopes of covering up signs of a recent fight. Authorities are now hoping the driver who ran over Jacobs's body will come forward and assist the police with the investigation into Jacobs's death. All charges of manslaughter will be dropped.

Wanda thought that leaving the scene of a fatality probably involved some very serious charges, so there might be a surprise waiting for that someone. Of course, Ryan must still consider that the person who struck and dragged the young man could be the same person who got into their vehicle and …It was too ugly to consider.

The paper went on to ask the public to be in touch with any information placing Jacobs in the area and then recapped his biography and mentioned memorial service information would be forthcoming.

Wanda was not prepared for the public to get in touch with *her*.

She was ignoring the telephone after a decadent Lance-prepared meal of handmade spring rolls and grilled boneless ribs marinated in sweet-and-sour sauce. The spring rolls were amazing, but the ribs were pretty tasty, too. There was rice, and Lance served pineapple chunks and fortune cookies for dessert. The new schedule, with Lance cooking Tuesday nights, was off to a delicious start. He had even volunteered to do the dishes, which was not part of the deal, and she was waiting for the "ask."

Wanda was also trying, for once, to write an early sermon. The landline ring was probably a poll, a robo call, or someone selling her something.

Lance came in from the kitchen holding the phone with two fingers as if it were a dangerous and unknown animal. "It's Mitch."

"Mitch who?" she mouthed.

Lance shrugged and dangled the phone like an exotic household pet. As soon as she took it, he vanished back into the kitchen, obviously thinking it was a "church thing."

"Hello?"

"Hi, Wanda? This is Mitch Allen."

"Hey Mitch," Wanda said. This might be the first time her favorite bar owner had ever called her at home. At least she knew Mitch to be a congenial conversationalist from her frequent visits to his newly opened establishment in Stone Ridge .

"This is awkward, but I have a question."

"Shoot."

"As a minister, you can legally keep things confidential, right?"

She did not like where this was going. "In theory, yes. In criminal matters, I am …less happy to have you tell me something."

"I read about police wanting information about that Jacobs kid. The paper showed a picture of him, and I realized I do remember him coming in here. He was young enough that I had to check his ID, and it was the same photo. He got into an argument that night. I had to ask them to take it outside."

"Here's my advice. Call the police."

"Listen, I've driven a few of my regulars home more than once. And I know it's a stereotype to watch out for ladies, but I do keep an eye on the ones who come in alone. This can be a rough place, but I make sure it's a safe one. That said, I will lose half my trade if they think

I'll call the cops on someone boasting about boosting a car, or taking home rebar or insulation from a job, or betting on dirt bike races in the woods." He paused. "So I was thinking that if you could come by, I could tell you what I saw and heard, and you could say that someone there that night told you in confidence and didn't want to be identified."

Wanda struggled with her conscience and decided that it would be all right with God if she did what Mitch wanted *without* mentioning that ten minutes after she told Ryan, he would show up at Laredo's, and his very presence would create the same bad press.

"I'm willing to listen, Mitch, but I still say to give your customers some credit. This is murder."

"You have a high opinion of my clientele."

"Well, I have been a customer myself."

"Good point. I'll have a tequila sunrise waiting for you. Thanks again, Reverend Duff."

"Make it a Shirley Sunrise. There's a sermon to write tonight."

"Okay, see you soon." He sounded relieved.

She hung up and grabbed her coat, then poked her head into the kitchen. "Lance, if anyone calls, you don't know where I am, which is Laredo's." She paused. "Unless it's the sheriff."

He raised his eyebrows. "A landline date? That's a new one."

That was an old one, she thought. "It's a pastoral call."

"Whatever you say." He winked at her, and she grinned back, rolling her eyes.

TUESDAY NIGHT WAS NOT HOPPING AT LAREDO'S. There were a couple of people at the bar and a few tables of sweethearts or pickups that were in deep conversation, but she could hear more noise from the next room, where pool and darts were perennial favorites. Wanda hoped that Luke Combs's "Beer Never Broke My Heart" was not going viral.

She peeked in on her way to a corner booth and saw Andy Soucek with a handful of darts. She waved and settled herself in.

A hand on her shoulder surprised her, but it was only Andy, come to give her a hug. "I can't stay to chat, but my friends needed a break from my winning streak, so I said I would pick up the next round."

"Andy, great to see you!" She checked her watch. "It's early for you to be dominating already!"

He threw back his head and laughed. "It's not my fault I don't drink. Some people swear they're better drunk, but I am the dart champion. The evidence doesn't lie." He pointed to his T-shirt. Someone had scribbled "Darts Champ: Laredo's Stone Ridge " across it in Sharpie. "I'm going to grab another orange juice and some beers. What can I get for you?"

"O'Doul's, or an orange juice if they don't have it." Mitch had a great house red he kept stocked. Wanda suspected not many others drank it, and she felt a little guilty about that, but she needed to keep a clear head today.

"You got it." Andy gave her a mock salute and headed to the bar.

By the time Andy had delivered the other drinks, Mitch still hadn't come over. "They switched to pool while I was gone, so I have a couple of minutes. Mind if I join you?"

"Please sit." Wanda waved him into the booth. "I haven't seen you for ages, and I have the coolest thing to tell you about dementia."

"Now that's a sentence I never thought to hear."

She laughed. "You need to Google 'the Restaurant of Mistaken Orders' in Japan. It is completely staffed by people with dementia, many of whom live in nursing facilities. Everyone who goes to the restaurant knows their order may be wrong, but all the food is delicious, so they don't care, and there is so much laughter and love. They have a bunch of YouTube videos, and it's just amazing."

"That sounds amazing. I'd like to visit someday," Andy said. "You know, you are the only clergyperson who doesn't treat them like children, and they stretch themselves for you."

She smiled, pleased. "In England, they've followed the idea with 'the Restaurant that Makes Mistakes.' I know it's just inspiration, but somebody needs to do it here."

He struck an over-the-top defense pose. "Whoa. Not me. I have enough on my plate right now."

"I heard you had less on your plate."

"That wasn't a lead into you asking about my breakup with Rye, was it?"

"Nope. That was a genuine nudge, because I think you have the imagination to make something like that work or be part of a team that does. But now that you mention it—"

"I didn't."

"You most certainly did." Wanda smiled. "You're a good one, Andy, and so is she. I think she's taking it harder than she lets on."

"She came by my house this weekend, and we talked again. She mentioned that she has feelings for someone." He took a sip of his juice.

Wanda nodded. "I did hear that much. I am a 'detective,' you know."

He smiled. "She's funny that way, isn't she? She's a loner who hates to be alone. She's been like that since she was in the second grade." He paused. "Since her mom left, I guess. As long as we've been friends, she's had this urge to push people away, but then she's afraid of being alone."

"Being abandoned by a parent at a young age can lead to that sort of behavior. She wants to be the one who pushes, not be the one who's left."

"I never thought of it that way."

Wanda shrugged. "Familial dynamics are sort of a specialty of mine. Speaking of which, how's Rachel doing?"

Andy glanced up, and when Wanda followed his gaze, she saw Mitch Allen standing behind her with his bald head and fresh shave, wearing a black shirt with a turquoise and silver bolo tie. He pulled off his apron to reveal a belt buckle to match. He looked like he had arrived from bartender central casting.

Andy stood. "See you at Fair Havens, Wanda." He smiled at Mitch and went to rejoin his friends.

Mitch slid in across from her. "Hey!" Mitch called after Andy, "take it easy on my regulars! I want them to spend money here, not lose it." He shook his head with a grin. "Andy Soucek is a great guy and a mean darts player. Not too shabby at pool, either."

"He's a man of many talents," Wanda agreed. "You should see him parent." She took a sip of her nonalcoholic beer and tried not to gag. She wasn't a huge fan of any beer, but this one was especially hard to swallow. "So what can I do you for?"

He seemed to relax. "That's usually my line." Mitch glanced over to the bar, out of instinct, Wanda guessed, because it was a quiet night, and no one seemed to need him. She raised her eyebrows at him.

"Two men got in a fight here. Turns out, one of them was that kid in the paper, Jacobs."

"That was what you told me on the phone. There must be more?"

Mitch nodded. "The older one was built like a football player. I don't know if I would recognize him if I saw his face, but his build was unmistakable. Stocky and strong, but no more than five foot seven. He kept using homophobic slurs, you know. 'Pansy' was the nicest thing he said." He shook his head. "I won't repeat the rest."

"Nasty stuff, though?"

"The worst. Thing is, I pride myself on, well, Pride, if you get my drift?"

"I do." Wanda smiled.

"I know this is a country bar, but I have a reputation." He pointed to a couple of flags above the door that she hadn't noticed before. "I'm not going to stand for that sort of talk in here, and neither are my regulars. If I hadn't gotten the older guy out of here, he probably would've gotten himself jumped."

"You didn't want to tell that to Sheriff Phennen? I don't get it. You know he'll come show around photos of anyone they consider suspects." She paused. "What you're not saying is you're going to make sure those customers won't be here when the sheriff is, the ones who helped you kick the aggressor to the curb. Because ... they aren't out?"

He was quiet for a moment. "Some of them are married," he said finally. "Some of them just want to keep things quiet. Their lives are ... complicated. I don't want to have to talk to the police."

"Is protecting your customers and your business more important than finding justice for a kid who was killed?"

She'd gotten to him, and he started to rise to his feet. "Tell the sheriff what you want—what you think is right—but I've got to protect my people. Some of them don't have any other safe place." He looked down at her pleadingly. "Could you tell me when you let him know?"

Wanda nodded, and Mitch gave her shoulder a squeeze before he excused himself to go back to work. She liked Mitch—a barman who was also a safe haven. No wonder she'd found this place last year when she was so lost.

She decided she'd call Ryan in the morning. She carried her empty bottle to the bar and let Mitch know. Something he had told her was tickling her memory, but she couldn't put her finger on it. Wanda felt her phone buzz in her pocket, and all thoughts of the case disappeared when she saw the picture Lance had sent of a bowl of popcorn and a pot of tea on the coffee table. She sent him back a string of nonsense emojis, just because she knew it would make him groan, and headed home so he could show her the first episode of his new favorite show.

24

RYE KNOCKED ON CLAUDIA'S OFFICE DOOR AT SEVEN forty-five. A few students were milling about in the greenroom before the start of the school day, their energy low. They seemed young to Rye this morning, like she'd caught them before they woke all the way up and put on whatever attitude helped them face the day. She was fond of these moments when she was allowed to see her students with their guards down.

She knocked again, but a voice spoke up behind her. "Ms. Ramirez is never in before eight because her classes don't start until eight thirty."

Rye turned to see Emma Reyes standing behind her. Emma looked terrible—if anything, worse than she had the night Rye had found her in the woods with Henry.

"I didn't know you were back in school," Rye said. "How are you feeling?"

Emma shrugged. It was a timeless show of resistance to authority. Rye had perfected her own nonchalant postures when she went to this school herself. "I'm okay. Thanks for not suspending me or whatever."

Rye knew full well that the reason no action had been taken against Emma and Henry was because of Ross's death. No one could stomach suspending a kid whose brother had been killed, and Emma had ridden the coattails of that sympathy.

They hadn't gotten off completely scot-free. Rye had been told they would be doing community service and attending drug and alcohol education classes. No pills or alcohol had been found on their persons, in either teen's car, or in their bedrooms, so they couldn't be charged for possession. Neither would talk about what happened, and although the rumor mill ran full tilt on speculation, that's all it was—rumor.

Rye had questions, but she doubted Emma would answer them. Her biggest was why Emma had not shown up on Rye's radar before last week. Henry was less of a mystery. His brother's death had obviously escalated behaviors he had been managing covertly for a while. From what she had heard, though, Emma was…difficult. She talked back, she hovered in the just-barely-passing zone, and she was mean. Students like that usually made themselves known to Rye's office before a cataclysmic event. Teenagers might think they were good at hiding signs of trauma, depression, anxiety, or abuse, but Rye had put together a great team to identify those who were struggling. Emma's name should have made that list.

"Henry is back, so my folks thought I should be, too. I mean, it's not like my brother died," she said with another shrug.

"How long have you and Henry been together?"

"Couple of months." She glanced at the calendar hanging beside Claudia's door as if to remind herself of the date. "Since just before school started." She looked back at Rye. "I've known him a lot longer, though. Ross used to date my older sister before he came out. They were together for, like, three years. Then he left for Brown, and she knew they would break up. She just didn't know it was because she'd been his beard." This was said with obvious bitterness.

Rye wanted to say so many things to that, but she settled for the most compassionate response she could think of. "That must have been hard for her."

Emma glanced up in surprise at Rye's gentle tone. "He broke her heart. And the guys she's dated since … I don't know. It's like she's trying to make sure it never happens again."

"Was she upset when you started dating Henry?"

"It was her idea. She said she'd always thought we had good chemistry." Emma shifted her backpack to her other shoulder to reach out for a compostable cup to use with the K-Cup machine. A few years ago, some teachers had made a push to install a few around the school so that kids couldn't use their need for coffee as an excuse for being late. Rye liked the idea, since it meant that those who took the bus or couldn't afford a daily Starbucks run could also have a caffeine pick-me-up if they needed it. Of course, the teachers had to contribute anything they wanted beyond the coffee and a shelf of tiny Coffee-Mate creamers.

It looked like Claudia had gone all out. There was a mini fridge under the counter, and when Emma pulled it open, Rye could see half-and-half, almond milk, and soy. Emma stood and pulled open the cupboard. She grabbed an unopened box of oat milk from the overflow shelf.

Rye looked closer at what else was on the shelf. "Carnation instant milk? Do people actually use that in their coffee?"

"I don't think so. Ms. Ramirez brought it in a couple weeks ago. Maybe she likes it?" Her tone conveyed quite effectively that old people—anyone over the age of twenty, presumably—were gross and incomprehensible to her.

Rye thought about Claudia's apartment—from the expensively stocked liquor cabinet to the ripe organic produce she'd seen on the counter. She didn't seem like an instant milk drinker. "I wouldn't have thought anyone would touch the stuff with all the options here."

"Maybe she got it when we did our cookie drive? We use the ovens in the culinary arts kitchen for the fundraiser every year. I know she ended up making a few extra batches when we ran short."

"Hey, Emma! Glad to see you back." Rye and Emma both turned with a start to see Claudia standing behind them, her coat slung over her arm. Rye had no idea how long she had been there. Emma grabbed her coffee and fled as the first bell for homeroom rang.

"This is a surprise." Claudia unlocked her office door.

Rye held up a small paper bag. "I brought donuts." She glanced down. "Well, donut. They smelled so good in the car that I ate one."

Claudia took the bag from her and sniffed. "It does smell incredible." Her face twisted for a second, and then she turned her head and sneezed hard. "Does it have cinnamon on it, by any chance?"

"Yours was glazed, but mine was cinnamon sugar. Why?"

Claudia handed the bag back to her. "I'm allergic to cinnamon. I'd better not risk it."

"Oh, no," Rye said, flushing. "I should have asked first. I'm sorry."

"I just like to be cautious. It's not severe, but it can give me hives, and with the show I can't afford to be scratching my skin to shreds."

"Of course. I'm so sorry."

"Hopefully it won't be a hardship for you to eat it yourself?"

"I'll manage." Rye watched as Claudia deposited her things and grabbed a mug from her desk to make her own cup of coffee. "I wanted to ask you a question."

"Shoot," she said, her tone cooler than usual.

Rye chickened out and decided to save her questions about Jonathan and Veronica for another time. "You scheduled the fall musical for Halloween weekend. Isn't that kind of kiss-of-death timing? These kids will be partying, and most of the adults in town will be walking little kids around or partying themselves."

"It was Mendoza's idea. I admit I argued against it. But this is the third year we've done it, and it's worked out well. The show is early—six thirty each evening, so it's done by eight thirty. Dollar-off admission for anyone in costume. And this year, since Halloween falls on the weekend proper, we decided to do *The Addams Family*. We've nearly sold out on every show. It is the place to be before heading out to a party. The cast and crew feel special. Or at least they did before …"

"Jonathan died."

"Yeah." Claudia added whole milk and a heaping teaspoon of sugar to her coffee and changed the subject abruptly. "The first month we had these, I bought flavored syrups. They were delicious, but the kids used them like water, and my budget could not keep up."

"I can imagine. That must have made you popular."

"It did. When I stopped, my stock took a dive." She smiled apologetically at Rye and brushed her hand across her arm.

Rye felt a shiver of desire where their bodies touched, but she couldn't shake a sense of unease. There was a distance between them now that she couldn't figure out how to breach.

"I'm sorry again about the donut," she said again.

The second bell rang, and Claudia turned back to her office. "I have to get ready for my first class, but let's talk later." She gave Rye's arm a perfunctory squeeze, then closed her door.

Rye stood there for a moment before she decided to make herself a cup of coffee. She hated the waste created by K-Cup machines, but she couldn't argue against the accessibility. A headache was forming behind her eyes, and she had meetings lined up all day. While she waited, she opened the cabinet to look at the powdered milk again.

Rye snapped a picture to show her dad. He'd get a kick out of it. They'd kept a box when she was a kid to use in his bread recipes, but she'd also seen Hardy reconstitute it to pour on cereal when they were out of the wet stuff.

Students started wandering in as she finished making her drink, and she hurried out, nearly scalding her tongue when she took a sip. Hopefully no one had noticed her spit take. She glanced up and saw Lance strolling toward her, a huge grin on his face.

"Careful, Ms. Rye," he said cheerfully. "Don't want anyone to slip." He pulled a wad of paper towels from his pocket to offer her, and she took them to wipe the ground at her feet. By the time she stood to thank him, he had disappeared into the greenroom.

25

RYE ALMOST MISSED WANDA'S TEXT ASKING TO MEET for dinner. She'd gone out to train with Camila for the New Year's mixed relay, and when she got back to the car, she had a dozen messages from her dad specifying what he needed her to pick up from the store for the evening meal. She was waiting in line at the deli when her phone buzzed again, this time with a selfie of Wanda holding up a ladle and making a quizzical face. Rye laughed and sent a reply that Wanda should join them for dinner at seven.

When Rye finally got home, the house smelled incredible. Her father had made slow-cooked pulled pork, and when she handed off the groceries he promised that homemade mac and cheese and a salad were forthcoming. She let him know to set an extra place and hurried out to her apartment to shower and change.

As she came in, she could hear laughter from the kitchen. She stood in the doorway for a minute. Hardy was at the stove stirring what smelled like butterscotch pudding, and Wanda was chopping vegetables and telling him about a clergy meeting she'd had earlier in the day. Rye smiled. The change in her friend since Lance had come to live with her—even with all that was going on with Jonathan Thorne and Ross Jacobs—was incredible. As Wanda turned to say hello, Rye could still see dark circles under her friend's eyes, but it was enough to hear the laughter in her voice and see some of her old confidence.

"It smells amazing, Dad," she said, dropping a kiss on his cheek and reaching in to pull out a ginger ale.

"Thanks. I'm glad you invited Wanda. I made way too much tonight, and she said Lance would be happy to help with any of the leftovers."

"As long as you leave enough for me to take for lunch tomorrow," Rye said. "If I can't make my colleagues jealous of your cooking occasionally, what's the point of sharing a kitchen?"

"Besides the excellent company, you mean?" Hardy asked.

"Of course," Rye said as she filled her plate.

"Hardy was telling me that you're training for a race at New Year's?" Wanda settled into a seat and accepted the ginger ale Hardy offered her.

Rye nodded. "Camila talked me into it. It's so much more complex than the relay we did last year. I wasn't going to do it, but she flattered me into it. Ana and Mike are doing the long hill runs, she's doing a fast section in the middle. I'm the patsy on the obstacle course. It culminates with me sledding down Garnet Hill." She paused to savor a bite of the pork. "I suspect we'll be one of the oldest teams. I have to compete against twentysomethings who have zero qualms about the danger of throwing themselves downhill headfirst to get a free T-shirt."

Wanda laughed. "Too bad a competitive streak doesn't run in this family," she teased.

"Oh, I fully expect I'll be picking Rye up from urgent care after the race," Hardy said. "She nearly broke my finger once when we were playing Spit. I have no doubt she'll make those kids work for their prize."

"You're exaggerating, Dad." Rye rolled her eyes.

"I had to wear a splint for a week."

"I guess I'm lucky we're usually on the same side, then. I really don't care about winning or losing—I just like to play anything, from softball to cribbage," Wanda said. "My sister inherited the competitive gene in our family."

"How is Mickey?" Hardy asked.

Rye glanced up. "How do you know about Mickey?" She looked back and forth between the two, noting their heated cheeks. Neither met her gaze.

"Wanda and I had dinner last week," he said. "When was it?"

"The night of the dance," Wanda replied.

"Oh, yes," he said. "I'd forgotten after what happened with the younger Jacobs boy. How is he?"

"Not great," Wanda said, just as Rye replied, "Not bad."

"He's back at school," Rye told him.

Wanda shook her head. "I visited his house with Lance. His mother is a wreck, obviously, but, even before Ross's death, I don't think she had much of a relationship with Henry. His dad is apparently abusive and homophobic, but Henry worships him."

"I thought you said he and Lance were friends," Rye said.

"They spent time together when Lance first arrived, but he's been steering clear of Henry since we went over there. I don't know what exactly Henry said, but it freaked him out." She paused, the expression on her face shifting. "You don't think he had anything to do with his brother's death, do you?" She looked at Hardy. "You're the expert."

He set down his fork and thought about it. "We know that someone killed him and then someone ran over him and didn't stop. We don't know whether they're the same person."

"I talked to Ryan about it recently. He'd been working on the logical assumption it had been one person, but when I suggested it could have been two, he let slip it was a possibility based on some of the evidence they'd collected." Wanda blushed when both Rye and Hardy looked at her.

"You've been talking to Ryan a lot recently." Rye kept her tone light, but she was watching Wanda carefully.

"I think—"Wanda paused. "I think he's worried about me. He doesn't have the first clue as to how to show it, but after what happened last spring, he's more on edge. The fact that I found Jonathan Thorne ... I don't know. He's reached out a few times. It's not like him."

"Has he asked about Claudia?" Rye asked.

"Yes,"Wanda admitted.

"Who's Claudia?" Hardy asked. He hadn't let the conversation slow him down, and his plate was completely empty.

It was Rye's turn to look anywhere but at her father. "A friend."

"You've never mentioned her before."

"I met her at school. She worked with Thorne," Rye said.

Hardy stared at her. "I know you and Ryan don't get along, but he's a good cop, Rye. If he came to you with concerns, then he has a reason."

"He found out that we were having dinner together. He knew it would tick me off if he pointed the finger at her."

"She worked closely with a man who was murdered," Hardy said. "In fact, he's dealing with two murders that are almost surely connected. He doesn't have time to mess around." He stared at her until she met his gaze. "And the fact that you think he does tells me you're not thinking straight."

"Let it go, okay? She didn't have anything to do with it."

"How do you know?"

"Because I know, all right!" Rye pushed back from the table. "I asked her."

"You asked a suspect whether they had any part in a murder, and they denied it?" Hardy replied. "How novel." He turned to Wanda. "Did he suggest to you why he wanted information about this woman?"

"No, he just said that he would appreciate it if I could pass along anything I heard about her."

"So now you're spying on me?" Rye asked.

"No!" Wanda sounded surprised.

"But you didn't tell him no."

"I was noncommittal. He was giving me information he might not have offered if I'd stonewalled him."

"But then you didn't mention it to me." Rye tried to keep the hurt out of her voice.

"You haven't said anything to me about Claudia anyway. I get all my news from Lance."

"You could have texted me, or called. You should have, the minute he asked you."

"Rye, you barely know this woman," Hardy interrupted, "and yet you're blowing up at two people you trust for bringing her up."

"You're attacking her for no reason!"

"The reason is that someone I happen to trust—with my life, more than once—is concerned she might be involved. And you seem to be fine with that," Hardy said. "I know you don't like Ryan, but you trust me, right? And I trust him."

Rye scowled. "Just leave it alone. I know you think you know everything, but you don't."

"You broke up with Andy, what, a week ago? Two?"

Rye stood up and left before either of them could see her anger dissolve into tears. She banged the front door closed and retreated to the barn. It was warm and snug—just one room, plus the bath—but it was hers. She threw the deadbolt before climbing up into her lofted bed.

Her shoes hit the floor with two consecutive soft thumps. Rye scooted back toward the ladder and looked down. They had landed on the floor, on top of the blanket from her couch. That wasn't right. She leapt down and landed softly on her feet. Now that she was paying attention, Rye could tell that someone had been in here. Several drawers were ajar. The light was on in the bathroom, and she could see her towel and robe on the floor.

There wasn't anywhere to hide here, so whoever had rifled through her things was gone now, but Rye couldn't slow the beating of her heart. Hardy never came in without her permission.

Rye paused. She'd come back to shower before dinner. It hadn't looked like this then. She would have noticed the bathroom in disarray at the very least. Had she locked it when she'd gone over to eat? She couldn't remember.

Her phone buzzed, and she pulled it out of her pocket. She had a text from an unknown number. She opened it to see a picture of her, clearly taken through her window in the last few minutes. With shaking hands, she called her father on speakerphone.

"Dad? Someone's been in here, and I think they're still outside."

"Door's locked?"

"Yes."

"I'm calling Ryan, then I'll be out."

"Dad, wait. Call him, then stay inside with Wanda. I don't want either of you to leave the house until the police get here."

"Rye—"

"I'm locked in and armed. Please. Just … stay put."

"SO YOU HAVE NO IDEA WHO MIGHT HAVE DONE THIS," Ryan asked, glancing around her home.

Rye shook her head. "No."

"Nothing's been taken?"

"Just my sense of security and well-being," Rye muttered.

"This is what comes of poking your nose where it doesn't belong."

"Is that why you asked me to spy on Claudia? Because that felt a lot like you were telling me to get involved."

"Forgive me for trusting you with a suspect in a murder investigation," Ryan said. "I won't make that mistake again, since you clearly can't handle yourself as well as I thought you could."

"You're just mad that Wanda was here having dinner with Hardy and not with you."

Ryan flipped his notebook closed with a snap. If his tone had been chilly before, now it was downright arctic. "We're going to run the number that texted you. It's probably a burner, but if we get a hit, we'll let you know."

"I'm sure you'll put your best people on it."

"My best people are working on murder investigations, but I'm sure my intern will be happy for the job." He turned to leave.

"Why do you suspect Claudia?"

Ryan glanced at her over his shoulder. "You know I can't tell you that. This is an ongoing investigation. Besides, you already made the speech about where you stand on helping me with this."

Rye walked past him and shut the door. She gestured around the room. "Maybe I'm rethinking my position. But if you have a murder suspect you want me to 'watch' and are willing to put me in danger to do it, I need to know more."

"Why the change of heart?"

Rye swallowed against the rising sense of unease that she was going to tell him the truth, but not the whole truth. "My dad. He said something tonight—"

"What?"

"He trusts you."

"Tell me what you found out that changed your mind."

"Claudia's girlfriend died of an overdose about six months ago. She told me that she'd asked Jonathan Thorne to be the woman's sponsor and that he'd refused."

Ryan studied her, then nodded once. "We have some emails she sent him over the summer."

"Threats?"

"Not exactly, but angry. And she knew about his allergy to milk. I suspect it wouldn't have been too difficult for her to capitalize on that knowledge."

Rye closed her eyes for a long moment. She could still see the grief and rage etched into Claudia's face. "She has a box of powdered milk in the greenroom—that backstage classroom with the student dressing rooms."

"You've seen it?"

"Yes. I was talking with Emma Reyes—Henry Jacobs's girlfriend?"

"I remember."

"Emma told me that she thought it was left over from the cookie drive a few weeks ago."

"Nobody drinks that stuff anymore, do they?" Ryan asked.

"The Drama Department has this huge fundraiser every fall, and the cookies are made at the school. They use the culinary arts kitchens and bake all day. It makes a lot of money for the program. I don't think the milk was for drinking. Probably dry milk was an ingredient in a recipe."

"By all accounts, Jonathan Thorne was extremely careful about what he ate," Ryan said. "He brought his own food everywhere."

"And an Epi-Pen?"

Ryan shook his head. "His husband told me Thorne wasn't great about carrying one. That's why he only ate food he prepared himself."

"Stupid of him not to carry the Epi-Pen anyway," Rye said.

"It would have saved his life," Ryan agreed.

"So you think Claudia tampered with his food?"

"She knew his schedule. She had access to the fridge where he kept it."

"Everyone who goes in and out of her classroom has access to that fridge, though," Rye said.

Ryan nodded. "Would everyone know he took a walk in the woods during the break between the last bell and the start of rehearsal?"

"Every day?"

"During his contract, yes, as far I've heard."

"Seems like they would, then. If it was part of his routine, students would know."

Ryan just shrugged. "Maybe."

"Is the powdered milk enough to arrest her?" Rye's throat felt tight.

"No. But I am going to swing by the school and confiscate it as evidence." He put his hand on the door.

"Ryan," Rye said. He glanced back. "Please don't tell Claudia you heard about it from me."

He stared at her for a long moment, then nodded once. "Lock your door after I leave."

"I'm going to stay with a friend tonight, actually." Rye glanced around. "I just need to grab a few things."

Ryan disappeared into the dark between her apartment and Hardy's house. Rye knew she could stay with her dad, but she needed a break. She grabbed her phone, a charger, and her work clothes and put them in her duffle bag. Then she tossed in a toothbrush and her pajamas and grabbed her keys.

She locked the door carefully on her way out.

26

CAMILA THREW OPEN HER DOOR AS RYE LIFTED HER hand to knock. Rye raised her eyebrows at her friend. "You weren't standing there for the last twenty minutes, were you?"

"No. The elevator dings loudly," Camila said. "It's my early warning system."

"Thanks for having me on such short notice." Rye put her duffle and laptop case down by the door.

"Please! Ana stays over all the time, so I always have sheets on the pullout couch." She smiled. "And I love having company."

"Is that a twin thing?"

"Probably." Camila held up a bottle of wine, but Rye waved it away. Camila put the kettle on instead and showed her friend the canister of ginger tea. Rye nodded, and Camila found two mugs. "I think Ana likes having her own place. I fought her on moving for a long time, and she kept relenting because she knows it's hard for me to be on my own. Eventually, though, I had to let her go." Camila poured boiling water over each tea bag, and handed Rye a spoon and a soy sauce dish she could use for the bag when she was ready. She flopped down in a recliner by the fireplace.

"She seems like she's pretty comfortable being alone," Rye said.

Camila nodded. "She always has been. When we were kids and had to share a room, Ana constructed this"—she waved her hands, slopping tea on her sleeve—"castle of blankets around her bed."

"Like a fort?"

"More elaborate. She would disappear into it all afternoon some days. She just needed space."

"You have three brothers too, right?"

"Four. One older, three younger. I think my parents were trying for another girl to even things up. Once Carlos was born, they gave up."

"Did you like growing up in a big family?"

"I loved it. My older brother, Marcos, is more like Ana, but my younger brothers are a blast. We got into so much trouble when we were kids. Ana and Marcos had to cover for us all the time." Camila laughed. "They were good about it, though."

"Do your brothers live in Denver near your parents?"

"Yes. And they've all produced grandbabies already. My parents are in heaven."

"Wow." Rye curled up in the corner of the couch and sipped her tea. Camila passed her a bowl of pretzels. "I can't imagine that."

"When we go to visit, it's total chaos. I love it. Here, I just try to keep my schedule busy. Now that Ana and Tyler have gotten serious, I don't see her nearly as much as I used to. We do have dinner every Sunday and Thursday. Those are our standing dates."

"Does Tyler come, too?"

"Sometimes. It depends on his shift. I like him a lot. I don't mind being a third wheel to them. It's company, not just one-on-one time, that I miss."

"He seems really nice. I've met him a couple times recently."

"After the dance?"

"Yeah. He came by tonight, too, to check the grounds with another officer. I didn't talk to him, though. Just Ryan." She made a face.

"I've invited Ryan to dinner a few times with Tyler," Camila said. "He's not that bad."

"So everyone claims." Rye ran her finger over the rim of her own cup.

"What's bothering you tonight? I know the stalker thing is scary, but you don't seem shaken up. It's more ... sad."

Rye forced herself to smile. "It's nothing."

Camila put her tea down and moved over to the couch beside Rye. "Is it Claudia?" There was a catch in her voice, but she cleared her throat with a cough.

"Is it that obvious?"

"A few days ago, you were glowing. Every time you saw her, your face lit up, and you got this look on your face ..."

Rye wiped her cheeks. "It's complicated."

"Isn't it always?" Camila asked gently.

"No," Rye said. "It's not. Or I want it not to be." She took the tissue Camila held out but made no move to use it. "Your brothers— They love their partners, right?"

"Of course, but everyone's life is hard in some way. Luiz and his wife both lost their jobs last year, just a few months after their third daughter was born. They ended up moving back in with my parents for a few months. And Marcos's wife makes way more money than he does, and even though my brother isn't a complete jerk, it bothers him sometimes. Carlos had to rush into marriage because his girlfriend was going to be deported, and Davi's oldest son has Down syndrome. It's meant a total lifestyle change for their family. My brothers are lucky. They found incredible people to share their lives with, but it's not happily ever after. It's just life, and instead of only pleasing themselves, they have other people to compromise with on everything."

Rye blew her nose. Camila handed her the box of tissues and then got up to find a trash can. "You're right," she finally said. "Of course it's never simple, but I've been in love before, and it did feel...easy. Sometimes, at least."

"What happened? How did it end?"

"With the first, I worked too much. I was just out of grad school. I had student loans, and I wanted to prove to myself that I could stay afloat and make an impact with my students. He was so supportive, and we had all the same friends. I don't know. It was fun." She threw her crumpled up tissues into the trash. "We'd been together about a year when he told me his boss had offered him a position in Copenhagen that he couldn't pass up. He'd been so supportive of my work. I couldn't stand in the way of his dream job."

"Did you try long-distance?"

Rye shook her head. "Neither of us wanted to drag it out."

"You said he was the first?"

"It took me about two years to get over him and the life we'd built together. When I met Leila, it felt like all the therapy had been worth it."

Camila leaned back, her cheek resting in her hand, studying Rye. "Was it?"

"For a while, yes. I was more stable when we met. I had a great position at a good school. I wasn't buried in debt. I'd had my heart broken, so I thought I knew everything about relationships." Rye paused, her fingers tearing a tissue into tiny pieces on her lap. "I still don't know when she started using. She must have found someone to prescribe her the pills, but she seemed fine. We didn't live together. I'd learned my lesson about that the hard way. It was important to me to have my own space just in case things went wrong."

"And something did?"

"She was in a car accident—she hit a family. Apparently she had oxycodone and alcohol in her system. The police asked me if I knew how long she'd been taking the pills, and if they were prescribed. I had no idea. When I went to her house to pick up my things, I found a couple of different prescriptions from doctors I'd never heard her mention." Rye curled into herself, resting her chin on her knees. "Her trial was a nightmare. She…she died in prison. The car she'd hit—there were two kids. I guess it's pretty well-known that in women's prisons, at least, killing children puts you at high risk for…incidents. Guards look the other way. I had to identify her body. It was…bad."

Camila reached out a hand and gently stroked Rye's arm. Rye "I'm so sorry."

"I took time off work. I got back into therapy, and it didn't help like it had the first time, so I found a new therapist. I went to Nar-Anon meetings just to listen. I had a string of really unremarkable one-night stands." Rye shrugged. "Eventually, I started to feel like myself again."

"How long has it been?"

"Seven years in January."

Camila nodded. "Was Andy the first person you've dated since? Like, really dated?"

"No. There were a few people in Austin. It was okay, but there was no spark."

"And with him?"

Rye finished her wine. "It felt safe." She shrugged. "I wished I was madly in love with him. He's a good person, and I know he would be a great partner, but whatever feelings we might have flirted with in high school are gone. He's just a friend that I'm lucky to have."

"So that brings us back to the woman of the hour." Camila's tone was light, but Rye sensed she was holding something back.

"I know she's not Leila, but I'm starting to feel like I can't trust my feelings about her. My dad, Ryan, even my friend Wanda—they all seem to see something about her that I can't. I don't want to believe that I could be so far off base again, but ..."

"Once burned, twice shy."

"When I'm with her, it's like having too much champagne."

Camila pulled a blanket down from the back of the couch and wrapped herself up in it. She handed one to Rye and helped her tuck it under her feet. "Is that love? Or infatuation?"

At the sound of a loud ding, both women turned to the door. "That's the elevator?"

Camila nodded. "Hard to miss, isn't it?" She sat up. "Funny, though. My neighbor moved out last week. I didn't think the landlord had finished painting and putting in new carpet yet."

"And you're not expecting anyone?"

"No."

Rye tensed and slid off the couch. She motioned to Camila to stay where she was as she went to the door. She pressed her ear against it, but there was no sound outside. After another minute, she eased the door open. When nothing happened, she stuck her head out and checked the hallway. It was empty except for a bright red glove by the elevator door. Rye walked over and picked it up, then carried it back inside. She hadn't seen it when she'd arrived, but she hadn't been looking, either.

"Yours?" she asked after she bolted the door.

Camila shook her head. "I look terrible in red. Not Ana's, either, and she's the only person besides you who's been here this week—at least who would fit a glove that size."

Rye arched an eyebrow at her. "Oh?"

Camila snorted. "The workmen across the hall? I haven't seen them wearing a lot of crimson leather accessories, at least not to work." She stood up and grabbed Rye's hand. "You're really freaked out, aren't you? It was probably just someone hitting the wrong button. The floors all look the same, so when whoever it was realized they didn't have the right one, they got back on. The glove probably fell out of their pocket."

Rye felt queasy, but she nodded in agreement. "Yeah, probably."

"Let's watch a movie." Camila patted the couch.

"Sure," Rye said after a moment. "Something stupid?"

"Definitely." Camila grabbed the remote from the coffee table. "I have just the thing."

RYE WOKE UP EXHAUSTED. THE COUCH HAD BEEN surprisingly comfortable, but she'd had a panic attack after Camila had gone to bed and tossed and turned, sweating, her stomach in knots, for most of the night.

When her alarm went off at six, she could hear Camila singing in the shower. She hit snooze and fell back into a dead sleep for eight minutes until it went off again.

The she dragged herself out of bed and into the bathroom, brushing her teeth before dozing under the warm water. She probably would have fallen fully back to sleep if the hot water hadn't run out, leaving her to finish washing up in the freezing cold.

Camila had taken pity on her and made a quick run for coffee and bagels. Rye couldn't stomach it yet, but she knew in an hour or two she would be profoundly grateful. She made up the couch and packed her things while Camila finished eating.

"I texted Ana that she didn't need to pick me up today, since you could give me a ride, but maybe I should have asked her to come get both of us," Camila said as they waited for the elevator together.

Rye had barely managed a word since she rolled out of bed, and she nodded blearily. "Maybe so. Do you want to drive?" She held out her keys.

"Sure." Camila walked around to the driver's side door and gasped. "Rye!"

Her friend's voice sent a shot of adrenaline straight through her, and she dashed to the other side of the car. It was covered with obscenities from bumper to bumper. Someone had used Sharpie to write a rainbow of misogynistic and homophobic slurs across the side of her white Toyota Corolla. There were even a few explicit pictures that depicted acts both sexual and violent in nature. Rye felt sick.

"Was it like this last night?" Camila asked.

"No." Rye sank down to sit on the curb. "I'd better call the police when I get to school. I'm sure they'll want to add it to last night's report."

"You're going to work? I think you should just drop me and head straight to the station." Camila looked at Rye, her face pale. "What if there was someone here last night? What if they followed you?"

"Camila—" Rye's voice sounded strained. "You're right. I need to go to the police station and make another report. If I brought this to you ..." She shook her head.

"I'm tougher than I look," Camila said, although her voice was low. "But just in case, I'm going to stay with Ana until you figure out who did this."

Rye nodded. "Do you need to grab anything so you don't have to come back here later?"

She shook her head. "I have a drawer at her place, and if I can't find anything to wear, her closet is well-stocked. Twins, right?" It was a feeble attempt at humor.

"Okay." Rye got into her car, then stopped before putting the key into the ignition. "Do you think it's too late for you to call Ana? I just realized I probably shouldn't drive away, just in case Ryan wants to send someone to take a look." She didn't mention that she was afraid to put the key into the ignition.

"No problem."

Camila called Ana while Rye dialed the station number she knew by heart. It was early enough that Ryan wasn't in yet, but the officer on duty told her to stay put after she explained that she thought the vandalism might be related to a break-in.

In five minutes, Ana pulled up with a familiar figure in the front seat. Tyler held the door open for Camila.

"Are you sure you don't want me to stay with you?" Camila asked.

"I'll be okay with Tyler here, but thanks." Rye reached out to give her friend a quick hug and got a longer-than-expected squeeze back. "I'll call you later, okay?" She felt

Camila nod against her shoulder, then pull away. Ana gave Rye and Tyler a little wave as she drove off, both women with matching furrows on their brows.

"I radioed the station when Ana told me what happened. I hope it's okay if I take your report?" Tyler's pen was already flying across his notebook page as he took note of the damage on her car.

"Sure," Rye said. "I assume you didn't notice this last night when you were looking for the intruder?"

"I would have seen it," he said. "I even checked in the backseat of all three cars when we couldn't find any trace of the perp. This must have been done after you got here."

Rye briefly outlined to him what had happened the night before and handed over the glove for evidence, glad she'd taken a picture of it to show Wanda and her dad. Tyler photographed the area and her car thoroughly. Rye eventually felt hungry enough to eat her bagel as she talked to her insurance agent.

"I think Ryan's going to want to talk to you about this," he said as he finished up.

"I should really get to work," Rye said. "Is there any chance I could ask you a favor, as a friend of a friend?"

He smiled warmly. "Sure. What do you need?"

"Would you be willing to take my car over to McKellan's garage for me? It's only a few blocks from the high school, and normally, I'd drop it myself and walk back, but I have back-to-back meetings starting in fifteen minutes."

He gestured to her to get in and walked around the passenger door. "I can definitely do that. I've used McKellan's since I got my first car. Should I just ask for a quote, or do you want him to start work on removing this and touching up the paint?"

"If he can squeeze me in, that would be great. I already sent photos to my insurance agent, and she said I should follow up with the police report later today so she can file that information as well. I just don't feel great about parking at the high school with the car looking like this. And let me give you some cash for a Lyft to the station."

"Don't worry about it," he said. "I left my car at the school last night when I met up with Ana. That's why she was giving me a ride this morning. I'll just walk back and pick it up when I'm done."

"Thank you, Tyler. I can't even tell you—"

"Hey," he interrupted gently. "I'm happy to help. You've had a rough time of it lately. This is the least I can do in my unofficial capacity of friend's partner."

After Tyler dropped her off, Rye barely had time to think about what had happened. In addition to her already full docket, two fights had been broken up before school, and she had to squeeze in time for disciplinary report or action. She didn't even have a chance to eat lunch, so when Claudia texted in the afternoon to ask if she wanted to grab an early dinner, Rye agreed.

27

WANDA WISHED SHE HAD A GLASS OF CHEAP RED WINE, but she refilled her glass with iced tea while making something to eat instead. She melted cheese on French bread and tossed on Trader Joe's Everything but the Bagel seasoning. Not exactly dinner, but she could simplify when Lance wasn't home. It was opening night of *The Addams Family*, and Lance hadn't even come home after school. Wanda was going to be late to the show if she couldn't find a way to tie off this telephone call.

"Are you even listening to me?" Mickey complained.

"Of course I am. I'm just grabbing dinner because I have to go to Lance's play in a couple of minutes."

"He won't notice you're not there. He's behind the scenes. He didn't even get a singing part, and he has a beautiful tenor voice. And he wouldn't care anyway. Trust me."

Wanda didn't. "He has a good voice?" She knew the answer, but she really wanted Mickey to say something nice about her son.

"I haven't heard him sing in years, but it's always noted as a real gift in his school reports. I do read them, you know."

Wanda sighed and tried not to sound as snarky as she felt. "Of course you do."

Her sister launched back into her own issues. All was not a Tuscan paradise with Enzo. He was young, and his eyes wandered. Mickey was getting tired of the daily skin care and body toning involved in trying to pass for twenty-eight instead of twenty years older. And every time she turned around, there was something they needed that was a major expense.

"A what?" Wanda started listening more closely, trying to remember everything Hardy had said.

"Well, he was short on the rent on our villa. We call it 'Casa dei giochi d'amore,' which means—"

"'House of Love Games.' Seriously?" Wanda shuddered. "So you paid the rent for one month?"

"Well, I paid the security deposit, first and last month, and next month. Four in total. And the rental car. After all, he knew I really wanted the convertible."

"With your hair?" It was a low blow, but Wanda was sure that Mickey, with her thin and fine hair, disliked having it windblown. She must be continuously using a curling iron.

"It's a *red* convertible. And also he gave me this beautiful broach today. It was his grandmother's."

"Mickey, stop. Give the broach back to Enzo now, tonight, or you could get into a lot of trouble. I know you like this guy, but he's setting you up for a major scam. Look how much he's already gotten out of you!"

"You're being melodramatic, Winnie. It's not a big deal."

"It is a big deal! He could easily accuse you of stealing a priceless family heirloom and use the fact that you don't speak Italian—not to mention having zero resources in the country to protect you—to take everything you have. You could go to prison there, and I would have no way to help you."

"He wouldn't do that. Enzo loves me." But Mickey sounded more like a petulant child than a woman in the middle of a whirlwind affair.

"I can't believe you don't see what's happening here."

"I think you're just trying to spoil my fun. You're probably sick of Lance already, and you just want me to come back so you don't have to deal with him."

Wanda clenched her teeth. "If you don't want my help, I can't force you. If you smarten up and realize that you're being taken in by this guy, call me. But right now I have better things to do than argue with you." She hung up, tears stinging her eyes. Mickey was infuriating, but Wanda knew from long experience that nothing she could say would change her sister's mind. Normally, Wanda tried not to let it bother her. With this, though— with Mickey gambling her life and livelihood—it hurt.

And on top of everything, now she was late. A cute jacket and a messy bun made in the car was all the fashion statement she could handle. Didn't matter. Talking to her sister had reminded her that tonight wasn't about her, and Lance didn't have a lot of experience with things being about him. She was going to get to this show.

WANDA WAS LATE GETTING TO THE SOCIAL HALL THE next afternoon, and Jessica Thorne was waiting when she arrived. Wanda had spent much of the previous evening groveling to Lance for missing the first act of his show. Eventually, she'd broken down and told him about the conversation with Mickey. She tried to present it neutrally, without her own fears overlaying the facts, but she decided he was old enough to hear Hardy's advice and predictions, and she could tell he felt anxious about his mother. They'd stayed up way too late eating ice cream and watching movies on the couch until they had both dragged themselves to bed, worn but mended, at least with each other.

Fortunately, Wanda had the best staff in the world. When she arrived at the church, Lisa was finishing centerpieces on the round tables. They were simple— yellow and scarlet maple leaves with fresh burgundy mums floating in flat bowls. Greg was helping Lisa out by playing a game of Guess Who? with her daughter, Lily, while Tony practiced on the baby grand. She had half an hour until the memorial officially started, but there were already a few guests pouring themselves coffee, soda, or water. She had passed food trucks in the parking lot on her way in—not yet open—and had made a mental note to grab something for herself after the party wound down.

Wanda had only just taken off her coat when Jessica was in front of her, her face red and her voice strident with anger. "What is he doing here?" Jessica whispered angrily. "Jonathan sponsored his brother, Ross, so I've heard plenty of stories about that little jerk."

Wanda followed her gaze. Henry Jacobs was on the other side of the room with a group of high schoolers. Many years of ministry had made Wanda as tactful as could be, but even she had a hard time biting her tongue when a thirty-five-year-old woman punched down on a kid, especially one who was obviously troubled. "Has he said something to upset you?"

"He shouldn't be here!"

"I can see that this is bothering you," Wanda said calmly, "and that you've heard some things about Henry that make you uncomfortable. If he causes any problems or says something inappropriate, we will ask him to leave, but at the moment he's just a sixteen-year-old who recently lost his brother. He is trying to deal with his grief, just as you are yours. I'm asking that while you're here, you try to extend a little grace to him."

"This is my party and *my* chance to mourn *my* brother. He has no right to come here."

Wanda held up a hand. "Jessica, I hear you. I do. But you did not ask that this be a private gathering. In fact, you enthusiastically encouraged an open invitation to the community. I have no right to remove him unless he acts aggressively or inappropriately. I promise I'll keep an eye on him. You should go greet your guests."

Jessica glared at her, then turned on her heel and stomped off.

"You have a gift for making friends, I see," a male voice said behind her.

Wanda jumped, then turned to see a vaguely familiar man with a glass of church punch in his hand. He couldn't have been more than five foot six, although that still gave him half a foot on her. His hairline was receding, and he gave off a hint of the same smell that had tipped her off to Lance's bender the other night. He clearly wasn't drunk now, but he had been, probably earlier today, and since it was still early, chances were good it was a regular occurrence for him.

"I'm Ben." He held out his hand. "We met at Stoneridge on the sad day when this young man died."

"Oh yes, you're the bus driver!" Wanda blurted out.

"That's me."

"Did you know Jonathan Thorne?"

"In a manner of speaking, yes," Ben said. "Must have been terrible for you, finding him like that." He saw her puzzled look, but before Wanda could ask, Ben explained, "I was still waiting on the team when the police showed up. I doubt you saw me—you looked pretty shook up—but I saw you and your dog—Whopper, is it?"

"Wink."

"Ah, yes, Wink. Talking with the police. Figured you must have been the one to find him."

She really should be getting the service going, but it hadn't occurred to Wanda that anyone else might have witnessed anything around the time of the murder. Her curiosity was piqued. "Did you see anyone? Anyone other than me?"

"Coming out of the woods, you mean?" Ben paused. "I had a pretty good view of it all, but I wasn't really paying attention until the cruisers started pulling in. I did see my son, Henry, and his girlfriend come out before the cops arrived. I know what they were getting up to, though." He winked, and Wanda felt slightly queasy. "Red-blooded American boy, that one."

Wanda didn't know what to say to that, so she just bobbed her head in acknowledgement. "No one else, though?"

Ben shook his head. "No. No obvious drug dealers, if that's what you're asking. Thorne must have brought his own stash with him."

"He didn't overdose," Wanda corrected. "It was in the paper. He died from anaphylactic shock. He had a milk allergy."

"That's what they got pressured into printing. Trying to protect that man's reputation, I guess, God only knows why. He was a drug addict. Trust me, I know." He leaned in, and the smell of drink grew stronger. "He and

my older son, they were close, if you know what I mean."
He touched the side of his nose as though he genuinely
believed he was being subtle. "Henry told me all about
it. Ross didn't think I knew what was going on, but I'm
no fool."

"You're Henry and Ross's father?" Wanda tried to
connect the friendly man she'd met on her walk with the
abusive homophobe Autumn Jacobs had told her about.
This conversation was making the leap a little easier.

He smiled again. It looked a little sharklike.

"I'm so sorry for your loss," Wanda said. She knew
Ross and his father hadn't been close, but still, to lose a
child was horrible.

Ben looked away and caught the eye of his younger
son. He waved Henry over. Henry reluctantly left his
friends and came to stand by his father.

He looked as though he'd shrunk three inches,
slouching by his father's side. "Hey," he said sullenly.

"Henry, nice to see you away from the pool," Wanda
replied. She turned to Ben. "He's a great lifeguard.
Always on top of things, even on the early shift when
I show up."

"Yeah, he's all right," Ben said, giving Henry's hair a
rough pat.

"Dad, let's get out of here." Henry tried to duck out
of the way as his father's hand moved to tighten on his
neck.

"It hasn't even started yet," Ben replied. "Don't you
want to hear what they have to say about the man who
got your brother killed?"

Wanda straightened. "What?"

"Can't be a coincidence, right?" Ben looked almost
jovial, his tone skirting the edge of teasing and menace.
"The two of them on the same day?"

"Let's just go, Dad, please."

Henry looked so uncomfortable that Wanda was about to escort him out herself, father be damned, when Ben released him and nodded. "You can drop me off for a drink on your way home. God knows I need one after this."

Henry practically dashed for the door. "See you, Reverend Duff," Ben said, giving her another wink.

Wanda was still staring after them when she heard Tony cough and begin softening the background music. That was her cue.

But not yet. Greg was heading directly toward them, and his normally easygoing demeanor was neither calm nor memorial appropriate. Tony half rose from the bench, but Greg waved him down.

"I have to go. Hopefully I'm not leaving you both in a lurch, but I need to get out of here," Greg said. His face was flushed, and he looked on the verge of tears.

Tony reached out and squeezed his boyfriend's hand. "Greg, what is it?"

"I'll tell you later, but I need to leave. Now."

Tony looked like he wanted to protest, but they were starting to draw attention. Wanda broke in. "Go down the hall and up the stairs. Head through the sanctuary. The front door will lock behind you." He practically ran. Wanda put her hand on Tony's shoulder. "Deep breaths, okay? He was scared, Tony."

"I know." Tony sounded panicked. "But of what?"

"I think the question is of whom," Wanda said, glancing around. Greg had been fine a few minutes ago. Someone must have shown up to cause that reaction. It was too crowded now to guess who it might have been, though. "Do you need to go?"

They could both see Jessica Thorne making her way over, and she didn't look happy. "No," Tony said quietly. "I'll play. He'll be there when I get home."

"Okay, if you're sure."

His shoulders relaxed as his fingers brushed over the keys. "Showtime, friend."

"Showtime." Before the folks leaving outnumbered the ones arriving, Wanda thought.

WANDA OPENED WITH WORDS OF GREETING ON BEHALF of the church and a brief explanation of the twins' birthday party that had become a memorial. Having mentioned Jessica, she invited Marc to be the first speaker after Tony played and Nicole sang "The Moon and Me" from *The Addams Family*. The students who had come to pay their respects were crying, especially the young man who played Festus. He had told Wanda when he arrived that meeting Jonathan his freshman year when he first got involved in the theater department had changed his life. At one point, Jonathan had kept him from ending it. He went from her over to Marc and shared the same moving words.

Marc's greeting and his memories were beautiful. Jessica was, well, the woman Wanda had gotten to know while planning the service. She was grief-stricken and also tactless, but by the end of her speech, she had moved many in the audience to tears with her memories of her brother. Wanda moderated the short memories and drew the gathering to a close with her standard civil funeral acknowledgement—that many believed Jonathan lived on because he had touched so many lives, and others had a faith-related expectation of a kind of reality after death, but for everyone, Jonathan Thorne was not gone but lived as an ongoing gift in the world. Nicole sang the reprise of "Something Different" from *The Band's Visit* in honor of Jonathan and Marc's first date.

Of course, none of this answered the questions surrounding Jonathan's death. Wanda still had no idea who could have hated this man enough to poison him on campus in the middle of a school week. His sister was openly distraught. His husband was intensely private in his grief. Meanwhile, his students and friends seemed completely devastated. Wanda just couldn't get a handle on what had gone so wrong for Thorne that someone had wanted him dead.

The memorial service might be over, but Wanda couldn't let his death go.

28

BY THE TIME WANDA FINALLY GOT IN LINE FOR PHO-
to-go, she was ready to turn off her hearing aids and
sleep for a week. The young people and a lot of the adults
were headed straight from the service to the show at the
high school. Lance would not be home, so Wanda set out
a bowl of candy for trick-or-treaters and a note saying
not to ring the bell because the dog would go bananas.
She had taken a cute picture of Wink in a costume a few
weeks ago that she posted underneath.

She was ravenous and devoured her soup in front of
the TV without even bothering to change out of her
church clothes. Her conversation with Ben Jacobs still
bothered her. She knew she'd better call Ryan and fill
him in, but she didn't have the energy tonight. She didn't
even have the bandwidth for Rye. Tomorrow, first thing.
Well, after church. Thank goodness she'd forced herself
to write not just her sermon but the whole service
earlier this week. Usually, she had a few things she was
scrambling to finish on Saturday nights, but not tonight.

Tonight, her brain was on overdrive. Andy sent her
a selfie of his championship dart win—unfair sober

advantage. He and Mitch were standing arm in arm holding up glasses of juice. She sent him back her hearty congratulations, then stared at the picture again.

Laredo's. Mitch had described the man who fought with Ross Jacobs as short, *built like a football player, stocky and strong*. He was describing Ben. Not Ben in the bus. Ben in the church hall. Ben the angry, bigoted father, picking on his son in public. Angry enough that it got physical.

Wanda felt sick. Maybe she was wrong. She could be. Maybe they got into a fight and then Ben had left, and that was when Ross was killed. Ben seemed like a nasty piece of work, but she still didn't want to even imagine...

With shaking hands, she pulled out her phone and searched for Ben Jacobs. When she added in "contractor," she found stories of his downfall. There were the allegations he'd skimmed money, mentions of his acrimonious divorce all over social media, even suspicions that he tried to burn the house down for the insurance. It was humiliating and ugly.

When she changed her search terms to "bus driver," she found his number in the Loyola Catholic High School directory. Funny that her brain had retained that detail—the name printed across the bus. Surely the school had not done a very good background check. Or they'd been desperate in this bus driver shortage for any warm body. No address, but a phone number. She reverse-searched it, knowing how proud Rye would be of her slowly improving techno-detecting. Sure enough, an address popped up. It was in Maplegate, a modular park right off Route 111. Locals, Laredo's, and Maplegate were in a direct line. She remembered the near miss that terrible night when she was driving out of the Locals parking lot. Could it have been him?

Wanda knew she wouldn't sleep. She had her tried-and-true method for brain erasure, but ever since Luke had confronted her, she couldn't shake the knowledge that she drank too often and too much as a means to escape her problems. It wasn't working. Maybe she should act instead.

AT THE LAST MINUTE, WANDA SWERVED INTO Laredo's. Mitch was there as usual, and busy. She couldn't ask him to go with her to confront Ben Jacobs, though his presence would be comforting. She waited her turn at the far end of the bar, and once he had helped a group of bikers, he turned to her.

"What can I get you, Rev?"

Wanda pulled out her phone and showed him a photo from the Loyola High staff page. "Is this the man you saw fighting with Ross Jacobs?"

He looked closely. "Definitely. Who is he?"

"Ben Jacobs. Ross Jacobs's father."

Mitch shook his head and whistled. "I've seen it before, you know. Family can make the worst enemies. There was real hatred there. Scary stuff. You tell the cops?"

She shook her head. "Not yet. I just wanted to know if you recognized him."

"I think you'd better call it in."

Wanda nodded noncommittally. "I know he lives over in Maplegate. That's close by, right?"

"Yeah, just up the road. Why?"

"I'm trying to get all the facts straight before the sheriff grills me."

"You used to come in to our original location with the sheriff once upon a time, didn't you? I wasn't bartending much back then. My brother Rodney was doing front of house, but I remember."

"We do have a history," Wanda said. "It's…complicated."

"Is that why you don't want to call him?" Mitch raised an eyebrow.

"Let's just say he doesn't always trust my instincts."

"He's a stupid man, then." Mitch snorted. "You want me to call?"

"I'm sure it will be fine," Wanda said. "I just want to drive by, see where he lives. Someone almost ran me off the road last week coming from that same direction. It's probably a coincidence, but I feel like I'll sleep better if I check whether he has a vehicle beside the truck."

"Just as long as that's all you're doing." Mitch's tone very much conveyed he knew BS when he heard it.

She smiled, accepted a to-go water, and thanked him for his help.

MAPLEGATE WAS A NEW AND SURPRISINGLY WELL-landscaped modular home park. The owners had worked around existing trees, so it didn't have the scalped look of many similar neighborhoods. Even in the dark, it looked comfortable—bikes left out on the lawns, a few garage doors open.

She found Ben's address and sat for a moment outside, her headlights off. What had she expected? It looked like a house. Small but neatly kept. Wanda could see a light on in the living room and the glow of the television. She was just getting ready to pull away when the door opened. Ben Jacobs stood there, beer in hand, staring out at her.

It would be strange for her to drive away now. Wanda got out and walked up the path. Ben had on jeans and a long-sleeved Henley tee, just a little too tight in the middle, although it showed off his muscular shoulders and arms. Maybe not an old football player, then. More like a former wrestler.

"Reverend Duff." He tipped his chin to acknowledge her. "Twice in one day. How can I help you?"

She hadn't come up with a plan on the drive over, so Wanda fell back on her greatest skill—pastoring. "I wanted to come by to offer my condolences. I was caught off guard earlier. I hadn't realized you were Ross's father."

"I was barely that," he said, but he stood aside, and she walked in.

The house was cleaner than she'd expected. A huge TV hung on one wall with a recliner across from it. The remains of his dinner were on a tray, and there was a beanbag chair in the corner, presumably for when Henry visited. Other than that, the room was bare.

"Can't really offer you a place to sit, I'm afraid." He had closed the door and now leaned back casually against it, one shoulder resting on the doorframe. "My ex-wife kept everything."

"Oh yes, Autumn. I met her." As soon as Wanda said the name, she regretted it.

Anger flashed across Ben's face. "I don't know what she told you, but it's lies. All of it."

"She didn't tell me anything," Wanda said cautiously. "She was just sad. About Ross ... and Henry, you know, what's happened to him since Ross died."

"She's ruining him. It wasn't enough for her to take my firstborn and turn him against me. Now she's got Henry messed up, too. She and Ross, ganging up on me, feeding that boy a bunch of lies."

"Henry is struggling. The drugs, his brother—"

"Don't tell me about my son!" Ben snarled. "You don't know him from Adam. That's my boy. Mine."

She held up her hands, trying to be placating. How had she managed to let him be between her and the door? "You're right. I don't know him well. But I can tell he needs help."

"He needs a backbone! Needs to learn to stand up for himself."

Wanda lost it. "Like Ross did? That was you fighting with him at Laredo's, wasn't it?"

"Who told you about that?"

"That's what happened, right? You were smacking around your son because he was worried that you were turning his brother into someone like you?" She stopped. Wanda could picture it. Ross thinking Henry was becoming like Ben, and Ben that Henry was going to be like Ross, with neither one caring who Henry really was. "What happened in the parking lot?"

"Ross got on his bike—twenty-five years old and he was on a damned bike, and in those girly bike tights with that flashing light on his— How could that be a child of mine?"

"And you?"

"I had to relieve myself in the bushes."

She shouldn't be disappointed, but she was. Wanda had thought this was the answer, that Ben had run him down in the heat of the moment. It was terrible, sick, but she'd hoped it was him, if only to have some closure. "So you just headed home?" She hesistated, then added, "Or maybe you were driving, and you saw that little light flashing up ahead. Maybe you sped up, thought you'd scare him, and got too close."

Wanda could see it all too clearly. Ben, drunk, speeding up until he was behind his son. At the right speed, he would barely need to nudge the bike to send Ross off the road. No damage to Ben's car. No real evidence except the body of his son.

He shrugged. "I followed him a ways. I was headed back here. He pulled off the road. I stopped, and he was fixing his shoe or something. I offered to give him a lift, and you should of heard what he said to me. Foul mouthed little—"

Wanda could only imagine, if Ross had inherited even a tenth of his father's disposition. "So you were going to help him?"

"I was going to give him a ride."

"What happened then?"

Ben laughed, but it was an ugly sound. "He was screaming at me. Calling me all sorts of names. I got out of the car and figured he and I just needed to have it out once and for all. He even got in a couple of good punches." Ben's face turned dark. "I had a right to kick that boy's butt, beat him so hard he couldn't sit for a week. Did it when he was a kid and he got out of line. No reason not to do the same thing again. And it worked. He manned up. Came at me for all he was worth." Ben massaged his fists as though he remembered bruised knuckles with fondness. He also looked like he wouldn't mind reliving the moment with another partner. "I hit him, and he went down. Hit his head on a rock, and he was out cold."

Wanda stared at Ben in horror. "Why didn't you call it in?"

"I'd had a few drinks. I've got two strikes already. If they came and gave me a breathalyzer, that would have been it for me."

"Why did you move his body into the road?" Wanda was guessing, but from the look on Ben's face, she'd guessed right. "You could have saved his life," she said. Even employing every pastoral urge she possessed, she couldn't hide her disgust.

"What kind of life would he have had?" Ben asked, but now his voice was soft, and he was moving closer. "Drug addict. Dropped out of school. Doing whatever he was doing with Thorne." He shrugged. "Ross peaked in high school." Wanda knew she had overplayed her hand. She inched back cautiously a few steps. The look in Ben's eye was calculating. "It was an accident. That's all. No reason for it to ruin my life, too. I have my teams to think about. Now those boys look up to me! They need me." He put one hand on her arm. Wanda felt a shiver run through it. "You understand, don't you?"

"It was an accident," she repeated.

"That's all. I didn't mean to do it, so there's no need to make a fuss, right?" His gaze was unflinching, and his grip had tightened enough to leave a bruise. "I don't want to have to make your life difficult. Not now that you and Wink have the boy to take care of. What's his name? Lance?"

Without a conscious thought, Wanda leaned into him, pushing Ben slightly off balance. The element of surprise was all she had in her favor, and she used it. Her knee shot up hard into his groin, and when Ben let go of her to grab himself, she headbutted him in the nose as hard as she could. He went down, and she jumped over him, beelining for the door.

Ben grabbed her ankle and held on, bringing Wanda to her knees. She kicked back at him hard, grateful for once that she was still wearing her church shoes. Wanda felt a high heel connect with something soft, and he screamed. She scrambled for the door. When she pulled it open, Tyler and Ryan Phennen were standing there, backed up by Jaz Malone.

Ben was bellowing like an angry bear as the brothers fought to get handcuffs on him. Jaz offered Wanda a hand up. "Glad to see you were paying attention in class," she said.

"Think I may have missed the lesson about avoiding potentially dangerous situations, though." Wanda wiped her face with the edge of her sleeve.

"Missed it or ignored it?" the younger woman asked, eyebrows up. "You're lucky you've got a friend like Mitch Laredo. He called it in, you know."

Wanda nodded. "Lucky he knows me so well."

Ryan was clearly furious with her. Wanda rather thought Hardy would be proud. She pulled out her phone and called Rye.

29

THE KITCHEN WAS COZY AND SMELLED OF GARLIC AS Rye, Camila, Ana, and Mike arrived, fresh from a vigorous training session, bearing baguettes from Harvey's. Hardy had, as usual, cooked enough to feed a small army, and even he seemed surprised when there weren't any leftovers to put away. They were just digging into Hardy's apple pie when Wanda called. Rye stood up to take it in the other room, since her father was in the middle of particularly raucous retelling of an old case.

"Hey Wanda! What's up?"

Her friend sounded shaky. "Rye? I had to call. Ryan's going to take my statement in a few minutes, but I wanted you to know first."

"Know what?" Rye took the stairs two at a time, closing herself into her old bedroom at the top of the stairs. "Are you okay?"

"I'm fine. Well, a little sore, but okay. The police apprehended Ben Jacobs, Henry and Ross's father, for Ross's death. He confessed to me."

"What?! Where? What are you talking about? Didn't you tell me his wife left him because he was abusive? Are you sure you're okay?" The questions came faster than Wanda could possibly answer them.

"I am, and yes, he is. I met him at Thorne's memorial service. Well, re-met. He was the bus driver from the day I found Thorne. I don't know if I even told you about that."

"I don't think you mentioned him, no."

"Well, when he saw me at the memorial this afternoon, Ben started talking about that day, and about his sons. Henry was there, too. The poor kid. He looked terrified. I don't know if Henry knows what happened or if he has other reasons to be afraid of his father, but it didn't sit right."

"Where are you now, the church?"

"Ben Jacobs's house."

"What? How—?"

"Take a breath, Rye! I'm trying to tell you." Wanda huffed a laugh. "I looked him up. The sordid details of his life are easy enough to find online, even for a Luddite like me."

"Lance helped, didn't he?"

"Just a little," Wanda acknowledged. "Ben Jacobs lost everything—his work, his family, his reputation. Started driving a school bus during that driver shortage we had a couple years ago."

"They must have been desperate if his dirty laundry had already been aired."

"They were. And as it turns out, he was even good at it. Connected with the kids. No complaints from families. It gave him a second start. I think if Ross hadn't come out, Jacobs would have just lived out that version of his life."

"But Ross did."

"At the end of high school, yes," Wanda said. "I don't know the whole story, but from what I can piece together, everything fell apart again. He and Ross were …Well, estranged is putting it mildly. Henry was caught between the two of them."

"Sounds like whatever was holding Ben Jacobs together was pretty fragile."

"Very much so."

Rye sat on the edge of the bed, attempting to absorb it all. "He killed his son and dragged him into the road to implicate someone else?" She shivered.

Wanda's voice was somber. "It's too awful. And tonight, at least, he wasn't exactly full of remorse." She sighed. "That may change someday."

Rye could hear someone say Wanda's name on the other end of the line. "Sounds like they need you."

"They do. Could you do me a favor?"

"Anything."

"Can you go check on Lance? Let him know what happened? I don't think I'll be home too late, but I'd feel better if he weren't alone."

"I'm on it," Rye said. "We'll see you later." She hung up the phone and went downstairs, grateful she hadn't finished her first glass of wine.

Her phone buzzed again. Wanda had texted her.

> *Forgot. Lance still at school. Reset of props*
> *should be finished soon. Could you pick*
> *him up in half an hour?*

Rye grabbed her jacket and left her friends in the capable hands of her dad, grabbing Hardy's keys on her way out the door.

> *On it.*

She texted Lance to let her know she would be his ride tonight and that she would explain everything to him over burgers and fries. He'd responded with a series of enthusiastic emojis and said he'd find her after he finished putting props away for the night.

Rye told him everything while he devoured a half-pound burger and she snacked on fries and a milkshake.

When she'd finished, Lance wiped his mouth. "My aunt is the one who deserves that T-shirt." He nodded at her chest.

Rye looked down. She was still Halloween-ing as Wonder Woman.

30

WANDA LEANED BACK IN HER CHAIR AND ACCEPTED the hot tea Jaz Malone had carried in to her while she waited for Ryan.

"How are you feeling?" Jaz asked. Her thick braids were pulled back into an intricate bun, and she had changed from her uniform into street clothes sometime after Wanda arrived at the station. That explained the drink. A few doors down from the station was the best tea shop, No Doze Cafe. Wanda treated herself to a chai every few weeks, and she knew Jaz's husband worked there evenings.

Wanda was glad she had sent Rye to get Lance, because this was taking much longer than she'd expected. The paperwork alone was daunting, and she hadn't even debriefed yet. "Better now," she said as she lifted the cup in thanks.

Jaz lifted her own and smiled. "It's not every day I see my training in action. Not that I approve of your vigilante approach—"

"I am not a vigilante!" Wanda protested. "I wasn't even planning to go inside!"

"Were you planning to call it in?" Jaz asked, one eyebrow raised. "Because your friend Mitch seemed to think it was unlikely."

Just then, the door slammed open, and Ryan stomped into the room. "Of all the stupid, pigheaded things you could have done—" He stopped abruptly when he saw Jaz. "I thought you left already."

"I came back," Jaz said. "Thought I'd sit in and listen to Wanda's side of the story."

Wanda tried to hide her grin, but apparently she was not quick enough.

"Do you think this is funny?" Ryan dropped a heavy folder on the table. He slid a notebook over to Jaz. She grabbed it and flipped it open to a new page, winking at Wanda while Ryan searched for a pen. Old-school. He would make Jaz log it on the computer.

"Not at all," Wanda said. "I think it's terrible. Ben Jacobs is obviously deeply disturbed, and I'm glad to know the truth, if only to protect Henry from him."

"Why on earth would you go into his house?" Ryan asked. "Why were you even there in the first place?"

Wanda sighed. "I shouldn't have gone in. You're right. That was stupid."

"Damn right it was!" he said angrily.

Jaz cleared her throat in the direction of her boss, and he clenched his teeth, taking a few slow breaths.

"I wasn't planning this. I drove to his house after I talked to Mitch, after he confirmed to me that Ben Jacobs had been in a fight with his son the night Ross was killed."

"Why?" Jaz asked.

Wanda shrugged. "I don't know." She kept her eyes trained on Malone, but she could practically feel the frustration pouring off her ex. "It's been tough since I found Jonathan Thorne's body. In my line of work, I see a lot of death, and it's not all peaceful. In fact, it often comes with a lot of ugly emotional baggage."

She paused, and Ryan took the opportunity to jump in. "But this has nothing to do with Thorne."

"That's not what Ben Jacobs said when I saw him at Thorne's memorial service. He implied the deaths were...related? I don't know. He didn't say anything about that tonight, but it was bothering me. Not knowing the truth has been bothering me."

"Of course," Jaz said. "That makes sense."

"It does *not* give you the right to insert yourself into a police investigation!" Ryan snorted.

Oh, my, Wanda thought. This was literally good cop, bad cop. "I know," she said to them both. "If I'd known how dangerous he was—"

"I think you can just assume, in the future, that anyone you suspect of murder is dangerous," Ryan said.

In was a sign that she genuinely was recovering a mental stability she had not felt in months that Wanda could not resist. "I'll remember that after I get my PI license," she said.

It looked like he might have a stroke, so she kept going in a more conversational tone. "Before I talked to him, I thought it might have been an accident. Jacobs knows I'm a pastor. I guess I thought maybe he would open up to me."

"He did that," Jaz said.

"Just didn't say what I was expecting to hear," Wanda replied. She finally looked back at Ryan. "I'm sorry. I didn't mean to worry you."

"That's not what this is about," he said, his face flushing.

"Then what it is about?"

"It's about a civilian thinking she can do what the trained professionals do! It's about you withholding evidence from the police for your own little investigation. Ben Jacobs could just as easily have hurt you as talked to you. Did you think about that?" Ryan was standing at this point.

"Hardy Rye believes I can handle myself. Why can't you?"

"Hardy Rye is not the sheriff anymore!" Ryan growled. "I am."

Jaz reached out and put a hand on Phennen's arm. "Take five, Sheriff. I can finish up here."

He stared at her for a long moment, glanced at Wanda, and then nodded, slamming the door closed behind him.

Jaz started to say something, but Wanda held up a hand. "If you're going to apologize for him—"

"You think I make it a habit of apologizing on behalf of white men who act like that?" Jaz laughed. "I was going to say, in the *future*, it might be more productive if you give your statement to someone a little less …"

"Biased?"

"Melodramatic," Jaz said.

"What makes you think I'll be here in the future?" Wanda folded her hands primly on the table and offered Jaz her most innocent ministerial smile.

Jaz just rolled her eyes. "Okay, let's start again."

31

WANDA HAD TEXTED RYE TO ASK IF SHE COULD GIVE Lance a ride home again, this time from the Sunday matinee since Rye was at the show anyway. Wanda hadn't gotten home until after midnight, and then she'd had church and a trustee meeting immediately afterward. She was dragging.

Rye was happy to help—and to have a chance to see Claudia to congratulate her on a great show. She'd been waiting around in the lobby, hoping to catch her on her way out, but after half an hour neither Lance nor Claudia had appeared. Maybe the cast and crew were still celebrating in the greenroom.

She pulled open the door to the auditorium—the squeak still mysteriously missing—and caught a glimpse of Lance as he carried props into the wings. She jogged down the aisle and hopped up on the stage to wave. Lance had his headphones on, but he waved back and squatted to get a cord untangled from a costume some student actor had shed for a fast change and forgot to return.

He pulled one away headphone from his ear. "I'll be done here in a few minutes."

"Sounds good," Rye said. "Did Wanda give you any more details when she got home last night?"

"She was asleep on her feet when she walked in. By the time I got up, she was heading out the door, but she seemed happy. Cocky, even."

"Hardy says she singlehandedly brought down Ross Jacobs's killer. Like, with ninja self-defense moves."

Lance stood up. "Seriously? And she's okay, right?"

Rye couldn't help but love this kid. "I think she's still riding an adrenaline high."

"Wow. Aunt Wanda's kind of a badass, huh?"

"Totally," Rye agreed. She was about to say more when she heard an argument in the wings. "Is that Henry?" she asked, her voice low.

Lance nodded. "I think so. He was helping me here a little while ago. I wonder what he knows about last night." They both stood listening as the conversation escalated. The couple must have thought they were alone.

"Why can't we take your car?" Henry asked. "I'm broke, and my mom says she's not buying me gas after what happened at the dance."

"I told you, I hit a deer," Emma said.

"Do you think I'm an idiot?" Henry's voice cracked. "It was the same night Ross died. Did you hit him after you left me at my dad's?"

Lance and Rye looked at each other. She put her hands to her lips.

"You saw the paper. Even if it was me, he was already dead."

"You killed him, and now my dad's going to take the fall for it! I bet Chloe helped you."

"I swear to God, Henry, if you tell anyone, I'll go to the police and say I saw you put that powdered milk in Mr. Thorne's smoothie."

"I just thought he would get sick. I didn't know—" He stopped, and Rye heard a little yelp of pain from Emma. "It was a joke."

"You know he and Ross weren't even together. Your dad lied." But Emma's voice sounded different than it had a moment ago.

Rye sprinted into the wings in time to see Henry push Emma against the wall, his forearm pressed against her neck. "You don't know anything."

Lance reached them before her, using his shoulder to tackle Henry. Rye shoved herself in between them, grabbing Henry from behind, since she hoped Lance would stop on his own once they were pulled apart.

Henry was larger than Rye, and he got in a gut shot that had her gasping for breath. As she staggered back up, she saw Lance come at him again. Henry was sweating, and his eyes were wild. He didn't seem to feel the blows Lance landed on him. He turned and grabbed a large vase from the props table, but he miscalculated Lance's speed, and the vase shattered against the wall by Rye's head. She raised her hand up to touch where a piece cut her.

Henry's rage gave him power that Rye was sure the boy did not normally possess. He grabbed Lance around the waist and ran him into the wall. As Lance staggered to his feet, Rye landed a kick to Henry's instep, took him face down, and sat on his back. He struggled hard against her, his nails gouging into her arms, but she kept him pinned as she glanced around.

Lance was holding a hand to his bloody lip. His long hair had come out of its bun and hung around his face. He looked pale and angry.

"Are you okay?" she asked. Lance nodded. "Then call the police."

Rye glanced around, alert for another attack, but Emma was nowhere to be seen.

RYE ZIP-TIED HENRY'S HANDS TOGETHER AND THEN looped another tie through the arm of a chair. She stood guard, refusing Lance's offer to watch Henry while she cleaned up some of the blood still oozing from her nose and the cut on her forehead. This was one of the situations she sadly received training for as a teacher and admin. All the fight seemed to have gone out of Henry, but she couldn't trust that it wouldn't resurge. She sent Lance to meet the police and lead them in, asking him to keep his phone out and ready in case he ran into Emma.

While she waited, Rye tried to keep straight everything she'd overheard, but her head was pounding from the knock against the wall. The adrenaline had drained away, leaving her exhausted and sick. She couldn't help thinking of Henry's mother, who had lost one son and now would lose another.

Henry looked up as though he guessed what she was thinking. There was no affect in his voice at all. "My mom can go live with my sister in Providence. That was her plan after I graduated anyway. Now she just gets to go sooner."

Rye met his eyes, trying to imagine what this kid had gone through. "Why didn't you go to the police after Mr. Thorne was found?" Rye asked. "If you had explained to them what had happened with the milk—"

"I didn't know I killed him," he interrupted. "I thought he'd OD'ed. That was what everyone said. I figured it didn't make much of a difference that I'd put a little of that powder in his drink. And then Ross ..." He started to cry, and the blood mixed with tears and snot on his face. "Emma said I should keep it to myself, that there was enough going on without admitting that we messed with Thorne."

"She helped you?"

"It was her idea. I did it, but she was the one who told me he was lactose intolerant."

"He was allergic to milk," Rye said. "It's different."

"I know that now." He shifted a little to try to wipe his face on his sleeve. Rye looked around and found a rag, probably used for painting, and gently dried his face. Henry winced. "I think Lance broke my nose."

"Not on purpose."

Henry shook his head. "No, I know." He sighed, and his whole body seemed to deflate. He seemed to be sobering up. "When the cops come, can they call my dad instead of my mom?"

Rye took a slow breath. She didn't want to be the one to tell Henry that his own father had been responsible for his brother's death. There was no one else here, though. She pulled up a chair in front of him.

"Henry, your dad was arrested last night."

"What? What are you talking about?"

"He confessed to—" She stopped. How could she say this in the gentlest possible way?

She didn't have to. "He killed Ross, didn't he?" Henry asked, his voice cracking.

"It was an accident." Rye didn't know if that was true, but she would give him a lifeline. "They got into a fight. Ross fell and hit his head."

Rye and Henry both looked up as they heard the door to the stage open and close. It didn't sound like the police. Claudia and Marc Dubois-Thorne emerged from behind the curtain, Marc's face twisted with hatred.

He jammed his finger in Henry's direction. "You killed my husband." He held up a wrinkled piece of paper. "And then you had the audacity to send this." Marc shook the paper in Henry's face. Then he pulled a small pistol out of his jacket.

Rye stepped in front of Henry. She held out her hand for the paper, and Marc gave it to her reluctantly. She only read the first few lines, but it was obviously a love note. She turned the paper over and saw Ross's name at the bottom. Over the original letter, words had been crossed out and awful slurs scribbled on it.

"I didn't send that," Henry said, his voice cracking. "I swear I didn't."

"Was he having an affair with Jonathan? How did you find out about it?" Marc's voice was low.

"Ross had a thing for Jonathan since they met in rehab. I don't think Jonathan knew about it, though," Henry replied.

"This is a love letter," Marc said.

"Ross never would have given him that," Henry said. "After our dad cheated on Mom ... He just wouldn't."

"How did you get this?" Rye asked Marc.

"I ... I found it in the box that Claudia gave me." Marc turned to glance where she had been, but she'd disappeared. The gun came up again, and Rye held her hands in the air, the paper dangling between them.

"Then anyone could have put it there," Rye said softly. "Her office is rarely locked, and students go in and out all the time. Plenty of them would have known that

Jonathan used the extra desk when he was working here."

"But who would have had access to the letter besides him?" Marc asked, glaring at Henry.

Henry paled. "Maybe Emma. She slept over sometimes, but my mom made her stay in Ross's room."

"Emma's sister dated Ross all through high school. Emma told me that Chloe was devastated when she found out Ross was gay, that she felt betrayed. Maybe Emma found the letter and thought she could cause trouble for Ross." Rye glanced at Marc. "This"—she held up the paper—"might have been her way of getting revenge."

"She convinced me I should use the milk powder in the greenroom to make Jonathan sick." He seemed dazed, in shock. "That night, she dropped me off at my dad's house after we found out about Mr. Thorne. I called to tell her she'd forgotten her backpack. Well, I texted her, but she didn't answer, so I called her because I knew she needed her notes for her Spanish test, and I didn't feel like driving them all the way to her place if she was still over on this side of town." He tried to reach up to wipe his face before realizing his arms were restrained. "She screamed. We got disconnected, and when she came back to the house, she told me it was nothing. A near miss." He dropped his head to his chest. "You should kill me," he said to Marc after a long moment.

Marc's hand had dropped to his side, but now, slowly, it came up and steadied. "Get out of my way, Ms. Rye. I don't want to hurt you, but I will."

"Just do it," Henry said hoarsely. "Please." He was trying to shuffle the chair to the side, going around her.

"No!" With both hands, Rye slammed Marc's forearm so the gun was pointed at the floor. She remembered her dad saying, *In close quarters, don't grab a gun. Untarget it. Gunshot in the foot hurts like hell but doesn't need a casket.* God, how old had she been when he was handing out this advice, eight?

"It's just a prop," Marc wheezed, holding his arm. "I just wanted to scare him."

She checked. He was telling the truth. It was a realistic model, and not something she would approve for use in any school shows, but definitely a fake.

The wings seemed to fill with police as Rye studied the gun. She found herself, abruptly, face down on the floor, her arms yanked behind her back, the gun pulled from her grasp. Somebody was already reading her Miranda rights when Ryan appeared in front of her.

"Why is it always you?" He reached down and removed the handcuffs.

Rye cautiously hauled herself to her feet and looked around. She didn't recognize the man who had cuffed her.

Ryan nodded to him, and the officer hurried off to help Tyler and Jaz. "Sorry about that. Brent and I were having coffee when the call came in. He's on the Lowell force."

Rye didn't think Ryan was all that sorry about the mix-up, but she let it go. She was too tired to argue with him right now. "It's fine. He saw a gun. Made the same choice I would have in that situation."

Ryan cocked his head, staring at her oddly. "And how do you know that?"

She shrugged. "I spent about six months at the academy before I decided I wanted to get my master's instead. My dad really wanted me to join the force, though, so ... I don't know. At least I learned enough to keep out of your way, right?"

"You are literally always in the middle of everything."

In that moment, Rye saw a flash of the old Rya—the young, repressed recruit who had parented his little brother and who had taken Rye's adolescent teasing with relatively good grace.

"I guess I am," Rye admitted. "I'll just remind you of who my father is—"

"And why you are the way you are," Ryan agreed. He shook his head and sighed, then gently took her by the arm and led her out to the ambulance where Lance was waiting.

32

When Rye got home after getting stitches accompanied by ER interviews with two detectives and a woman from social services, Hardy was waiting for her. He came down the steps of the porch as she climbed out of Tyler's truck.

"I'll pick you up tomorrow afternoon, and we can go get your car before round two with my brother," Tyler said. "I asked them to fast-track the paint job."

"Thanks, Tyler. I really appreciate it." She waved a half-empty bag of peanut M&Ms at him with a smile. When he'd offered to give her a lift home, she'd discovered that his pickup was a candy shop and Halloween rolled into one, and she'd picked the treat that seemed to have the most nutritional value.

Hardy gave him a wave and then reached out to envelop Rye in a huge hug. She hung onto him, the strain of the afternoon overtaking her.

After he fed her a bowl of soup and rolls, Hardy gave her a tour of the new motion-activated lights he'd had put up on the house and barn, as well as the security camera he'd hidden in the eaves above her door.

"That might be overkill," Rye said. She leaned against her dad and dug for her keys.

"Maybe," Hardy agreed. "But I made an account for you anyway."

"I mean, the kitchen window does look right at my front door, which you've now lit up like Times Square," Rye pointed out as she unlocked her door.

"Lots of people have nosy neighbors. Just a fact of life. Besides, you probably shouldn't invite anyone over who you're ashamed for me to meet."

Rye rolled her eyes but smiled. "It was a long day. I'm going to lie down for an hour, but then maybe we could eat dinner together? I know it's my turn to cook, but—"

"I have a chicken pot pie ready to go, and there will be an enormous pan of brownies waiting for you."

"Thanks, Dad. Will you lock the door on the way out?" She gave him another hug. "And feel free to stare at my door while I'm sleeping."

"Oh, I was planning on it." He left, shutting the door gently behind him.

RYE TOOK HER TIME IN THE SHOWER, TRYING TO WASH away the aches while keeping her bandaged face dry. She was dressed in fleece leggings and a plaid shirt she could button up rather than tug over her head when she collapsed on her couch.

It was dark outside when she heard the knock on her door. At the same moment, her phone chimed.

> *There's a young woman at your door.*
> *Dark curly hair.*

Thanks, Dad. I've got it. She opened the door for Claudia, twisting a hair band around her braid as she did.

"I'm sorry to bother you," Claudia said. "I didn't know if you'd want company." She held up a bottle of wine.

Rye studied her face. Claudia looked almost as exhausted as Rye felt. "I can't drink tonight"—she gestured to her bandages—"and I have dinner plans with my dad, but come in." She felt the familiar rush of blood to her face as Claudia brushed past her into the room.

Claudia perched on the edge of the couch. "I just wanted to come see how you were doing."

"I'm fine."

Claudia studied Rye's face, from the bruises on her cheeks to the small stitches that went almost to her ear. "Oh. Good, I guess." She pushed a stray piece of hair back. "I also wanted to apologize for running away. Again."

"Marc had a gun. It was smart."

"I didn't know he had it till he pulled it out. I didn't even know he owned a gun. I wouldn't have—"

"I know. I'm fine. And as it turns out, it was a fake." Rye studied Claudia. She looked pale and tired, and a part of Rye wanted to pull her in close and be the one who kept the world at bay.

"You keep saying you're fine, but you aren't."

Rye sighed. "Claudia, I can't do this right now. I can't unpack what just happened. I can't begin to apologize for believing you might have had something to do with Jonathan's death."

Claudia looked shocked. "What?"

"When I found out about your girlfriend, and Jonathan refusing to sponsor her, I thought—"

"You thought I killed him?" Her hand over her mouth, her eyes filled with tears.

"You were so angry. And then someone broke in here and defaced my car."

"And your first thought was that I had something to do with that? Why?" Claudia asked. "What happened to being honest with each other?"

"I thought you might be worried that I suspected you, that you were trying to scare me off," Rye said softly. "I didn't want to believe it. I don't think, in my heart, that I did believe it. But I've been wrong about people I care about before."

"You don't trust me." It wasn't a question.

"I didn't." The words stuck in Rye's throat.

Claudia nodded. She stood up and wiped her eyes. "I should have known this was too good to be true."

"I'm sorry, Claudia. This is my thing. It has nothing to do with you."

"Of course. The 'it's not you, it's me' defense. How refreshing."

"I think," Rye began, her fingers brushing Claudia's sleeve, "that it was also too soon. For you. I know a little about that—"

She was interrupted by another knock on the door and a simultaneous buzz from her phone. She glanced down.

Andy and Rachel.

Her cheeks flushed. "You've got to be kidding me."

"Were you expecting someone?"

Rye shook her head and opened the door. Andy glanced past her to the red-eyed Claudia.

"I'm so sorry. I should have texted first." Andy seemed to register her face for the first time. "Rye! What happened? Are you okay?"

"It's a long story." She reached up to rub her throbbing temples and winced as her fingers brushed the bandage. "Would you like to come in?"

He glanced from her to Claudia. "This is a bad time."

"It's been a bad day," Rye said. "But you've come all this way."

"I don't know if we're about to make it worse or better." Andy ushered Rachel inside with him. He shut the door, and the four of them stood awkwardly in the small room.

Rye wondered if her dad had gotten out his long-range binoculars yet or if he could see her making introductions easily enough from his spot by the window.

"Claudia." Andy stretched out his hand. "I've heard such nice things about you."

"You talked about me?" she asked Rye.

Rye shrugged helplessly. "Only nice things."

There was another awkward silence. Andy broke it by reaching into his pocket and pulling out a phone. He handed it to Rachel and left his hand on her shoulder. "Go ahead," he told her.

Rachel mumbled something. Andy cleared his throat and gave her shoulder a little squeeze. "Fine," Rachel said. "I'm sorry."

"For...what?" Rye asked.

Rachel blushed. "I took Andy's key and came in here the other night. I was just ..." She sighed. "I was mad at you."

"He has a key?" Claudia asked, at the same time Rye repeated, "For what?"

"You broke up with Andy, and you didn't even come to say good-bye to me," Rachel said. "And the other night, you came over, and I thought you were at least going to come in and say hi, and you didn't."

"I'm sorry," Claudia interrupted. "When did you break up with him?"

"Like a second ago," Rachel said.

Rye closed her eyes. The difference between a ten-year-old kid and an eleven-year-old tween was a swiftly raging river of attitude-adjusting hormones. "Let me get this straight. You broke into my house? You took that picture of me?"

"I thought you would text me back, and then I could tell you that I left a note." She pointed to a blank piece of paper on the table by the door.

Rye stared at it. It took a minute before the pin dropped. "You wrote me a note in invisible ink?"

"Yeah. That was, like, the most fun thing you ever showed me how to do. Well, that and how to properly kick a boy in the ... you know."

Rye picked up the paper and walked over to her lamp to hold it under the bulb. The letter filled both sides of the paper—no easy feat using the lemon-juice-and-water technique Rye had shown Rachel. The room was silent while she read it. When she was done, she put the paper down carefully and turned back to Rachel.

"I'm sorry. Andy and I should have thought about how you might feel. I didn't think you even liked having me around."

"You're not good enough for my cousin," Rachel said. Andy let out a strangled sound, but she went on. "But I think you're okay." This time, Rachel sounded sincere. She wrapped her arms around Rye, and Rye tried not to wince as she squeezed her bruised abdomen. "I didn't mean to scare you."

"How come your cell number came up as blocked?" Rye asked her.

"It's a phone my dad gave me." Rachel's father, Eric, was awaiting trial for second-degree murder, attempted kidnapping, assault with a deadly weapon, and multiple drug violations. "I guess it was one of his old burners. Andy just got me a plan for it last week."

Rye looked at Andy and shrugged. It was stupid, but maybe not as dumb as a few of the things they'd done at Rachel's age.

"Did you vandalize my car, too?"

"What?" Andy blurted out.

Claudia put up a hand. "That's my fault."

"You wrote those things on my car?" Rye asked.

"No!" Claudia said. "Emma did." She let out a deep breath. "Earlier this week, I was talking to Gerard Mendoza about the fact that Jonathan hadn't overdosed. Some people knew and some people didn't, and Stoneridge had become a rumor mill. Marc called me to talk about it, and I wanted to be sure Gerard knew because he had been so upset. I mentioned to Gerard that you had been approached by the sheriff and that he wanted you to keep an eye out for suspicious behavior around school."

"How do you know it was Emma?"

"I caught her hanging around just after that conversation, and when the police showed me the photos of the graffiti on your car, I knew it had to be her. I busted her last year for doing the same thing with lipstick in one of the dressing rooms. I caught her red-handed, and she still tried to deny it. She has a distinct way of writing her Fs, though."

"That's certainly a letter that was prominently featured on the side of my car."

"They haven't found her yet, have they?" Claudia asked.

Rye shook her head.

Another knock at the door made them all jump. There was no accompanying text, so Rye moved carefully, gesturing Andy and Rachel back toward the bathroom with Claudia. She lifted the edge of the curtain, then dropped it and swung open the door. Hardy stood there holding a casserole dish with hot mitts, a Tupperware container under one arm.

"I thought you might be ready for dinner," he said to Rye.

"Mr. Hardy!" Rachel dashed over to him and gave him a careful hug before pulling the container of brownies out from under his arm.

"Hey, Bug," he said, setting down his dish on the coffee table. "What are you doing here?"

Rachel glanced up at Andy, then straightened her shoulders. "Apologizing," she said.

Hardy nodded approvingly. "Glad to hear it." He opened the lid of his dish, and the scent of his homemade chicken pot pie filled the room. "I hope you can all stay. I always make too much for just the two of us."

Claudia and Andy both looked to Rye, and she nodded, trying to decide if this was the most awkward dinner she'd ever had. Her belly growled so loudly that she decided not to worry about it. She helped herself to a heaping bowl.

"No bread?" she asked a little mournfully.

The knock on her door was perfectly timed. Hardy stood up to let Wanda and Lance in. Wanda looked a little worse for the wear, but she carried two fresh baguettes from Harvey's. Lance had a large fruit salad and a quart of mint chip ice cream. Wink just wagged his tail.

"Any room at the inn?" Wanda asked.

Lance grinned. "It's a little early for Christmas jokes, isn't it? Don't you have any Advent puns? Thanksgiving witticisms?"

Rye held up her hand to wave the chunk of baguette she'd already grabbed at him. "Don't tempt her!" She scooted over so that Wanda could come take the seat by her on the couch, and when her friend sat, Rye handed her a brownie.

"Life's too short not to eat dessert first."

Wanda sighed and leaned against Rye's shoulder gently. "You know me so well."

She took the proffered brownie in one hand and the bowl Hardy handed her in the other, balancing the latter carefully on her knees. Lance was already most of the way through his first serving, and Rye wondered whether Andy still had a metabolism that could keep up with him. She couldn't help but smile at the puppy dog eyes Rachel was shooting at Lance. That was a feeling she remembered from middle school.

"Claudia?" Wanda whispered to Rye as she wiped her mouth. Rye had put on the TV so Andy could show them YouTube videos from the Restaurant of Mistaken Orders while they ate.

"That's her."

"She looks a little—"

"Fragile?" Rye suggested, having watched her father grill the young woman for several minutes before Andy tactfully found the entertainment for everyone.

"I was going to say overwhelmed, but same difference."

"Hardy Rye can have that effect on people."

"That he can," Wanda said, covering up a sudden flush of her cheeks with her napkin. "What's the story with you two now?"

"What's the story with you and Ryan? I heard he asked you out for an apology dinner and you said yes."

"Who told you that?"

"Hardy has his sources."

Wanda grabbed another brownie. "I can handle a free meal and a little groveling. He owes me."

She patted the pillow beside her, and Rye pulled her legs up and tucked them under a blanket. It wasn't long before they were both fast asleep.

Rye roused herself to grunt good-bye as her guests left, listening as the cars pulled out. Hardy whispered to her that he would install Lance in Rye's old bedroom, and when they left, Rye fell gratefully back into a dreamless sleep.

33

WHEN RYE WOKE UP, WANDA WAS GONE. SHE'D LEFT A note saying Hardy had called the school to say Rye was not coming. He was driving Wanda home, since she had a parishioner in the hospital to visit before her not-a-date with Ryan Phennen.

Rye squinted at her phone. It was still dark outside, but it was a little after six, and she'd fallen asleep early enough that she couldn't go back to bed now if she tried.

She flipped on the TV and let Netflix pick something to play as she got changed and brushed her teeth. She took an Aleve for the throbbing in her face and was getting out some eggs to make breakfast when there was a knock on her door. Rye sighed and shuffled over to open it.

Emma Reyes stood in front of her. Rye was so shocked, she didn't say anything for a long moment. The young woman wasn't dressed like a fugitive on the run—just the opposite. Her dark hair was pulled back in two neat French braids. She had on maroon pants that complemented the plaid in her knee-length wool coat, and her scarf was perfectly wrapped. Emma was clearly channeling a more clean-cut version of herself, which Rye thought was a brilliant move. A greasy teen skulking around in a hoodie would immediately draw the attention of the police. This young woman would do the opposite.

"Ms. Rye?"

"What are you doing here, Emma?"

The girl fidgeted. "I wanted to tell you that Henry is innocent." She looked as if she expected Rye to let her in out of the freezing morning.

Instead, Rye wedged herself between the doorframe and the door and stared at Emma. "If you have information that will help him, you should talk to the police."

"They won't believe me. They think I'm a manipulative little drug addict."

Rye raised an eyebrow at her. She'd perfected the move over years of teaching, and it didn't fail her now.

"I'm not!" Emma insisted. "I've only taken pills, like, twice, and that was because my sister said it would be fine. Chloe gave them to me and Henry. She said they would relax him, let him have a little fun after Ross ..."

"So you never took them before Ross died?"

She shook her head. "No. Only after I ..."

"After you hit his body," Rye said softly. She didn't like this girl, but Emma was a kid, and she wasn't going to rub it in and make things worse.

Emma nodded. She glanced away and blinked a few times. "I thought I killed him," she said in a low voice. "I was so freaked out that night. Driving too fast. We'd put a little milk powder in Mr. Thorne's smoothie, and then he died. But I did the research! It was just a sprinkle!"

"Some people have such severe allergies that a sprinkle is enough, no matter what the Internet told you."

"But Mr. Thorne told us it wasn't. He said when he was a kid, he'd had milk by accident once or twice—just a sip—and he'd gotten sick but not needed his Epi-Pen."

Rye sighed. "That doesn't mean his allergy didn't become more severe as he got older. That happens to a lot of people, you know."

"But it wasn't …" She stopped, clearly frustrated. "If you'd seen how little we used …"

"What about the letter? Why did you give Ross's letter to Mr. Thorne?"

"Not to him! I sent it to his husband, like, weeks ago. I told you about my sister? Chloe knew she lost Ross because he loved Mr. Thorne, who acted like he didn't exist."

"That must have been awful," Rye said.

"It wrecked her. She dropped out of Bard. Now she just gets high with whatever guy rolls up on her."

Ross and Jonathan. Both named responsible for the emotional destruction of women. Emma and Claudia, both angry about it. Angry at Thorne.

"So you mailed Marc Dubois-Thorne a love letter that Ross wrote but never sent?"

"Ross didn't even know it was missing. Maybe he never looked in the drawers in his old room."

"Maybe he's just a good actor," Rye suggested.

Emma shrugged. "I don't know. He would have blamed Henry, and Henry would have told me."

Marc had been so angry backstage. And he'd said the letter was in Jonathan's things. Clearly it hadn't been, unless Jonathan had grabbed the mail on his way to school and left it there.

"When exactly did you send the letter?"

"A month ago. Maybe longer." Emma clenched her hands into fists. "Right after Chloe asked me to go with her to a clinic in Manchester." She looked as young as she'd costumed herself to be. "She cried the whole way home."

Rye stared at Emma. It wasn't Ross's fault that breaking up with Chloe had sent her careening away from college and whatever dreams she'd had for herself. He hadn't deserved to die just because a girl he used to love got an abortion with only her little sister for support. But Rye couldn't say for sure that if she had been in Emma's position she wouldn't have wanted to extract some sort of revenge.

"Whose idea was the milk powder?"

"Henry doesn't have ideas, really. He just goes along—with me, or with his dad."

"What are you going to do now?"

"I was going to take these," Emma said, pulling a prescription bottle out of her pocket. It looked like she had been rubbing at the label, because the words were illegible.

"But you didn't kill Ross. Emma, think. He was already dead." Rye held out her hand. Emma handed the bottle over reluctantly. "You aren't responsible for that."

"I should have stopped. I should have called the police."

"Yes," Rye said. "You should have."

"Aren't you going to tell me it's all going to be all right?"

"That's up to you," Rye replied. "You have more choices than whatever's in here, though." Rye shook the bottle. "You haven't done anything yet that you can't come back from with therapy and support."

"What are you talking about? We killed Mr. Thorne. If I turn myself in, I'm going to prison."

"You definitely made a mistake. You absolutely endangered his life. Whether or not you were responsible for his death…That's still up in the air." Rye stared at her. "But if you leave Henry to take the blame for all this, to carry the guilt of whatever happened without your support or the truth as only you can tell it …"

"I thought you were supposed to make me feel better," Emma said.

"What makes you say that?"

"My friend told me you helped her. That you would understand."

"Here's the thing. I think the best way to help my students is to show them the truth, as best as I understand it, and allow them to make decisions based on what feels right to them," Rye said. "You were trying to protect someone you love, but you went about it the wrong way. I think you try to do the right thing, and even though it feels like it's all gone wrong, you have a chance to keep trying."

Rye thought about all the problems she'd run away from when she was Emma's age. She had left so much unsaid, so many wounds open to fester by leaving town without saying good-bye. Rye knew she hadn't earned the forgiveness Andy or her father had given her. She was just fortunate that they loved her enough to see past her mistakes. What she deserved was the reception Ryan had given her, and continued to give her—distance and barely disguised annoyance. She wasn't the same person she had been at seventeen, but had she really proved to anyone who'd known her then that she had changed?

Rye shook her head to clear these thoughts away. This wasn't about her. "If you take your own life, or run away, you have no chance to repair anything. You'll always be the manipulative little drug addict. Is that who you are?"

"No," Emma said.

"Then prove it. Show me that you can do hard things, and I'll help you any way I can."

Rye closed the door and leaned against the edge of the couch, listening as Emma's footsteps on the gravel faded away.

Maybe this kind of waiting and trusting was what Wanda called faith. Rye looked at her calendar. It was November 2, Dia de los Muertos, Day of the Dead. Of reconciliation.

34

WANDA TRIED ON TWO SHORT-SKIRTED, SPARKLY dresses that she had worn to many a disastrous date over the last few years. Tonight, they felt too tight and itchy. Since Lance had arrived, she hadn't gone out, and honestly she hadn't missed it. Having his company, and seeing Rye, Hardy, Tony, and even getting to know Greg felt like the balance she'd been missing. Too bad it had taken two murders to make it happen.

When Ryan asked her out, though, Wanda couldn't bring herself to say no. She would probably regret it, but a part of her wanted to hear him acknowledge her help on his cases. An actual thank-you was probably too much to expect, she mused as she clipped her hair back from her face.

She settled for black pants, a silky royal blue blouse, and the gold-and-blue parrot earrings from her trip to Mexico that complemented her original royal blue hearing aid covers. Ryan had once mentioned it made him feel old to date someone with hearing impairment. He'd meant it as a joke—or so he claimed afterward when he saw how upset she was—but the comment had led directly to their most recent split. If he couldn't love all of her, he couldn't love her at all. That's what she'd told him, and it was true.

He'd been so wound up for the last few weeks, though, that for her own sake, she needed to make peace with him. Wanda knew from experience that leaving things unresolved with Ryan ended poorly. She blushed just thinking about the last time they'd tried to make up. But tonight would be different. She had no intention of making that mistake again.

When Ryan arrived, he was ebullient, as he always was after closing a big case. Most of their reconciliations had happened during just such a high, when he was unfailingly charming, funny, and almost mischievous. Tonight was no exception. He wore a sharp navy suit, and he'd put in the tiny gold hoop earring that she loved. He never wore jewelry while working, but she had seen his extensive collection. Understated, and all in gold to bring out his tawny complexion, he had slim-chained bracelets, tiny studs, and delicate hand-wrought necklaces he picked up from local artisans.

But the little hoop was her favorite. It made him look like a roguish pirate, a fact that Wanda had once confessed, and not in a police report.

She tried to concentrate on her food instead. Wanda twirled the cheese on a generous bite of eggplant parmesan and asked, "So how's my dancing partner, Ben Jacobs?"

"Remind me not to get in a fight with you," Ryan said, his fingers brushing against hers. "Seems like Jaz teaches more than the basics."

Wanda studiously ignored the shot of heat and shoved a large bite into her mouth. "She's the best teacher I've had."

"You've taken a lot of self-defense classes? I thought you were more into peace, love, and yoga."

Wanda rolled her eyes. "I meant for anything. She's incredible. I suspect any of her students could hold their own, many of them probably better than me."

Ryan raised an eyebrow. "Good to know. If I see a vigilante uprising, at least I'll know who's training them."

"Maybe you should be recruiting from her class. The force could use a little more diversity, don't you think?"

Ryan nodded. "Not a bad idea, actually. Maybe I'll ask her if she wants to put up some flyers about the class in community meetup places and then talk to some of the promising young students about the police academy."

Wanda hid her surprise. Sometimes Ryan could be so off-putting that she forgot he was a liberal guy. They'd first met while protesting for immigration reform, back before he'd become sheriff, and when they'd dated that first year she'd been in awe of the fact that she'd found someone as passionate about human rights as she was to whom she was also wildly attracted.

She studied his face as he ate. Becoming sheriff had changed him. Hardy Rye's accident and abrupt retirement had come as a shock to the community, and they hadn't been enthusiastic about his replacement. Ryan had been trying to prove himself for almost two years now, and the strain had brought out all his failings. Not as an officer of the law—she had to admit he was good at his job—but vain about his success, quick to anger, resistant to even the gentlest criticism, and sullen when stressed. He'd also burned a few bridges when he was new, and he remained bitter that those same people wouldn't get in line now that they saw he was here to stay. At least until the next election.

"What are you thinking about?" he asked.

Wanda blushed and shoved another bite into her mouth. "The Jacobs family," she lied when her mouth was mostly empty again.

"I hope you're not wasting any tears on them. Especially Ben Jacobs. He's strategizing with his public defense lawyer to get the charge down to manslaughter. If he pleads to it, she can argue that he was emotionally incompetent and ask for antihomophobia therapy and AA and hope to get out in seven. He knows how to play the good guy, and he is tough enough to survive." Ryan shook his head. "And, Wanda?"

"What?"

"Watch out when he gets released."

She felt a chill. "Has he had visitors?"

"Not his wife, and of course not Henry. But before he got sent to county, the daughter from Rhode Island came and offered money for bail. He refused but asked her to clean out the house and set it up as a rental. She said she would have much preferred to bail him out so he could handle all that."

"You got this information how?"

"How do you think? Jaz, the kind, the empathetic, the listening ear. By the time she left, that woman knew the cheapest, best self-storage, and she had a two-week temporary town dump pass and the cell phone number of someone Jaz knows at a rental agency who will check out the applicants and make sure her father's savings account is connected for necessary repairs."

"What do you know? Renting houses so a murderer can make money."

"Not a murderer. An accident, right? That's what his pretty lawyer is going to say."

"Dragging his son's body into the road?" Wanda felt ill just thinking about it.

"Panic and alcohol," Ryan said. "Trust me, after being accused of skimming money from his own business, he still got a job at a Catholic high school. Ben Jacobs is a man who knows how to sell the best version of himself."

"Unlike his son."

"Henry is on suicide watch. The plan was to send him to a secure adolescent mental health center for full evaluation. We were ready to transfer this morning because we're not set up to handle a kid. Then an anonymous donor sent money for ten days at a well-established private facility instead of the state-run one. All the diagnostic work, time for individual sessions, the whole nine yards."

"That sounds wonderful," Wanda said. "Suspicious, though, don't you think?"

He shrugged. "I didn't see the family asking any questions. Autumn Jacobs seemed grateful someone else wanted to take care of it."

"But why would someone do that? Unless they felt guilty."

"If you're thinking of Emma Reyes's family, you're barking up the wrong tree. They still haven't found their daughter, and the last thing they'd do is help out her murderer boyfriend."

"I just ..."

"You just don't like to let sleeping dogs lie." Ryan pulled out his wallet and handed his card to the waiter as he passed. "It's over, Wanda. I know it's not what you'd like to hear, but the guilty parties are in custody. We can't change that just because one of them is a sixteen-year-old kid who didn't get enough hugs."

Wanda knew for a fact that one of Ryan's many issues was that he had been just such a sixteen-year-old. She knew a case like this one, with an abusive father and two brothers in turmoil, hit too close to home for him.

Ryan pasted on a smile. "Before you start treating me like one of your parishioners, yes, I'm still in therapy, and no, I'm not sure if it's working."

"And you don't want to talk about it."

"No more than you want to talk about why you haven't touched your wine tonight."

Wanda pushed her glass away without thinking. "Truce, then."

He held out his hand and pulled her out of the booth. "Truce."

The warmth of his hand in hers as they walked out of the restaurant took all of Wanda's attention. And when he kissed her at her door, it took considerable willpower not to invite him in. She didn't have quite enough not to pull him back as he started to walk away, kissing him once more on her own terms. At least, that was how she reassured herself as she let herself in.

She said good night to Lance, sitting at his computer with the air of someone who of course had not been peeking through the curtains a moment earlier, and went to bed alone.

RYE CALLED BRIGHT AND EARLY THE NEXT MORNING. Wanda groaned as she rolled over to answer, regretting her decision to use "Joyful, Joyful" as her ringtone. It had seemed cute a decade ago. Now she mostly left her phone on vibrate, but at night, when parishioners might call with an emergency, she put the ringer on high.

"What do you want?" she grumbled, burying her head in the pillow.

"Good morning to you, too. Late night?"

Wanda rubbed her face. She'd forgotten to wash up last night, and by the taste of her mouth, she hadn't brushed her teeth either. She'd gone without a drink for almost a week before her date with Ryan, and she wasn't used to being with him without being buzzed. This thought reminded her that she should probably find a meeting if she was going to try to keep her sobriety. Triggers were an addiction's best friends, as she well knew from years of counseling others. "I guess so."

"How was your not-a-date?"

"Informative." Wanda sat up and took a long drink of water. "Apparently, an anonymous donor is paying for Henry Jacobs to go to a pricy private adolescent psychiatric treatment facility."

"You told me his family doesn't have money. Couldn't pay for the funeral without a GoFundMe."

"Hence the anonymous donor part."

"Emma's family?"

"Ryan says no. They don't want anything to do with Henry. Certainly not while their daughter is still on the run."

"She came to my house," Rye said. "Says she and Henry barely used any of that milk powder, and that for what it was worth, she Googled it first to make sure they wouldn't kill him."

"What?!" Now Wanda was awake. "Are you okay?"

"I'm fine."

"Did you call it in?"

Judging by the long silence, the answer to that question was no.

"She also admitted to sending that letter to Marc DuBois-Thorne," Rye finally said. "She found it snooping in Ross's old room a few months ago. Emma says she sent it over a month ago, which doesn't jibe with what Marc said. She's an angry kid, but I just don't buy that she and Henry set out to murder Jonathan or run over Ross."

"I don't either," Wanda confessed. She rubbed her temples. "Ryan is convinced it's all been wrapped up with a nice bow, but something doesn't sit right with me."

"Me neither. But if his death wasn't a result of the prank, who killed him?"

"Could he have eaten someone else's food by mistake?" Wanda asked. "I know he was careful, but maybe he was in a hurry?"

"Or maybe someone switched his food with look-alikes?" Rye mused.

"That wouldn't be a mistake, though."

"Do you really think it was one?"

Wanda sighed. "No. I just can't see who would have done this."

There was a long silence. "I don't want to believe it could be Claudia. But she and Marc were the most likely to know about the allergy, where he kept his food, when he ate …"

"When he would have gone for a walk," Wanda finished. "Having met Claudia, I agree with you, though. I don't think she would have done it that way. I know she has a motive, but my gut says that if she were going to kill him to avenge her girlfriend's death, she would have done it sooner."

"In the heat of the moment?"

"Exactly."

"At the very least, she would have shielded her students from it," Rye agreed.

Wanda swung her feet to the floor, and Wink jumped up out of the blankets. "So that leaves Marc."

"He could have done it, Wanda. You didn't see him the other day with Henry."

She shook a couple of Advil into her hand and followed them with a long swig of water. "I know you said he creeped you out, but every time I've met with him, he's seemed devastated. Like he's truly grieving Jonathan's death."

"Plus you like his dog, so how could he be the killer?"

"I didn't say that!" Wanda protested.

Rye snorted. "People with nice dogs can be murderers, you know. He threatened a sixteen-year-old with a gun."

"A prop, but I see what you're saying. The cozy house might be his stage?"

"I'm sure you've seen plenty of crocodile tears in your line of work," Rye said. "I know I have."

"What are we going to do about it, though?" Wanda asked. "Ryan is done. He's not going to listen to me if I suggest that Marc might be guilty."

"Not even if you suggest it right after a passionate night of lovemaking?"

"Lance told me that kind of phrasing was much worse than just saying someone hooked up, and now that I've heard it from you, I have to agree. And he most definitely did not spend the night."

"Lance texted me. I happen to know you made out with the sheriff on your front porch."

Wanda did not manage to stop herself from making a little noise of surprise.

"You live with a teenager now," Rye said. "Nothing you do is private anymore."

"But why did he text you?"

"I'm going to go out on a limb and say that whatever's happening with his mom and her sketchy boyfriend probably has him more freaked out than he wants to admit. He may not know your history with Ryan, but he's a smart kid, and one who's seen a maternal figure make a lot of poor dating decisions."

Wanda groaned. "It's too early in the morning to get psychoanalyzed."

"But not to discuss murder? Good to see where your boundaries lie."

Wanda twisted her hair off her neck. "Yes, I kissed Ryan, and yes, it was great. It's always great, which is why I've made this mistake so many times" Wanda paused. "Also, I've never really kissed him sober before."

"Wait, what?"

"I've been drinking for years, and whenever he and I have been together, I would drink more. I'd be hungover, or I'd be buzzed, or we'd have a glass of wine with dinner. With our schedules, we rarely saw each other during the day or on weekends. We never were serious enough to live together, and honestly, he almost never spent the night. It was...casual."

"But now...it's not casual?" Rye sounded confused.

"No. Now, I'm not drinking."

There was a long silence while Rye processed this information. "Like, ever?"

"That's the goal. I'm new to this, but...I'm going to try."

"That's awesome. Can I ask why now?"

Wanda sighed. "Lance. And, I don't know. It's just time."

"You have come alive in the last few weeks," Rye said. "I've never seen you so happy."

"I haven't felt this good in a long time," Wanda replied. "Now let me take a shower so I can wash my bad decisions off."

"What are we going to do about Marc?"

She turned on the water to let it heat up. "I'll ask Tony if he knows anything. He and Jonathan were friendly, although they both had so many gigs outside of school that I don't think they were closer than that. Maybe he has some insight that might help."

"Call me after you've talked?"

"I will," Wanda said. "And thanks for telling me about Lance texting you. I don't want to mess this up."

"I know. I've got you."

35

TALKING TO TONY HAD SEEMED LIKE THE SAFE CHOICE, but the chance didn't come till Friday afternoon, and Wanda felt anxious as she sat waiting for him in Harvey's with a flat white coffee and a plate of croissants. She and Tony had seen so much less of each other since he and Greg started dating, and although she knew some of that was on him—new relationships always took on a big role—she was also to blame.

Tony had always had an active dating life, but he never seemed to settle down with anyone. He wanted to, she knew, because he had told her so about three million times and described the children he would have once he did so, but he seemed to attract bores, cheaters, and those looking for casual relationships.

Greg was different. She had noticed right away, even before Tony told her that he was seeing someone. His energy had shifted, and instead of coming in with a hangover and epic bad date recaps, he seemed content. Relaxed. In love.

Although Wanda didn't know Greg well yet, he seemed like an unexpectedly perfect match for her friend. She couldn't quite put her finger on why, but they were in sync. Whatever had been going on last Saturday when Greg needed to leave the church, Wanda was confident they had resolved it. She was happy for them both, but she recognized jealousy when it walloped her in the gut.

She and Tony had been the victims of bad Internet dates for so long, but they'd also been in it together, so it hadn't felt quite so discouraging. Even when she'd been kissing Ryan last night, a part of her was doing it because she was tired of looking for the right new partner. She wasn't even sure that person existed anymore. But when she'd seen Tony and Greg together, hope bubbled up. Ryan might not be a good choice, but he wanted her. He touched her like she was precious, and he knew her. That wasn't nothing.

Hating her hearing aids and thinking she was damaged goods because of them was something. Also the temper. The misogyny. The list went on ...

As she watched Tony hold the door open for Greg despite the sleety rain coming down, she felt tears prick her eyes. Ryan had never looked at her the way Tony looked at Greg, with such tenderness. That was what she was missing—a partner who brought not just love, but peace and joy, too.

Tony gave her a kiss on the cheek and dove into a chocolate croissant and conversation. "I'd say good day, but you look like you've been through the ringer already. Rough morning?"

"No worse than usual." Wanda took a sip of coffee and smoothed her hair back into place.

"So does that mean you're ready to hear my plans for a six-church Epiphany choir concert?"

"That sounds more like something next-week Wanda would like to talk about."

Greg laughed. "I told you she wouldn't say no outright."

"She also didn't say yes," Tony argued.

"Take the win," Wanda said. "Trust me. I'm probably the easiest person you'll be selling that particular idea to, but even I don't have the brainpower to consider it right now."

She looked up as the bell jingled over the door. Jessica Thorne walked in, and before Wanda could take evasive action, she detoured over to the table.

"I just wanted to thank you again for the service," she said, then did a double take. "Greg?"

Greg looked pale as he dropped the menu he'd been holding. He gave her a wan smile. "Jessica."

She leaned down to hug him, but he pulled back abruptly. Jessica looked nonplussed, and Wanda could feel Tony bristling beside her. "Sorry for interrupting," Jessica said after a moment. "I'll see you around." She turned and left without getting a coffee. Greg let out a long, shaky breath when the door shut behind her.

"What was that about?" Wanda asked.

"I'm …" He glanced at Tony. Tony gave him a nod of encouragement and squeezed his hand. "Remember the other day when I was helping you set up for the memorial service?"

"Of course!" Wanda said. "I owe you at least a dozen croissants for all you've done for me this month alone." Tony put a hand on her arm. She glanced at him, and he shook his head.

"Marc Dubois and I dated. Before he met Jonathan, obviously." Greg paused, his fingers rubbing a worn spot on the edge of the table. "He was … abusive when he didn't think he could control me. When I tried to reach out to family or friends. When I got my job at the library." Tony leaned closer to his boyfriend as if he could change the telling of this with proximity. "Marc was better at hiding his rage than anyone I'd ever met, and I came from a family with plenty of anger issues. I was with him two months before I saw that side of him for the first time. It was cold, calculated punishment that he meted out when I didn't fit his perfect image. That was more important than anything." Greg blushed. "I ... Well, I am attractive."

"Yes, you are," Tony agreed.

"But it's more that I fit with the beautiful house, the gorgeous, unusual dog, and, most of all, I don't threaten his social dominance." He took a deep breath. "I didn't know Jonathan personally. I knew about him. I try to avoid people who trigger my old behaviors, but I met Jessica at a library function, and we hung out a few times. When she invited me to a party her brother was hosting ..." He trailed off. "She texted me the address, and that was it. I ghosted her. I couldn't risk her even mentioning my name in front of ... him."

Wanda stared down into her coffee. "He must be very good at hiding it, because I didn't catch a whiff of it over the last few weeks."

"Greg, show her your hand." Tony's voice was gentle.

Greg lifted his hand palm up. There were scars. "I borrowed some money from his wallet. I should have repaid him, but I forgot. Marc accused me of stealing and put my hand on the high burner on the glass-top stove to punish me." Greg looked straight at Wanda. "I went to urgent care and then stayed overnight at the head librarian's house. Maureen wanted me to call the police, but I knew he would just say I'd had too many glasses of wine and forgot the burner was on and put my hand there by mistake."

"He didn't come after you?"

Greg managed a weak smile. "Sometimes an uncle who's failed out of anger management half a dozen times isn't the worst thing to have."

"He drove over and told Marc if he ever came near his nephew again, they'd never find his grave," Tony added.

Wanda shuddered. A bully always recognized a bigger bully. "You didn't get the police involved?"

Greg shook his head. "Marc had a hundred ways of convincing people that what he did was their fault."

"So he has no police record," Wanda said slowly. "No history of abuse attached to him?"

"Not unless someone else filed one before me." Greg wiped his eyes, then reached out and took Wanda's hand. "Is it my fault that his husband died?"

"What do you mean?" Tony asked. "It was some kid, right?"

Wanda looked from Tony to Greg. "You don't think so, do you?"

"That boy served himself up on a silver platter. Marc would never pass up an opportunity like that," Greg said. "What always triggered Marc was when his perfect life was disturbed. He's got the great job, house, the beautiful clothes … and he likes a Pygmalion."

"A what?" Tony had clearly not heard this part before.

"Like Eliza Doolittle in *My Fair Lady*? Like me. I was a recovering alcoholic—someone he could rescue and shape as his own. It's no surprise to me Marc ended up marrying an addict." Greg shook his head. "I should have said something. Reported him. I could have at least found a way to warn his husband."

Wanda shook her head, looking out the window. This wasn't going to be a light snow. "They were married for years, Greg. Jonathan knew. He knew, and, for whatever reason, he stayed. We can't know what their relationship was like, how abusive Marc was, or what power dynamics were at play, because we weren't there. It's not your fault or your responsibility." She could tell he wasn't convinced. "We don't even know for certain what happened. But I can tell you this. Marc said he moved out for a few months because Jonathan wouldn't go to rehab. That was a window, and for some reason Jonathan Thorne didn't take it. If he couldn't leave when the door was wide open, there was nothing you could have said to change his mind."

Greg took a deep breath and let it out slowly. "I went back for my things when Marc had to stay in the city overnight for work, so maybe you're right. There was a lot we owned together, but I left it. I still wish I'd been brave enough to do something about it."

"You may still get your chance," Wanda said. "If you want it."

Greg looked at her and nodded. "I'll do it."

"I don't even have a plan yet," Wanda said.

"I do. And I am not waiting. I'm going now. See you at home." Greg leaned over and gave Tony a kiss.

Tony rested his forehead against Greg's. "I'll come with you."

Greg squeezed his hand. "It's okay. I can do this." He stood up and pulled his jacket on. As he opened the door, the sound of the wind made everyone in the cafe look up.

Wanda got Tony another latte. She started to speak, and he jumped up, sloshing coffee all over the table.

"What is it?" she asked, alarmed.

"He's gone there. Greg's gone to Marc's. I know it."

"No. He's gone to the police station to give a statement. He wouldn't go to Marc's alone. It's sleeting. Visibility is like an inch."

"He used to live there. He knows the way," Tony said, pulling on his coat. "When I met him, I thought, 'Here's this hot guy who reminds me so much of someone.'" He stared down at her. "You. He reminds me of you, Wanda."

She scraped back her chair. "Let's go."

36

LANCE KNOCKED ON RYE'S HALF-OPEN OFFICE DOOR. She glanced up from the paperwork she was trying to finish. She had fallen behind the last few weeks, and with the holidays coming, she needed to clear the backlog.

His face was drawn in concern, though, so she closed her laptop and gestured for him to come in. He closed the door behind him, but he didn't sit. "Can I help you, Lance?"

He looked as though he was having second thoughts, then slid down into the chair across from her. "I don't know if you're the right person to talk to about this."

Rye waited, but he didn't offer more. "About what?"

He twisted his long fingers around the straps of his backpack. "I was coming in to wash up after packing up props, and I saw Emma Reyes talking to Ms. Ramirez."

"Here?"

He nodded.

"Did they see you?"

Lance shook his head. "They were in Claudia's office. Emma was trying to convince Ms. Ramirez that they needed to confront Mr. Thorne's husband."

"What do you mean, 'confront?'"

"I don't…That's just what I heard first. Ms. Ramirez said something about Emma having no proof, and Emma said that's why they needed to do it, that he would never just confess. She seemed really upset."

Rye stood up. "Is Claudia still here?"

"I think so."

"I'm going to check it out. Can you call the station and make sure an officer is alerted?"

"Already done," Lance said. "I called on my way to you. But the officer is coming here. She said I should try to keep an eye on Emma if I thought I wasn't in danger, but when I went back into the greenroom, she was gone."

Rye pushed away from her desk. "I'm going to follow up."

"Can I come with you?" Lance asked hopefully.

"Absolutely not. I want you to head out front and find the officer. If you see Emma, text me."

THERE WAS A CAR IN MARC'S DRIVEWAY. WITH THE sleet coming down, the November afternoon was dark as night. Tony pulled Wanda's car over to the verge where they couldn't be seen from the house.

"Why don't you make the walk as long as possible?" Wanda was already damp and chilled from the dash from Harvey's to the car.

"Car trouble is our alibi and an easy departure. We might not need to be seen at all if that's not Greg's car."

"Can't you tell from here?"

"Cars have never been my thing. You know that."

"Color, at least?"

"Dark blue, I think. Or gray." He paused. "Or green?"

They pulled their hoods up and trudged toward the car. Tony peeked in the window.

"It's not Greg's. Let's go," Tony whispered.

The motion detector lights came on, and Wanda and Tony both jumped. The point must have been to blind unexpected visitors, and it worked. As they shook their heads to clear the stars, Wanda heard Marc say, "It's a little early for caroling parties from the church, isn't it?"

RYE STARTED TO JOG WHEN SHE SAW CLAUDIA DOWN the hall, heading for the doors to the teachers' parking lot. "Claudia! Hey!" Claudia picked up her pace, forcing Rye to break into a full-blown run to reach her before she left the building. "Hey!" Rye put her hand on Claudia's arm. "Stop for a minute, please."

Claudia turned toward her. "I'm sorry, Rye. I've got to go."

"Why? What are you and Emma going to do to Marc Dubois-Thorne?"

"I'm not doing anything to him."

"I know Emma was here," Rye said.

"There was no stopping her," Claudia replied. "I tried. So I called and left a message for Marc to warn him that she was coming, then—"

"You what?" Rye dug in her pocket, but she'd left her keys with her bag in the office. "C'mon. We do need to go." She gave Claudia a gentle shove out the door into the freezing rain. It seemed to change Claudia's mind.

"What? Why? Shouldn't we call the police to report that Emma was here?"

"Already done." Rye spotted Claudia's headlights flash and picked up her pace. "But Emma thinks that Marc killed Jonathan, right? Because of a letter she sent to him more than a month ago."

"What? No. Marc found that letter here when he picked up Jonathan's things, remember?"

"That was a lie. Can I drive?" Rye's fingers nervously tapped at her leg.

Claudia looked as though she wanted to say no, but she handed Rye the keys and slid into the passenger's seat.

"You weren't the only person on Emma's reunion tour. She showed up at my house on Monday. I told her to turn herself in or I would." Rye put the car in gear and reversed out, feeling the tire slip as she did so. "I know. I should have hauled her in myself, but I wanted to give her a chance to do the right thing. It was a mistake, but now you've warned a murderer that a seventeen-year-old girl is coming after him."

The weather had gone from bad to unbelievably bad in the last half hour. The roads were too slick for her to go even the speed limit by the time they reached the edge of town. Claudia kept quiet as Rye got off Route 119 and navigated the dark road out to the Thorne-Dubois house. Claudia tried to call Lance on Rye's phone to tell him to redirect the officer who came out to investigate at the high school, but there was no answer.

She was on hold with the duty officer when her phone died.

"Do you have a charger cable in here?"

Claudia shook her head. "No, sorry. Really old flip phone. Need to update. This thing barely holds a charge, and … no service."

"Well, that's just great," Rye muttered.

"I think we should turn around. Let's find a gas station or something. We can call the police and tell them what's happened."

"And how long will that take?" Rye brushed wet hair out of her face. "If Emma makes it to Marc and he knows what she thinks he's done, he could do anything to her and call it self-defense against a fugitive who killed her husband." She glanced over at Claudia, who sat rigidly beside her. "You don't have to get out of the car, okay?

Claudia just shook her head. "This is a bad idea, Rye."

"If you think of a better one, let me know."

"PLEASE, COME IN." MARC STOOD BY THE FRONT DOOR, his face in shadow from where Wanda and Tony stood getting soaked.

There was nothing else to do. Wanda had to walk carefully to stay upright, her eyes glued to the ground. She noticed small boot prints leading to the house. Marc must have company—whoever the car belonged to, she supposed. Wanda was just grateful it wasn't Greg and that they wouldn't be alone with Marc. After all, he had no reason to think they suspected anything.

"Sorry to bother you, Marc," she said, slowly navigating her way up the steps. "We skidded off the road. I remembered your house, and …" She pointed in the direction of their car. It was, indeed, off the road.

He gestured to the front door. "Come inside." The front hall and stairs were in shadow, lit only from the fireplace in the living room. Marc waited while they removed their coats and, at his insistence, their wet boots. Wanda glanced around but didn't see evidence of visitors. Theirs were the only jackets dripping on the coatrack. The house was silent.

Wanda reached over to flip on a light, but nothing happened.

"Power's out," Marc said. She jumped, startled by how close he was standing behind her. He clicked on a flashlight to show them the way.

"Oh, of course," Wanda said. "This weather is terrible. I hope your guest is able to stay the night."

"What guest?" Tony asked, glancing around.

"The car outside? That's not yours." Wanda threw Marc a forced smile. "My nephew pointed out your electric Porsche before the memorial service. I guess he'd noticed it from the funeral home the other day. He was very excited about it."

"Please. Sit." Marc herded them into the lovely living room, and they sat where he gestured. There were several candles lit. He turned off the flashlight. "I did have a visit from someone you know, in fact."

"Greg Engstrom?" Tony blurted out.

Marc looked genuinely surprised. "What about Greg?" There was a look in his eye. Predatory.

Tony paled but seemed at a loss for words.

Marc smiled coldly. "What did Greg tell you about me? I haven't seen him since ... Well, I should pay him a visit. It's been too long."

"Stay away from him." Tony half rose, and suddenly there was a gun pointed at the middle of his forehead. He sat down very carefully.

Marc hadn't removed his jacket when they'd come in, and Wanda realized he'd been hiding the gun there. But why? What reason would he have for arming himself against a minister and a church organist?

Unless he'd needed it before they'd arrived.

Marc looked Tony up and down. "So you and Greg are together?" He barked a laugh. "You're not exactly an upgrade, are you?" He slid his hand along Tony's shoulder and tightened when he reached his neck.

"Greg used to be fun, you know. He wasn't always the stick-in-the-mud librarian. We used to party so hard he couldn't remember his name the next day." Tony looked terrified as Marc leaned down to speak directly into his ear. "Then he went too far. That's when I sent him to rehab. It doesn't look good for me to be with someone who can't control himself, does it?"

"That's not what he told me," Tony said softly.

"Well, he's a liar, isn't he? And ungrateful. Can you believe he wanted to trade all of this to get a new job and start seeing his family again? Have you met them?" Marc made a face. "They live on an actual farm. Nothing charming like you'd scroll on Instagram, either. It was disgusting. And his uncle is a thug, a Scandinavian thug."

Wanda glanced around for something she could throw at Marc, but everything in his house was soft and fluffy.

"They're total homophobes, too, of course. They turned their backs on Greg when he came out, you know," Marc continued. "But he kept saying that they had changed. That he wanted to give them a second chance."

"Sounds like you don't really miss him," Tony said.

Marc squeezed Tony's neck and gave him a shake. "You don't get it. I do the leaving. Greg doesn't get to have his fairy-tale ending after making me look bad. Ross didn't, did he? Talk about a nasty family. And Jonathan's family was even worse than that. Jess! What a piece of work. I'm going to interview the dear kinfolk before I get a new boy toy."

Wanda realized that as soon as Marc had started talking about Jonathan, Tony had relaxed a little, even with the gun in his face. Anything to keep him from worrying about Greg.

"What was wrong with Jonathan?" she asked. "He didn't party. He loved you."

"Not enough," Marc growled. "When that kid threw himself at Jon, he was flattered, charmed."

"But Jonathan didn't do anything, right? It was just a one-sided crush."

"Kid's dad took care of him anyway, didn't you hear? I owe the guy." The gun dropped a little. Marc clearly did not view them as a threat—more of an inconvenience. "But I wasn't going to let a second man walk away from me. Jonathan wouldn't take my hints, though. He cut himself when he was an addict. I think he liked the pain."

Tony's face had gone completely white, and all Wanda could think was that she had managed to put another one of her close friends in danger. The rift between her and Lisa had been bad enough. It would be unbearable if it spread to Tony, too—not that she would blame him.

Marc actually chuckled. "So I sent him to the Milky Way." Wanda felt sick. "Milk powder is magic. I put it in everything, easy. Not taking any chances." A thump sounded from above them. Another thump, louder. Marc glanced up, his face suddenly flushed with anger.

Wanda shifted closer to the fireplace. If she could grab the poker, she might be able to do some damage.

"Just what do you think you're doing, Reverend Duff? Do you really think you could hit me with that poker before I shoot your friend?"

Her fingertips brushed the metal, and she heard the gun being cocked. She pulled her hand back. "Marc, don't do this. No one can tie you to Jonathan's death right now, but if you shoot us in your own home—"

"You're right. It's far too messy," he said, coming to stand in front of her. "And this rug is my favorite. There are much cleaner ways to take care of this problem." Another thump from upstairs. Marc glanced up. "Paddy? Guard."

The enormous dog came over and started to growl. Marc tucked the gun into his waistband and let the dog handle security. He slapped duct tape across their mouths and wound it a few times around their arms and the chairs. He pulled a hearing aid out and stuck it in his pocket. She prayed he would not see the one in her left ear, covered by hair.

At the sound of car tires crunching on snow outside, Marc looked up and swore. "You've got to be kidding me." He walked to the window to peer out. "What is Claudia Ramirez doing here?"

Wanda felt her heart leap. If Claudia was here, maybe—

"And that *insufferable* vice principal." He slammed his hand against the wall in frustration before turning to glare at them. "I'll be back to deal with you." He snapped his fingers at the dog and repeated, "Paddy. Guard."

The dog growled like a train coming out of a tunnel and started to drool on their feet. A lot.

As Rye carefully rounded the bend, the trees thinned. If Claudia hadn't been giving her directions, she would have missed it. The house was barely a dark patch in the storm. A car was parked in the driveway, so Rye pulled in behind it and turned off the engine.

"What do we do now?" Claudia asked.

Rye was already opening her door. "Stay here," she murmured. "I'm going to check to see if that's Emma's car." She shivered as the sleet immediately soaked through her sweater. She hurried over and peeked into the window of the Camry. The backseat was littered with graded papers and what looked like a semester's worth of gym clothes.

Emma wasn't inside. Rye pulled at the door handle, and it opened. She stuck her head inside. She felt rather than heard the movement behind her and twisted as the door slammed hard against her shin. Rye screamed and pulled her leg toward her just as the passenger door was shoved shut again. She fell back, banging her bandaged head against the mirror. Lights flashed in front of her eyes, and the pain on pain was so intense that bile rose in her throat.

She sat up but almost blacked out as the blood rushed away from her head. The noise of the storm made it impossible to hear what was happening. Rye swallowed against another wave of nausea and opened the door just enough to slip out. There was no way Rye was going to stay here waiting for Marc to come back and finish her off. She slid away from the car, the ground sheer ice beneath her feet.

Her father's training came back to her. *Stay low to the ground. Don't move unless necessary. Use your ears, not your mouth.* At age twelve, she'd barely managed to absorb this sort of stuff, but now it felt like second nature. If she couldn't see him, he couldn't see her. Probably.

Marc was stumbling back to his house. Rye glanced at Claudia's car, but she could barely make out its form with the blowing snow. This was her chance. It was dark, and Marc must have thought she'd passed out when she hit her head or he would have come after her again. Rye followed him, moving as quickly as she could against the buffeting wind until she judged that she was close enough to jump him. She'd forgotten about her head.

She managed to grab him around the waist, and Marc howled with anger as he went down, slamming his face on the edge of the stair. She climbed onto his back and got a grip around his neck, but his skin was wet and slippery, and Rye could barely focus through her own pain. He wriggled away and was up faster than she expected. He grabbed the front of her jacket and hauled Rye to her feet, shoving her against the porch railing. Her head hit the post.

Stars exploded in her vision.

Marc lashed out hard, catching the edge of her ribs. She moved with the blow by instinct and was able to use the momentum to grab him again. He had at least six inches on her, but he was slight, and she used her lower center of gravity to her advantage, plowing him over into the icy slush.

Tripping was her new signature move.

She tried to catch her breath, but her chest burned. Faintly, Rye thought she could hear someone yelling. Claudia? She shook her head to clear her ears and immediately regretted it. She couldn't hear any better than before, and now there was a bell reverberating in her skull.

Rye looked up as light hit her face. Not a bell. A horn. Rye staggered to her feet as the patrol car, its lights flashing red and blue, skidded on the gravel, headed straight for her. She closed her eyes, waiting for impact, but instead the world exploded.

Her eyes flew open. The patrol car slammed into Claudia's, which plowed into Emma's Camry, causing all the cars to fishtail out of control. Rye staggered up the steps to the front door, away from the wreckage. She twisted the brass knob and fell into a warm, dark entryway.

The last thing she remembered was a tongue licking her face.

37

"TELL ME AGAIN WHAT YOU WERE DOING HERE?"
Wanda wasn't sure whether the sheriff was talking to
her or Rye. Probably both of them. He was not pleased.

An ambulance had taken Emma to the hospital after
they found her bound and gagged in the bedroom
upstairs. Paramedics treated Rye and told her to go
to her own doctor for a more thorough checkup in
the morning and to set an alarm for every three hours
through the night—or, better yet, have someone stay
with her. Apparently, that perfunctory advice cleared her
for Ryan's questioning, although she looked as glazed as
Wanda felt now that the adrenaline had left her system.

Ryan glared down at them. "It seems logical that one
person, Mr. Engstrom, came into the police station
to give a statement, and that his statement would be
enough for me to come check things out here, and yet
it seems like whenever you two are involved, a simple
arrest becomes a carnival."

Wanda rolled her eyes and handed Rye a cup of hot
chocolate. She looked like she needed the sugar. "Marc

was packed to move. Didn't you see those suitcases in the hall?"

"I did, and I would have seen them just as well without you coming over here and getting yourself kidnapped."

"I didn't get kidnapped." Rye offered him a wan smile. Ryan snorted.

"Paddy-pup remembered my treats." Wanda reached into her damp coat pocket and pulled out a few Milk-Bones. "Besides, whatever Jonathan and Marc trained that dog to guard against, I'm betting it wasn't human."

"It was rabbits." Claudia spoke up. She was sitting close to Rye, her hand rubbing absently up and down Rye's arm. "They have a lot of trouble with animals in the garden during the summer. Jonathan told me. They trained Paddy to bark whenever he saw one and to guard the vegetable patch when he's outside." She shook her head. "That dog doesn't have a vicious bone in his body. He never would have hurt you."

Ryan growled. "Marc would have done that with his gun."

"Was it loaded?" Rye asked.

Ryan stared at her, then at the weapon still waiting to be marked as evidence. He pulled on some gloves and checked. "Empty," he said.

"Marc's a lawyer," Rye said. "He knows there's a different charge if the gun is loaded, right? He didn't need bullets, because once Wanda and Tony were tied up he could have easily overpowered them or just dragged them outside to die of exposure. He could come back later and untie them, tell you some story about their car breaking down. They slip, fall, maybe hit their heads. He could pretend he wasn't even home when it happened. Besides, he certainly would have used a loaded weapon on me if he'd had one."

Ryan, Wanda, Tony, and Claudia just stared at her.

"What? I can think of at least five other ways he could have killed or discredited them without it tracing back to him. Same with Emma. Deranged teenager stalking him. At worst, he could have claimed self-defense. The only reason he got caught was because we all piled on. If any one of us hadn't shown up, it would have been easy to pick the rest of us off, especially in weather like this. The cold would have confused time of death, and the sleet would wash away physical evidence."

"Which is why *none* of you should have been here," Ryan said through gritted teeth.

"What makes you think he wouldn't have found a way to do the same to you?" Wanda asked. "Yes, you have superior firepower, but he was obviously comfortable acting outside of any moral or legal code. If you'd come here alone tonight, maybe we'd be reading about your accidental death in the paper tomorrow."

"We're done here." Ryan flipped his notebook closed. "Ms. Ramirez, I expect to see you at the station giving your statement tonight." She nodded. "You are not to speak to Prudence Rye, Wanda Duff, or Tony Tomeo until you have made your statement. Is that understood?"

"Yes, sir." Claudia saluted him. Then, she flipped back her drenched hood, turned, and kissed Rye long and hard. She gave Wanda and Tony a wave and left, Rye staring after her, clearly baffled. Apparently Claudia's car was not a totaled car-sandwich.

Wanda suppressed a snort of laughter, and Ryan turned back to them.

"The three of you had better be in my office tomorrow at nine a.m. I don't care what you are supposed to be doing," he said, cutting off objections that were clearly forming. "If you feel up to it, tonight is better, while the details are still fresh." He stared at each one in turn. "I do not want the glamorized version of events, either. We've had enough melodrama. Understood?"

Tony made a small harrumph but nodded. Rye and Wanda just stared back at Ryan.

"I think he's talking about the kiss," Rye whispered to Wanda.

"Yours or mine?" Wanda asked, and then she began to giggle hysterically.

Ryan just turned and stomped out of the house into the storm, leaving the cleanup to Tyler and Jaz.

WANDA THOUGHT THEY ALL LOOKED AS TIRED AS they felt as she drank a steaming cup of tea Lance had pushed into her hands when they finally got home. Tony had called Greg when they'd gotten in and left after he hung up. Wanda gleaned from him that Greg was not happy Tony hadn't trusted him to go to the police and, on top of that, had put himself in danger. She hugged him tight and sent him home with one of her parishioners who'd been plowing her street of the now slushy snow when they'd arrived. Glen was happy to do them the favor, and she felt better knowing Tony wouldn't slide off the road.

While she and Rye compared stories, Lance fixed them scrambled eggs and toast with a side of pumpkin pie he had apparently stress-baked while waiting to hear from them. It was delicious, and Wanda helped herself to a second piece to be sure Lance knew how much she appreciated it, and him.

Lance watched them across the table, his own cup of tea in front of him. "Honestly, I'm just glad Henry isn't a murderer. Reckless, yes. Bad taste in women. Definitely. But not ..." He trailed off. "Also, I found out my boss—

you know, Mr. Fairchild? He's the one who paid for the detox and psychiatric care for Henry. Mrs. Jacobs told me when I went to check on her."

"You went to see Autumn Jacobs?" Wanda asked.

He shrugged. "She kind of reminds me of my mom. I brought her a casserole and met Henry's half sister. I think Melissa will take care of her." Lance took a sip of his tea. "Anyway, I am really glad for Henry. I guess Mr. Fairchild is on the board of directors and had some pull. Pretty decent thing for him to do."

"That was very generous of him," Rye said. "And of you, to go check on Henry's family."

"His mom said the place is nice. Henry told her the group meetings are good, too. No one knows him or what happened with his brother. He's sort of ..."

"Anonymous?" Wanda offered.

"Exactly." Lance yawned. "Do you two need anything else?"

"Go to bed." Wanda leaned over and gave his arm a squeeze. "Thank you for feeding us."

He came around and dropped a kiss on Wanda's head. "'Night."

His door had just closed when the doorbell rang. Lance stuck his head out of his room and yelled down, "Oh, I forgot to tell you that Ms. Rye's dad called earlier. I told him you'd probably be here soon." The door slammed again.

She winced. "I'm surprised my phone hasn't been ringing off the ..." Her eyes widened.

"Didn't you tell Ryan that you left your phone at school?" Wanda stood to answer the door. "Like, hours ago? Before you were attacked by a cornered murderer, which your father probably heard about on his police scanner?"

Rye sighed. "I'm just surprised he didn't break the door down to get in here."

RYE PUT HER PLATE IN THE SINK AND SNAGGED A TO-go container to help herself to another piece of pie while her father made nice with Wanda. By the time he stomped down the hall, she had drained her teacup and was ready to go.

Hardy just gave her a look. She slid past him to hug Wanda. "Call me tomorrow before we see Ryan?"

"I will," she said. "Don't be too hard on your dad, okay?"

Rye glanced behind her. Her father's face was an unreadable wall. "Aren't you supposed to say that to him?" She jerked her thumb in Hardy's direction.

"I already did." Wanda handed Rye her coat. "Play nice, you two."

"A pleasure as always," Hardy said to Wanda as he stepped past her and followed his daughter out into the snow.

It was warm in the car, but Rye could feel her teeth starting to chatter as she pulled her damp coat tighter. She was tired, and the meds the paramedics had given her were starting to wear off. Her head throbbed. Hardy tossed her a fleece blanket and got into the driver's seat. Rye wriggled out of her coat and stuffed it into the back seat, wrapping herself up as best as she could with her seatbelt on.

She didn't realize she'd dozed off until Hardy turned the car off and got out, slamming his door behind him. He came around to the other side and helped her out. The sleet had changed to snow, but the ground beneath was slick, and Rye appreciated his steadying arm as they carefully made their way to her front door.

While Rye got changed into flannel pajamas, Hardy made up the couch for himself. She didn't have the energy to protest, and the paramedics had told her not to sleep alone. A small part of her wished Claudia could be here instead of her father, but this was all right, too.

He didn't say a word until they were both tucked into their beds. "Lab tests came back on the food Jonathan Thorne took to school on the day he died. There was part of a brownie with a milk-based protein powder in it, and the bread for his sandwich was made with powdered milk."

"Just like you used to make for me."

"Common enough recipe. Autopsy showed he ate some of both."

"It must have been right before he headed out for that walk," Rye said.

"Apparently his husband stopped by and asked if Jonathan wanted to take a quick walk, since Marc was supposed to leave for New York early the next morning. A mini date."

"But nobody saw him? Nobody suspected him?" Rye asked.

"Emma Reyes did, but she thought her prank had killed Jonathan Thorne, so she never came forward to say she'd seen them arguing in the parking lot that day. Later that night, she was involved with the hit and run and says she forgot all about it."

"I believe her," Rye said. "She would have said something if she thought there was anyone else to blame."

"I agree."

They lay there in silence for a minute. "How do you know all this?" Rye finally asked.

"You think I was going to sit around twiddling my thumbs after that girl showed up at your house?" Her father snorted. "I'll give you this, Rye. You come by that curious nature of yours honestly."

"Do you know why he did it? Why he killed his husband? Wanda and Tony told me about his history, that he was abusive, but it seemed like whatever was happening between Marc and Jonathan was working, at least by some definition of the word."

"The letter," Hardy said. "You told me that Emma said she sent the letter a month before Jonathan's death. The envelope was postmarked late September."

"Because of what happened with her sister ..."

"What happened with her sister?"

"Nothing good." Rye rolled over to take some pressure off her sore leg. "But no one deserved to die over it."

"No one ever does."

38

IT WAS A WEEK BEFORE RYE WAS CLEARED BY HER
doctor to resume training for the New Year's race with
her friends, and she was told that under no circumstances
should she sled or do anything else that might result in
another head injury for at least six more. It was easier
to abide by that advice, since the snow had melted and
been replaced with unseasonably warm weather. Besides,
that doctor's appointment took place on Friday the
thirteenth, and the whole fall had been bad luck.

On the Saturday morning before Thanksgiving,
Camila and Rye raced laps on the track while Mike
and Ana completed their long run on the hilly cross-
country track behind the school. Rye was rusty and stiff
when she started, but after a couple of hours gossiping
with Camila, she even felt ready for stair running. In the
past, Rye had the advantage in that event, but Camila
had clearly put in the hours. Losing only pushed Rye to
work harder, though, and by late afternoon, soaked in
sweat, she could beat Camila up to the top of the stairs
about a quarter of the time.

"Good thing we have school off next week," she said as they watched Ana and Mike wind down the trail to the track from their seats at the top of the bleachers. She finished her water and tossed the empty bottle down toward her backpack. Last year, the school district had moved to giving the entire week of Thanksgiving off, and Rye could not be more grateful after the month she'd had.

"Mendoza looks like he needs at least that long to recover." Camila leaned into a deep stretch. "Have you talked to him?"

Rye shook her head. She wasn't sure what Ryan had told him, but she wasn't about to fill in the details. "He's been in triage mode with parents. The last two weeks at work have been nothing but meetings with him, on the phone with even more parents, sending email updates—it's never-ending."

"Makes you wish for a couple of kids smoking a joint in the bathroom, huh?" Camila nudged her gently with her shoulder.

"I'd kill for some straightforward disciplinary action," Rye agreed.

"Poor choice of words, but I know what you mean."

"By the way," Rye said, "I handed in my contract to Gerard yesterday."

"You signed it?" Camila squealed. "Five years? You'll really be here for five years?" She turned and wrapped Rye in such an enthusiastic hug that it knocked them off balance and off the bench.

Camila was lying on top of Rye, hers eyes glowing and her cheeks flushed. "I guess you're not sick of me yet?" Rye asked. The cement was cold against her back, but she felt curiously unwilling to move.

"Not yet," Camila said, and dropped a kiss on Rye's nose before standing gracefully.

Rye scrambled to her feet with significantly less agility, her cheeks hot. She busied herself finding a sweatshirt to pull over her sweat-drenched tank top and retrieving her water bottle from where it had fallen under the bleachers.

Rye could feel Camila's gaze on her. "What?" she finally asked.

"Do you want to talk about what happened?"

"Not really, no."

"Because it's too fresh, or because it was so traumatic that you want to repress it until those feelings explode out of your control?"

"Do I have to choose just one option?" Rye stood and pulled Camila to her feet. She raced down the steps, Camila overtaking her at the last step with a leap to the sidewalk. Rye grabbed her bag and slung it over her shoulder. "Listen, when I'm ready to talk, it's you I'm going to call, okay?"

"I'll hold you to that." Camila gave Rye another hug before running off to join her sister.

WHEN RYE GOT HOME, HARDY WAS SITTING ON THE porch eating a piece of pie with Andy. Rachel was messing around with an old bow and arrow set Hardy had dug out of the basement. Her target was a stack of hay bales. From what Rye could see, the girl had some natural talent—either that or archery was still a PE unit requirement in fifth grade. She hit the mark more than she missed.

Rye climbed out of the car and waved at her dad before walking over to Rachel. "You're better at that than I ever was. How long have you been practicing?"

Rachel beamed. "I just started a few days ago. Your dad told Andy it was okay if I came here some days after school instead of going to Gram's."

"If you don't watch out, he'll have you baking bread and checking the fluids in his car before too long," Rye said with a grin.

"Really? You think he'd teach me?"

Rye thought back to when she was eleven. She had preferred to spend her spare time at Andy's house to avoid her dad's lessons. "If you ask him, he'll teach you just about anything you might want to know."

"Like self-defense?" Rachel glanced at the bruises that lingered on Rye's temple.

"Sure, as long as you don't expect him to go easy on you." Rye smiled. Another five years of this really wouldn't be so bad. "Hey, do you know if that pie is up for grabs?"

"It is," Rachel nodded, "but it's pecan."

Rye's face fell. "Oh."

"Andy mentioned that you hate pecan pie," Rachel said as she aimed at her target again. "I think he might be mad at you."

"Did he say why?"

"Not to me."

"Oh?" Rye raised an eyebrow.

"I heard him tell your dad that you were being reckless and stupid, and that you do that when you have a crush on someone who's totally wrong for you."

Rye blushed. "Was that a direct quote?"

"No." Rachel let the arrow loose. It hit the top bale of hay squarely in the center. "I didn't want to hurt your feelings, though. The rest of the stuff he said was, you know. Boy stuff."

"Boy stuff?"

Rachel shrugged and let another arrow fly. "Yeah, like how he was sad you weren't making good choices, and how he should have known better than to date you when you always do stuff like this." She rolled her eyes. "Boys are so dramatic. He's known you forever, so if he doesn't realize that you might get into trouble to help people, it's his problem, not yours." She ran over to collect her arrows.

Rye glanced over at the men on the porch. They appeared to be absorbed in serving coffee, but she wasn't fooled. Her father had the hearing of a man half his age, and Rachel's voice carried.

To be fair, there was a lot of truth in what Rachel had overheard. Andy had every right to be angry with her for a long list of reasons. It still stung, though.

Rye shook her head and blew the men a kiss, then dropped her bag to get a refresher lesson on the bow. It couldn't hurt to have a few more tricks up her sleeve, just in case a little more of the right kind of trouble came her way.

39

WANDA WATCHED LANCE PICK UP HER COAT AFTER IT slid off the radiator where it had been drying. He fished out the car keys and hung them on one of the hooks he had installed by the door.

The keys were available for either of them as long as Lance checked in first to be sure Wanda didn't need the car for work. Next to the board, there was a new whiteboard calendar. as well, where both had started filling in work hours, appointments, and meetings to make sharing one vehicle a little easier.

Wanda watched the chips—one white and one red—drop from the folds of her jacket and fall to the floor with a clatter. Lance picked them up and turned them over in his hand, smoothing his fingers across them before tucking them back into her pocket.

He came across the kitchen and snagged the still-hot carafe of coffee. "Need a refill?" He poured himself a cup.

Wanda nodded. "It's afternoon decaf, just so you know."

Lance made a face. He was liberal with the sweet creamer and brought milk over for her. "So who took you to a meeting, Mitch or Greg?"

Wanda took a sip before answering. She'd been all ready to identify the white chip as representing her commitment to sobriety and the red marking her first month of sobriety, but he already knew. He also knew, somehow, that she'd been too afraid to go alone. "Greg. I like him and trust him. His boyfriend is my one of my oldest friends, and he's a drunk like me." There, she'd said it. "Mitch is a huge friend to alcoholics, certainly for a man who runs a bar."

"And he has those expensive mocktails to show for it."

"Mitch is not shy about asking someone whether they really want a drink if he knows they're trying not to, which is as unusual as running a queer-friendly country-and-western bar in the first place. But he's not an alcoholic, and Greg …" She drifted off.

"Got it."

"I went twice. It was good, but I'm not sure I'll go back." No one had really said anything at the meeting that she hadn't told people herself countless times before.

"Can I tell you what my therapist used to say to me after I'd skip an appointment?"

"Please."

Lance looked down at the table. "He'd say, 'Look, this is going to be hard, and at some point, you have to be the one to decide if you're worth showing up for.'"

Wanda studied the young man sitting across from her. When she'd prayed for companionship, and for strength in walking a path rife with other people's sorrows and challenges, she'd thought she was asking for a partner. She had been searching for love and support in the wrong people.

She smiled. God did enjoy laughing at her plans. "So you're saying I should keep going to meetings."

"I'm saying maybe you still feel uncomfortable with the whole idea of being vulnerable when you're used to being the one in control. But if you don't go, you have to do all the work alone." Lance smiled. "Well, not all alone. But you know."

"I guess you're right. I can give it a few weeks. Maybe try a couple of different meetings and see if there's one that clicks."

"It worked for my mom."

She put down her cup carefully. "Mickey went to AA?"

Lance nodded. "She started when I was ten. She still goes to meetings a couple of times a month. Or she did until she left for Italy."

"She's been sober seven years?" Wanda hadn't realized Mickey's drinking had gotten out of control. Of course, she hadn't realized her own had either, so that was really no surprise.

He shook his head. "About six years. It was tough for a while. I don't know if you knew that Grandma came to live with us for a year."

"I do remember that. You were ten, right?"

"Yup. Mom and I were both having a really hard time. For the record, your mother is not warm and fuzzy."

"No, she is not." Wanda grimaced.

"But it did the trick. Mom was desperate to get her to leave, and Grandma wasn't going anywhere until Mom was sober. So I guess it worked."

Wanda had never known any of that. She vaguely remembered her mother moving in, but Mickey had told her it was because Mom had needed help, not the other way around. Their mother had moved from Mickey's into assisted living, so Wanda had no reason not to believe her sister. "I'm sorry I didn't know. I'm sorry I wasn't there for you."

Lance shrugged. "Me, too. Now that I know you, I think I would have liked moving here sooner, but my mom needed me."

"And what does your therapist say about parenting your own parent?"

"Oh, he said plenty," Lance said with a smile. "And I'm working on it."

"Good. Me, too."

"Speaking of Mickey, she called last night."

"That's great. You haven't heard from her for a while, have you?" Wanda tried to ignore the sinking feeling in her gut. She stirred more milk into her coffee.

"Nope. I guess the school hasn't tracked her down to complain about me yet."

"So how is she?"

"She is staying in Italy 'with some changes,' whatever that means. She didn't go into details. Anyway, she's not coming back for a while."

"I'm sorry you won't get to see her for Thanksgiving or Christmas. I am happy to have you here, but ..." Wanda took a deep breath. "I would pay for you to fly out and see your dad for a holiday, if you'd like."

Lance laughed. "He and his family have their own traditions, and it's always so awkward for me to be there. I like his kids, but it's much nicer if I visit another weekend instead."

"We can make that happen," Wanda promised.

"Thanks. Honestly, I'd rather have a low-key Christmas with you."

Wanda grinned, knowing that Lance didn't have a clue that low-key Christmas and clergy were utterly incompatible. She wondered whether he would prefer costuming reluctant sheep for the pageant or baking a hundred mini fruitcakes.

"Low-key sounds like the perfect way to finish this year."

HARDY RYE'S
VEGETARIAN CHILI

1 can black beans
1 can kidney beans
1 can diced tomatoes
½ chopped onion
1 chopped green pepper
1 minced jalapeno
3 cloves minced garlic
1 Tbsp. chili powder
1 tsp. red chili flake
1 tsp. oregano
½ tsp. salt
½ tsp. pepper

Add to the Crockpot. Cook on high for an hour. Cook on low for 3–5 hours.

1 can corn

Add 1 hour before serving.

sour cream

shredded cheese
green onions
salsa
olives
tortilla chips

Top with any or all of the above. Serve with cornbread to good friends and strangers who will become friends.

AUTHORS' ACKNOWLEDGMENTS

OUR FIRST HEART-HUGGING GRATITUDE IS TO BEN Miller-Callihan for his ongoing encouragement, promotion, hand-holding, and particularly for his serving as sensitivity reader for hearing concerns in *Death in the Woods*. We are also grateful to Courtney Miller-Callihan and the Handspun Literary Agency community of writers, where we feel at home, as well as for the resourcing and new friendships that have come from "Sisters in Crime."

During the in-between time, when we needed moral support in transitioning from first novel to second novel in a series, we felt a little fragile, and we want to acknowledge some special people. Many simply said, "We want more," encouraging us to write three free, not-so-bloody short stories set in Stone Ridge. Thanks also to the women who gathered at Pilgrim Lodge Outdoor Ministry Center in Maine for an entire weekend spent reading and discussing the issues in the book, as well as the places that invited Maren to lead "Holy Clue! Mystery Novels and Faith-Based Detectives" workshops. Among book groups visited (you know who you are), one hosted *Death at Fair Havens* at its first meeting back after the three years they missed because of the pandemic, and one started a new book club with it. Finally, thanks to so many who responded to our social media push to get *Death at Fair Havens* in public libraries everywhere so that people could read Rye and Wanda for free.

Continuity and character building is always blessed by Beta Readers, and *Death in the Woods* was no exception. Nancy Hardy, Don Tirabassi, and Dea-Sue Pelletier were wonderful. The amazing editorial skills of Brain Mill Press are so deeply appreciated. They are such a strong team, they moved a fictional building twenty miles. We are deeply appreciative of the technical and promotional assistance of David Mankin and Jennifer Gray.

Our family supports us so much. The gifts of time, patience, to-die-for advice, and did I mention...time? To Donald, to Matt and Julia, to David and the boys— you are the best! Thank you.

ABOUT
THE AUTHORS

Maren C. Tirabassi's forty-two years' experience in mainline ministry shape Wanda Duff's professional life (but not her personality). Tirabassi is a former Poet Laureate of the city of Portsmouth, New Hampshire, and has published twenty-two nonfiction titles, as well as poetry and short stories in fifteen anthologies.

After teaching and working in early education for a decade, Maria Mankin has published six books with Pilgrim Press and has contributed to several anthologies. She is also a coauthor of *Circ*, a mystery set in Skegness, England, published by Pigeon Park Press, and *Pitching Our Tents: Poetry of Hospitality*. She is a regular contributor to Living Psalms, a collection in which the Psalms are reinterpreted in poetry and art as a reflection of God's work of justice and compassion.

CPSIA information can be obtained
at www.ICGtesting.com
Printed in the USA
LVHW030454080723
751847LV00002B/135

9 781948 559829